IN THE BUSINESS OF LOVE

IN THE BUSINESS OF LOVE

Book Two in the Taking Chances series

KATIE BACHAND

MINNEAPOLIS, MN

ISBN **978-1-7334326-7-2**

FIRST EDITION

Author Image by: Studio Twelve:52

In the Business of Love is a fiction novel. Names, characters, places, incidents and plot lines are used fictitiously and are a result of the author's imagination. Thus meaning, any resemblance to persons alive or deceased, buildings, establishments, locals, or events is coincidental.

For every friendship.

"A friend is someone who knows all about you and still loves you."
— *Elbert Hubbard*

"There is nothing I would not do for those who are really my friends. I have no notion of loving people by halves, it is not my nature."
— *Jane Austen, Northanger Abbey*

Ready for your close up?

Start by following Katie on Facebook, Twitter, and Instagram.

Then use **#inthebusinessoflove** and tag Katie in a picture of you and your copy of *In the Business of Love.*

You'll be entered to win random prizes and get fun messages from Katie!

In the Business of Love

PROLOGUE

How was it possible that the sound of her mom and dad arguing from the kitchen made it all the way up the stairs, through her closed door on the opposite end of the house, and over the sound of Tom Petty blaring on her radio?

Casey slid off the side of her bed and wedged herself between its sturdy white wooden frame and the blue paisley-patterned wallpaper, then covered her head with a pillow to drown out the screaming voices. The muffled tantrums barely made their way through the feathers, but somehow they crept in.

Ian and Linette Saunders were having one of their bad nights, filled with endless yelling and blaming. Average nights were filled with silence at the dinner table, followed by the nightly news or one of the two shows they actually agreed upon (*Law and Order* or *Survivor*–it didn't escape Casey both shows usually displayed some form of torture).

Good nights were a rare occurrence, but when her mom had a work event or dinner out with friends, there was a sense of normalcy–happiness even. She would talk to her dad about her day over a box of steaming pizza and she'd get to pick the TV show or game they played.

Casey lowered the pillow and let her eyelids close as she leaned her head against the wall. She could sit there for hours trying to block out the strained voices of her parents. Or, she thought, she could escape.

She pushed herself up using the side of her bed and the window frame, then crawled across the bed to the cordless phone on her nightstand and dialed. With every ring she sent up a silent prayer, *please be home, please pick up.*

"Hello?"

Casey felt herself relax when she heard the calming sound of Raymond Thomas' voice answer her call.

"Hi, Mr. Thomas, it's Casey."

Casey cringed as her mom's screech reached through the phone, only to be outmatched seconds later by the booming sound of her father's retort.

"Hi Case, are you looking for Grace?"

"I am."

Casey could hear the smile in Raymond's tone as he said, "Let me run and grab her, she's just finished with her homework. I'm sure she's ready for a friend."

"Thanks, Mr. Thomas."

The sound of footsteps and Grace mocking her brother–that she had a phone call and William hadn't received a call from Rachel yet–had Casey grinning in spite of her parents' anger echoing throughout the house. They both knew their friend Rachel was more in love with William then she imagined Romeo and Juliet had been with each other, but that didn't stop them from giving Grace's brother crap every chance they got.

"Case!" Grace happily sang into the phone, but the happy left as soon as she heard the background. "Oh no. They're at it again."

Grace didn't have to question what was going on anymore. She knew from years of experience her friend's parents would fight for hours. Their seemingly unlimited ammunition had the ability to take them straight through the night.

"At it again," Casey confirmed, and looked at her door. Over the years her feelings during her parents' epic fights had changed from sadness to irritation. Irritation was easier, but she also felt it changing her. With the sadness, she held onto hope. With irritation, she became closed off and distant. Her guard was constantly up, and she slowly let the idea that she would be alone for the rest of her life harden in her mind. She would keep her friends close, but love and life with a man, a partner with whom she was supposed to commit her life to, would never happen for her. She wouldn't let it.

Not if this is what happened when you did, she thought to herself grimly as she listened to her mother's voice rise in a crescendo of bitterness.

"Do you want to come over? Dad already said it would be okay. Just stay the night and we can get a ride to school with William tomorrow." Grace's words caused Casey's mind to start calculating.

Casey looked at her computer and thought about the work she was going to try and get done tonight. She had finished her homework too, but had plans to hack into her English teacher's computer to change her grades again. She did *not* do well on their latest *Scarlet Letter* paper and had to change that. Subjectivity was hard, facts were more her style.

Anyway, if she thought her parents were mad now, she didn't want to see them when they found out she got a B. Perfection was a rare topic her parents tended to agree on–when it came to her, that is.

Her thoughts paused as she felt the angry dagger of her mom's voice pierce her heart as she screamed, "When Casey graduates, I am done!"

"Good riddance," her father spat, sounding dejected.

The finality in her dad's response twisted the dagger.

Casey breathed deeply and tried to hold the tears that had welled in her eyes from falling.

"Yes," she said, a whisper into the phone, "*please* get me out of here."

Without a moment of hesitation, Grace replied, "We are on our way. Ten minutes."

"Thanks, Grace."

"Anything for you. See you in a few."

When Casey heard a click and a dial tone she placed the cordless phone back on its base, packed books and binders into her school bag, then shoved in pajamas and an outfit and struggled to close zipper. She took one last look at her computer and decided her grades could wait–or she could sneak onto Grace's computer when everybody was sleeping.

Casey scrawled a note telling her parents she'd gone to school early knowing they wouldn't check on her until morning, then looped her book bag around her shoulders, hopped back over her bed, opened the window, and climbed out.

The trellis on the side of the house served the Tuscan-style home her parents had built years earlier well, and it served as an escape for Casey to climb down. Hopping the last two feet onto the front walk, Casey made her way to the end of the driveway to sit on the curb and wait.

The neighborhood was quiet. And though she'd had the thought many times before, she was certain *this time* the silence had never sounded so good.

Casey knew if she looked back she would see the glow of the kitchen lights and the silhouettes of her parents deep in their argument. So she looked out instead.

The houses were all different. Some craftsman style, some modern, some that looked as if they should be on a New England coastline, or the Italian countryside. Though, most of those had direct access to the lake.

One day, she thought, she was going to own one of those houses. So she could hear nothing but the peaceful sound of water rippling against a lazy beach.

Casey closed her eyes to see if she could hear the lake tonight, but the only sound she heard was an old Jeep engine rumbling closer. She didn't open her eyes, but it was enough to make her smile.

She was saved.

Before William's jeep could slow to a stop, Grace jumped out of the passenger side door and ran toward Casey.

Casey felt Grace's arms wrap around her and couldn't remember anything that had ever made her feel so safe. William climbed out once he put the Jeep in park and walked around to the embrace, cocooning them both, squeezing so tightly both of the girls laughed and let out squeals as they tried to wriggle free.

Gradually their arms all fell and one by one they filed into the Jeep so William could drive them home.

—

Casey walked into Grace's room and threw her bag onto the top bunkbed–*her* bunk. Years ago, Lydia and Raymond Thomas had agreed to put bunkbeds in their house so she and Rachel would have a warm bed to sleep in whenever they stayed the night. If her computer hadn't been at her parents' house, she would have moved in with Grace a long time ago. It was more of a home than her parents had even given her.

"I called Rachel," Grace said as she walked in and closed the door behind. "She's coming, too."

Casey eyed Grace and tipped the edge of her mouth up in a grin, not saying a word.

"I know," Grace responded with a smirk of her own, reading Casey's mind. "She just wants to see William. But I made her promise no boy time, until after girl time."

"You're a real hard-ass, Thomas."

"Don't I know it," Grace said, as she tied her hair into a blonde knot on the top of her head. "So, I'm not going to ask you to start until Rachel gets here, but I am going to ask how you're doing?"

Casey crawled onto the pink, teal, and purple geometric shapes of Grace's comforter, and stared at the ceiling. It was a simple question with so many not simple answers. So the easiest answer was, "Fine." Casey turned her head. "I'm doing fine."

The doorbell saved Casey from Grace's narrowed eyes and further explanation–for the time being.

A quick three knocks and a flowery voice sang from the other side of the door. "Hello sexy ladies, anybody in there?"

Casey and Grace stole amused glances at each other before Grace replied, "In here, and ready for you so we can get started."

Rachel bounded in with flushed pink cheeks and daydream eyes.

"You couldn't go ten seconds, you're mush," Casey said, disgusted. "So much for no boys until after girl-time."

Rachel floated over to the bed and fell in a spin next to Casey, an act that had Grace laughing.

"How am I supposed to say no when the *cutest* guy in the world traps me outside for a *holy shit* make-out session before I can even set one foot in the door?"

Casey ignored Rachel and looked toward Grace. "We've lost her. There's no hope. And, she's pathetic."

"*She* is right here," Rachel said while bumping her hip into Casey. "And you haven't lost her, she just happens to be in love." Rachel turned and her face grew serious, "Now, tell us how you're doing."

"I-"

"How you're *really* doing," Rachel added, cutting Casey off from her standard *'I'm fine.'*

Casey stared at the ceiling and felt Grace sandwich her next to Rachel, then linked their arms together. She thought about it as the three of them lay in a row.

She was, of all things, confused. Why would two people agree to a life together only to fight all of their time away? How could two people who had at one point in their lives been in love enough to make a vow, dedicating their lives to one another, hate each other so much? When would they see the way they acted toward each other was making their own child feel so unloved?

Casey sighed. "I feel…thankful." She looked from Grace to Rachel. "Thankful that I have you. Because I know no matter what happens, here, I'm loved. And I'm learning from my parents' mistakes. I'm never going to get married, no matter how much I think I love somebody, I won't do that to them or myself."

Grace stole a sad look at Rachel. They didn't say anything else, just laid with their arms intertwined, and snuggled in a little closer.

Casey relished the feeling of warmth between the friends she knew she could always count on, and thought, with friends like this, she'd never need a man to marry anyway–she had all the love she needed right here.

CHAPTER 1

Casey swung into the Thomas and Jane LLC building a little after eight and sauntered into her new office. The unexpected perks of the Wallace Corporation joining forces with her best friends' company lent wonderfully to her schedule. She could enjoy an early cup of coffee with Grace at the Bistro, work on her own ventures while cozied up at their corner table, then climb the stairs to her consulting assignment–integrating the two companies' different technologies.

Who would have thought all these years later Grace would be running her own company and Casey would be in the perfect position to help her out?

The project was massive, but so was the paycheck. And after some great negotiating, she had the authority to build her own teams to handle the workload. Casey only had to plead her case once when she wanted to hire a *former* hacker to handle security. In the end, she won out with the expectation that she keep a watchful eye on the frightfully brilliant teenager.

Casey stood outside her glass-paneled door and stared at her reflection.

Well, she thought, *there was* one *downfall.*

Her tailored dress pants and crisp oxford shirt were a little too preppy and a little too far away from her usual jeans or sweatpants. But, she had to admit, her butt looked good in the fitted forest green trousers. And the velvet chunky heels did give her a nice lift. Her red hair was twisted securely in its signature bun–some things weren't worth the effort. She nodded once in approval, figuring she looked professional enough.

Pulling the door open, she walked into the office filled with screens, cords, boxes of routers, laptops, and empty diet Mountain Dew bottles overflowing from her recycling bin.

Hmm. Either she was going to have to cut back on her intake or talk Maggie into scheduling an extra pick up.

"Some people eat real food for their meals, but I suppose, to each their own."

Casey didn't have to turn around; she was able to match the smooth voice to the tall, well-dressed man.

"Travis, good morning. I didn't realize you were so interested in my eating habits." Casey turned as she responded and presented a sweet, forced smile that matched the sound of her words.

Travis smiled and welcomed the sarcasm he knew he'd find, and took in the firecracker of a woman he'd been unable to resist since she first walked into Wallace Corporation for her interview. She hadn't given an inch when asked to compromise on the technology they should use to upgrade all of their systems, and she had given even less when Travis eluded to the two of them sharing dinner, a coffee, or even small talk in the break room.

The former made her perfect for the job. The latter was what sealed the deal with his buddy, Luke Wallace, who gave final approval when it came time to hire for the position. Travis was certain Luke made the decision to approve not only based on Casey's skills, but also in knowing she would drive Travis crazy while she was there.

"I'm interested in a lot of your habits." Travis paused only for a second, but long enough for Casey to scowl. "The main one being the integration. How are you managing?"

Casey dropped her green canvas satchel on the corner of her desk–the only free space she could find–and looked up, irritated at Travis' response. She didn't want him to be interested in her habits–work or otherwise. She was doing her job and doing it pretty damn well. As for her personal life, things were easier at a distance.

Besides, with some space between them, she wouldn't have to smell his spiced cologne, see the smile lines crease at the edges of his lips and eyes, or listen to his voice as it coolly delivered compliments or witty remarks. And he was smart. Smart enough to keep up with her.

He was, Casey realized, *herself*–but in an extremely handsome and manly package. *That* was even more irritating.

"Everything is going according to schedule," Casey clipped. "Andy and his team have the new environment secure and it's been tested. It can handle more load than we would ever need from it. Theresa and her team are ready to make the switch to the new platform. All of the backups have been done, we have a final backup scheduled for Friday evening. All of the announcements have gone out letting everybody know they won't be able to log in beginning at nine Friday night. They will be able to get in again Monday morning beginning at six. We'll send out additional daily reminders, and a final right before cutover."

"That's actually ahead of schedule." Travis' tone was serious.

"Is that a bad thing?"

This time, Travis grinned at her irritation. "No, just pleasantly surprised at your efficiency."

Casey began to speak to defend her work, but he went on, catching her off guard.

"I knew you were the best, but I'm beginning to think you're priceless."

Casey's mouth hung open at the compliment and forced herself to close it.

Really? she thought, what was she supposed to say to that?

"Thank you." Casey let the stale words fall out. She intended them to be a little more combative, but Travis left her no choice but to be nice. The ass.

"You're welcome. Have a good day, Casey."

Travis knocked twice on her door frame and smiled on his way out.

"For the love of sanity," Casey whispered angrily as she threw an empty green bottle toward the door.

"Yikes!" Grace squealed, stopping in time to let the bottle fly in front of her face and into the hall.

"Shit! Sorry." Casey plopped in her chair and sank.

"Rough morning?" Graced asked as she slid into a chair across from Casey after placing the stack of boxes that were using it carefully on the floor.

"Travis was just here."

Casey watched Grace's eyes grow wide with amusement. "Ah yes, Travis. He's just so terrible, isn't he?"

Casey scowled her response.

Grace gave a teasing smile. "You do realize you have to work with him for another three years?"

"Yes." Casey rolled her eyes and went on looking for something solid to build her case on. "He's just so...nice."

"I like to think that's a description that fits nearly everybody that works here. You don't seem to have a problem with the rest of them."

Grace was leading her on and she knew it.

"Yes, but not all of them look like him. The stupid model-looking, good-smelling, nice-shoed jerk."

Grace pinched her lips together trying to hide her smile. She had accomplished what she set out to do this morning so she figured she could move on.

"Want to grab lunch today?" Grace asked, changing the subject.

"I like lunch," Casey admitted begrudgingly, not wanting to leave her anger behind so quickly.

"Great, what time?"

"Ten minutes?" Casey responded, wanting that precious distance from Travis and his allure as soon as possible.

"I tend to eat later than eight-thirty in the morning, but if I could I would make an exception for you. Unfortunately, I have meetings until noon. Want me to swing by when they're over?"

Casey sighed and accepted. She should probably do some work and earn the generous paycheck she was receiving for the job.

"Yes."

"Perfect! See you in a few." Grace chirped her reply, not thinking twice about the one-word, bland answer she received from Casey. They'd been friends too long to read into the delivery.

Casey huffed out a breath then pulled her laptop out of her bag, clicked it into its stand, powered it on, and smiled.

Now *this* she could do.

She could tune out the world around her and build an infrastructure that would make even the geniuses in the Silicon Valley jealous. She slid her earpieces in, selected her favorite Zeppelin playlist, and got to work.

CHAPTER 2

Casey trudged through the March blizzard cursing Minnesota, the weather gods, and the meteorologist. The gods for making it snow, and the meteorologist for telling her she wouldn't see a day without snow for another three days.

When she swung the Bistro door open she was greeted with an empty room and a blazing fire.

"I love you," Casey said in a sigh as she moved toward the warm flames with outstretched arms.

"I love you, too." Aimeé stated her response in a low French purr.

Casey shook her head and pointed to the fire, then said, "But I do love you, even more than this fire."

"For that, you will receive the first choice of wine. Second bottle goes to Grace since she's prepping for wedded bliss."

"Seems acceptable. I would like a crisp Pinot Grigio so I can pretend it's warm and sunny outside. I'll let you pick the poison."

Feeling the warmth from the blaze moving through her, Casey peeled off her black jacket, houndstooth scarf, and wool mittens before meandering to their table.

It might have been freezing and snowing outside, but Aimeé had already transformed the Bistro into a picturesque spring scene. Little white vases held happy, white and yellow flowers with leafy green stems as a garnish.

Casey settled in and pulled out her laptop. She might as well work and check her schedule before the rest of the girls got there. She opened her Matchme.com calendar, and the feeling of dread was immediate.

Has it already been a year?

"No, no, no," Casey whined as her head found the top of the table.

"Ah, how I remember fondly the agony of a man. Lucky for me it worked out in the end." Grace came up to the table and set herself in the chair across from Casey. She went on, "What did Travis do to you now?"

Aimeé joined them at the table with the wine and poured as she and Grace exchanged amused looks.

"It's not Travis," Casey said flatly, "It's fifteen million men and women across the United States. And the team of leaders that help me run the most successful dating site in the world."

Casey couldn't help the pride that seeped into her words, but she was still crabby. The worst part was she'd have to keep up the lie she had told the executives and the board.

"I don't feel bad for you one bit," Rachel said as she swooped in, snagging a glass of the liquid gold Aimeé had just poured and placed on the table. "You're a multi-millionaire with two houses, and you get to work with Grace. I work with child terrors who forget the last day of school is three months away, not three days."

"Aww, Rach." Grace stroked the arm of her pretty, petite friend. "Money doesn't make you happy either, just look at Casey."

The laughs were quick but Rachel wasn't done with her pity party. "Really? Casey makes more in two weeks than I do in a year. Let that sink in."

The three women stared at each other and tried to do the quick math in their heads, then moved their looks from one to the other before slowly nodding.

Without taking the time for compassion Aimeé agreed, "Yes, I think you're right. Okay, you don't have to pay for drinks tonight."

Rachel thought about the offer, then nodded. "Done. I'm no longer upset. What's going on with Match Me that has you so grumpy?" she said, turning her concern to Casey.

"Our spring and summer events are starting. This Friday we are having our annual kick off meeting. So I'll be sitting in front of a screen full of people who think that *love* is the best thing in the world."

"Love *is* the best thing in the world," Aimeé said simply, while pulling up her own chair, joining her friends as she did every Thursday evening.

"You know, I agree," Grace said holding up her nicely diamonded ring finger, the gem sparkling in the warm light.

"Why do it if you don't like it?" Rachel asked Casey, knowing that loving what you do was more important than the paycheck you received. Though at the moment, Rachel was only half on board with that logic.

"For some reason love is a great business to be in. People will do just about anything to fall in love–the lunatics." Casey shook her head, then paused, knowing that wasn't the real reason, and her face paled.

"And…" Casey continued slowly.

"Spill it out," Aimeé encouraged.

"It's 'spit it out.'" Casey assisted Aimeé with the English slang, then hid behind her hands and let her muffled words escape through her fingers. "They think I have a boyfriend. A *serious* boyfriend."

Laughter filled the room as the girls' heads fell back, holding their glasses of wine high ensuring they wouldn't spill. Their free hands holding their stomachs and wiping tears from their eyes.

"They think you *what?*" Rachel exclaimed as she tried her best to compose herself.

"See this," Casey pointed to her friends, "this is not what friends are supposed to do. You're supposed to be supportive and understand that I think love is a sham. And completely realize why it's so hard for me to have to pretend to have a boyfriend."

"Why are you pretending to have a boyfriend at all?" Grace couldn't help but wonder why Casey would even consider it. She liked the thought of a man in her life even less than actually having one.

"Three years ago board *kindly* suggested I use Matchme.com to find myself a significant other." Casey's mocking tone held an edge. "I was," she searched for the word they had used, "unsuitable representation of the company I created."

Casey scoffed and took a sip of her wine as she recalled the conversation with the team, led by Carrie Bolden, the blonde that seemed to be overly invested in the staff–getting along particularly well with the men. Why was it she always seemed to flock to them rather than the women?

"They can't really expect that from you, right?" Rachel looked around, then back and forth between Grace and Casey, the two that would know more about business expectations than she ever would.

"Technically, no," Casey began, but her eyes fell after looking to Grace who was reading her mind, a mirror of her own expression.

"But the board can, for the sustainability of the company, choose the leadership." Grace said it as if she was reading from a manual.

"That cannot be true. It's Casey's company, is it not?" Aimeé's concern was apparent.

"We're a publicly traded company. When we made that transition–when I agreed to that transition–I put most of my fate into the hands of others. I needed to, so I could start other ventures and work on other things."

At the time, Casey knew going public was the best decision for herself, the staff that had worked by her side day and night, and ultimately the customers. But now? After three years of keeping up the charade of having a boyfriend, it seemed terrible.

At one point, they were going to want to meet him. And unfortunately, she felt her excuses were reaching their expiry, and the team was getting restless.

"What will you do?" Grace asked the question for everybody at the table.

"Head to the lake, have the meeting, and pretend for as long as I can." Casey shrugged. "Then, I'll have to come up with something."

'The lake' was the affectionate term used for Casey's home on Lake Minnetonka. And it didn't slip past the girls, as each of them loved the house, *and* loved visiting the house.

"Um," Rachel began, "I have all the faith in the world in you, Case, and I don't mean to shift the conversation, but…"

Casey sighed, knowing where the conversation was headed. If she didn't know her friends truly loved her, she'd be hard-pressed to believe they were friends with her because of that love, but rather *the lake*.

"Did you say you were headed to *the lake?*" Rachel smiled, knowing she had Casey.

"I might have."

"When?" Grace pressed.

"Early tomorrow morning."

"I'm coming!" Rachel cheered, and threw her hands in the air.

"Me, too!" Grace agreed, not caring that they hadn't received an invitation from Casey, and knowing Luke was slated to help Travis pack up his room since they were selling his loft.

Then they looked to Aimeé.

"We've been having some…" Aimeé decided not to dive into The Bistro's financial issues quite yet, so she opted for a sliver of the story, "employee issues. But I can ask Christopher to come in during his shift to check on things. So yes, I am in as well."

Casey did have to agree it was like a mini vacation when the four of them got together at the lake over a weekend.

She thought through her schedule and glanced at her laptop that still sat open on the table. Closing it in a single motion she held her straight face.

"My last meeting ends at two." Casey let the corner of her mouth turn up, then watched her three best friends cheer and lift their glasses.

It was hard to be so damn cynical when you were surrounded by the best women in the world. And, at the end of the day it wasn't hard to admit it would be a really great weekend.

CHAPTER 3

Casey groaned when her alarm clock blared and startled her out of a wine-induced sleep.

"Why?" Casey moaned, covering her eyes, and pressing on her head where the ache was building.

The Thursday night ritual was a beloved event. Never missed, never a plan broken. Though many times they vowed to leave the second bottle of wine corked, it never quite worked out that way.

Casey rolled out of bed, slid on her decade-old slippers, and shuffled sleepily to the kitchen. She opened her medicine cabinet, then the fridge, and washed the aspirin down with a cold swig of her cherished Dew. The sweet burn of carbonation tickled her throat and watered her eyes. She wondered if there was a better feeling in the world–aside from sex, adding the criteria to her thought.

Thinking on the topic, today was the day. She would face her company and their expected pressure on her love life.

'When will we meet your boyfriend?' 'Has he hinted at popping the question?' 'It's been three *years.'*

People were nauseating.

Sure, she created a massive, successful dating website, but that didn't mean *she* had to partake in the business of love.

Casey's head fell forward and her wavy copper curls fell over her face. She sighed then inhaled the sweet scent of orange blossom that lingered in her hair from its wash the night before, and felt resigned. She'd have to tell them the truth. She prided herself on being honest, and it was time she stopped pretending to be something she wasn't.

17

What she was, was great at her job. Great at pairing qualities in people that nearly promised relationship success. And she could put it into writing, then into an algorithm, then into code.

Maybe her team at Match Me wouldn't approve of her love life–or lack thereof–but they couldn't deny her ability to provide one for their customers in a perfect match.

Yes, she would tell them the truth. They needed her. And that was that.

Casey lifted her head, turned, reached back for the green bottle, then marched to her city loft bedroom to get ready for the day's work and the weekend to follow.

—

The drive out of the city always felt like she was heading on a road trip across the country. The sun coming up behind her glistened off freshly fallen snow, giving the open road ahead a sparkle. The farther she drove, the more frosted trees she saw. And in just a couple of weeks the snow would be melted and she would be surrounded by green grass and budding trees.

When Casey's phone rang she saw *Ian Saunders* appear on the dashboard of her Range Rover. She couldn't close her eyes to make it go away, so she simply groaned, then accepted the call from her dad and tried not to sound like it was the last thing she wanted to do to start her day.

"Good morning, Ian."

A long time ago Casey had started calling her dad by his first name. It was around the time she'd learned he was dating somebody who wasn't her mother. She was younger then and didn't understand the intricacies of the relationship, but it had hurt nonetheless.

Her mom had moved out by then and had moved on to her own boyfriend. But her parents were still married. That's what she didn't understand. And she couldn't quite explain why she was only mad at her dad.

Perhaps it was because she had still respected him. When her mom had left, she left everybody behind, including Casey. Her dad always made sure to care, to call. But as the years passed, she never returned to the affectionate title her father used to own. So when he responded, she heard a bit of the hurt in his voice at being called by his name.

"Hi, Casey. How are you? How was your week?" Ian asked, as he did every Friday, his voice filling the vehicle over the Bluetooth speaker.

At the very least, her dad made an effort, even if the blueprint was the same every time.

"Doing good. Heading to the lake now. I have some Match Me meetings today that require my attention. How are you?"

Somewhere over the years their conversations had become cordial, and their interest in each other's lives had become normal.

Those first couple of calls she took after years without speaking had been harder than she ever imagined they would be. She'd be forever grateful those times had passed.

"Yeah, we are doing good here. Pamela and I will try and make it to a play downtown this weekend. She likes those." Ian continued without hesitation, as the conversations about his long-time girlfriend now came naturally, "You could, well, you could join us if you wanted?"

The invitation didn't surprise her, as he'd been offering for her to join them for the better part of two years. What did surprise Casey, was that for a moment, she considered it.

"I–thanks for the invitation–but I'm having the girls at the lake this weekend." Casey didn't usually explain, but something inside her wanted her dad to know this time it wasn't because she didn't want to, it was because she couldn't.

"Oh sure, no problem. How are the girls doing? I haven't seen them since…"

The pause was her dad trying to navigate the terrible years and probably hoping he didn't just navigate himself into an awful memory both of them would rather leave behind.

"Since graduation." Casey helped out, offering a lifeline. It had been her college graduation when they had all been together last.

The girls were invited. Her father showed up knowing she was in the 2008 graduating class. There weren't student lists, no valedictorian announcements–since MIT didn't have them–just faith that Casey would be there. It marked the first time her dad made an effort to reconnect with her. His pride in her was stronger than whatever discomfort reuniting after four years of not speaking would cause.

"Graduation," Ian confirmed, and cleared his throat uncomfortably, wondering how far he could carry the conversation, "I'm still proud of you. A 5.0 from MIT. My brilliant girl."

19

"Yeah." Casey still wasn't good at accepting his praise. "Thanks. Well, I should probably get inside." Casey eyed the stretch of highway before her and immediately felt the guilt of the lie.

"Right, of course. Ah," Ian held her on the line and struggled to get the next words out, "have you heard from your mother?"

"No." The answer was sharp and finite. "Goodbye, Ian."

Worry and sadness breathed audibly through the phone and her dad relented. "Goodbye, Casey. I love you."

Casey tapped her finger on the steering wheel to end the call without a response, and forced her breath come and go in heavy waves as she tried to keep calm.

Why would she hear from Linette Saunders? *Whitley.* Linette Whitley, Casey reminded herself. Her mother wasn't quite as delicate as her dad when it came to moving on. And why would *he* care?

Linette had married the man that had made her unfaithful and started a happy family of her own. One filled with new children that apparently deserved Linette's time, attention, and love. A new family that was so wonderful Linette could forget she had Casey at all.

Casey didn't have to be an IT whiz to learn about Linette's new family either. She simply had to log into every social media platform out there and see the obnoxious, happy pictures everywhere.

Images strewn all over social media of her mom laughing as she hugged her three young daughters, looking at them as though they were the light of her life. Or, when the daughters weren't present, the photos were of Linette and her husband jet-setting around the world, holding champagne glasses high in France and rare bottles of wine in Italy and Spain.

The funny thing was, the happy pictures her mom was flaunting online for the world to see, looked eerily similar to the ones in photo albums she'd looked at as a child. She went through them endlessly as a young girl and could almost feel the laughter of her mom and dad when they were dating, the happiness during their fairytale wedding, and the ecstasy of their honeymoon shortly after. Images of building their house close to–but not on–the lake, then standing proudly on the doorstep when it was move-in day.

The happy pictures continued through their first pregnancy. Casey would stare at herself as a sleeping baby in her mom and dad's arms with their hospital gowns still tied around them. Their smiles tired, but so full of joy.

Then the pictures stopped.

Casey pulled into her long drive, parked, then allowed herself to press her hands to her eyes as the memory recall was forcing a new ache in her head.

The pictures had stopped when she was born. They had been happy—until she had happened.

Casey opened her eyes and shook her head slowly. Well, maybe she wasn't a good baby, had been a troublesome child, and a teen who was more interested in computers than sports or boyfriends, but she was great at being a friend. And at her job.

The looming craftsman-style home that sat before her was proof of that. She was a genius when it came to computers and coding, great at working hard, and good at juggling multiple ventures. So maybe she wasn't good at being a daughter, but she was damn good at working and she would enjoy the enormous fruits of that labor.

The tiny loft in downtown Minneapolis was efficient and necessary. This? Casey looked up at a house that was probably more suited for a Colorado mountainside or a Lake Tahoe retreat, and grinned. This was excessive and *utterly* over-the-top *un*necessary.

Creamy white, gray, and brown rocks stood as sturdy pillar bases and accents surrounding the home. Deep espresso brown siding wrapped every inch of the four-story house except where large windows were strategically placed to ensure every angle offered a luxurious view.

Casey could have gone through the garage but she climbed the steps to the wrap-around porch and walked along the wooden panels until she reached the back of the house.

The view of the lake was breathtaking. A low line of steam formed over the frozen water as the morning sun from the east lightly kissed the far side of the lake.

Turning to move inside, Casey reached for her keys in the side pouch of her laptop bag, then unlocked the wide French door that sat in a wall of floor-to-ceiling windows looking out to the lake.

It had only been a week since she'd last been home but it didn't make the welcome any less warm. She flicked the switch to the rock-framed fireplace that centered the room and rose to the two-story paneled ceiling.

As she turned she took in the kitchen that was remodeled with Aimeé in mind. If she had to stop working at the Bistro, Aimeé could pack up her entire operation and move it here. Casey moved through the sitting room that was Grace's favorite place to lounge and read the stacks of books lining the walls. And as she moved, she saw the little breakfast nook that led out to a small framed porch, where she would be sure to find Rachel sipping coffee and looking out, romanticizing the view.

Other parts of the home were remodeled for comfort, for parties, or to ensure whomever stayed the night had a nice place to lay their heads. And Casey agreed, the bedrooms were exquisite. Hers especially. But it wasn't her favorite place in the house.

Casey turned the corner and stood looking through the paneled glass doors that led to her office.

This, she thought, was for her. She pushed the doors open and immediately relaxed.

Two rugged, chocolate-colored couches paralleled each other, and she smiled as she walked between them to the front of her desk. The desk was an expansive six-foot executive desk that provided the perfect base to three sleek monitors. When she was sitting at her desk, she had all she needed right in front of her. And when that wasn't enough, the wall to her right had six screens mounted in two rows of three.

Typically, she used the screens on the wall for monitoring the businesses she wasn't dedicating her time to that particular day. So today, while she worked on Match Me, she would be monitoring her Thomas and Jane, LLC dashboard and email. And of course, she would put the bottom three monitors on local and world news channels. Just in case she wanted to do a little digging into world markets.

On that topic, Casey thought, "I wonder." Mumbling to herself as a curious look came over her face. She slowly maneuvered to the other side of her desk, flipped on the fireplace that sat directly behind her, then sat in her chair, and made a smooth turn to face forward.

She knew she shouldn't, but…

Casey connected her laptop to the monitors and slowly lifted the top, debating her next move.

Technically she wasn't supposed to look into her friends' lives without their permission, but in this case, she wondered if one of them might be in trouble.

Aimeé had never been very open about her finances, and when they had been in France for Grace's birthday last May, they learned there was more to Aimeé's grandmothers' death than she was willing to share. Casey's concern had started then.

But she respected that boundary. Family was delicate. She knew all too well. But if Aimeé was in trouble, and asking Christopher–a childhood friend and local police officer that had taken a liking to Aimeé–to look into it, maybe she could lend a hand.

Casey logged in and authenticated herself three times before she hopped from one IP address to the next, ensuring if anybody happened to be watching, they couldn't trace the hack back to her. She found Aimeé's bank records, then dug into the data. Her fingers flew over the keys quickly and surely.

Eyeing the time, Casey determined she had exactly ten minutes of digging before she'd have to get ready for her call. So she scanned, filtered, searched account balances and discrepancies, and filed the information away so she could come back to anything that piqued her interest later on.

Casey sighed when she catalogued at least five numbers on Aimeé's bank statements that looked to be suspicious from one month to the next and backed out of the account without anybody, or anything, knowing she'd been there at all. Reaching blindly into her bag, she stared at the scenic mountain view her laptop background and found the unopened bottle of diet Mountain Dew, and evaluated what she saw as she sipped.

The cash flow fluctuation from month-to-month for the Bistro had always been consistent, peaking where it should in the winter and summer months. But the expenses, payments made, coming from Aimeé's business account looked off. She could look at personal bank accounts, but when it came to her friends, those were off-limits–that was her own rule.

Casey entered a couple commands on her keyboard and within seconds Match Me calendars, folders, and applications sprang to life on her monitors. She clicked open her video monitor to get a look at herself before she joined the call and decided the view was good enough. The makeup and collared shirt she threw on that morning would suffice. She looked down and arched a brow. Her ragged jeans were comfortable, but that's about where their appeal ended. So she would stay seated.

Within minutes everything she would need for the call was at her fingertips. Monthly customer reports, financial reports, company employment satisfaction surveys, and details for their upcoming spring and summer events. And, scanning the *Magical Match* emails, she couldn't help her exaggerated eye roll at the ridiculously excessive success stories of people who had found love using her site.

She was happy for them, sure, but let's face it, not everybody got engaged on a beach in Hawaii to a man that looked like Ryan Gosling as he presented a five-carat princess cut diamond ring. It would attract more desperate-for-love members, but it would also be setting them up for unrealistic and improbable expectations. She supposed that's what the marketing team was shooting for.

Casey dialed into the team call and turned her video on. When she did, faces from around the state and across the country sprang to life. She smiled at the group of men and women sitting before her and greeted them.

"Good morning, everybody. How are you all doing today?" Casey didn't have to force herself to be nice, since she genuinely liked most of the crew.

"Good morning." The team echoed their responses, then sat and stared as they waited for the remaining seats to be filled.

Casey noted Carrie Bolden hadn't joined the call yet and didn't feel the least bit guilty when she hoped she'd be absent.

It wasn't that she didn't like Carrie, she just found her completely obnoxious. Maybe it was the fact that Carrie seemed effortlessly put together and conversation came easy to her. Maybe it was because if Casey hadn't found Carrie so...whatever she was, she might actually think she was nice, funny, or even *like* her.

Just as the thought entered her mind it fell away. She scowled when she saw Carrie's video feed brighten the screen.

"Good morning!" Carrie's voice practically sang out the words. "It's so good to see all of your beautiful faces today!"

Oh for shit's sake, Casey thought, *really?* 'Beautiful faces?' Yeah, there was no way they would ever be friends.

"Casey, it's so good to see you. How are you?" Carrie directed her attention to Casey alone.

"Carrie," Casey's labored response came out with the appropriate level of enthusiasm, "I am great. How are you?" The smile she plastered on almost hurt to maintain.

"I am doing just so well. We are all so lucky in this life, aren't we? Great family, great friends, great jobs."

The 'great jobs' comment got the room to chuckle.

"I do want to get down to business, Casey. I think I see your calendar is booked completely today so we'll only have you for a few more minutes."

"Unfortunately, yes. I have to meet with our technology leadership for the remainder of the day."

"Okay, we'll take what we can get then," Carrie continued, not wasting any precious time. "As you all know, we have three major events coming up. One, we'll have our April Escape at Casey's house to go over all of the final details for the Spring Fling Conference, and ensure everything is in place for the Love Gala in June. Casey, is everything set for April? Do you need anything from us?"

"Everything for April Escape is scheduled."

"Great! Then there is just one more topic."

Here we go, Casey thought. It's now or never.

"We've discussed image and branding with our marketing executives and we really think it's important for the company, and our customers, to see their creator as a living example of what we represent. We would like to meet your significant other and would be *over-the-moon* pleased if he could join all of our events this year. Because…"

The pause made Casey nervous.

"We'll be featuring *you* in a series of articles and promotional materials!"

Casey blinked, unable to speak.

They what?

Carrie took this as her cue to continue as the cheers and mumbling from the rest of the team subsided. "You have the right skills, the right drive, and quite frankly the right look. You're exactly the type of person we would choose for an advertisement, so we are going to use the best representative for it.

"A powerful, successful woman balancing life, work, and a relationship! Isn't it wonderful? Now if we could just get your boyfriend to pop the question! Wouldn't that be perfect for timing!" Carrie giggled like a school-girl.

Casey slid her eyes to the email still open on one of her screens, then stared at the couple on the beach. She wasn't those people, nor did she want to be, but it sounded like the decision had already been made. *Shit.* So much for putting an end to her lie.

"So," Carrie nudged, "will we meet him in April?"

"Ah," the word dragged on as she tried to quickly think of something else she could say, "sure."

Sure! Casey yelled inside of her head. *That was the best you could come up with?*

"Great! We are all so looking forward to meeting him."

Then Casey saw it. Something that had been missing from Carrie's left hand before today. The thin gold band almost went unnoticed, but when Carrie had moved a strand of her blond hair away from her face, she saw it.

"Carrie, why didn't you tell us you were engaged?"

The color drained from Carrie's face. Casey almost felt badly for asking the question. *Almost.*

"It's nothing at all." Carrie brushed it off. "Just a decorative band, nothing more."

Casey watched Carrie look down and move on to the next subject without reverting her attention back. She wondered how Carrie could be so outgoing, but so secretive. That wasn't her style. So, Casey danced her finger in circles over her mouse and thought, maybe she'd look.

After excusing herself from the meeting Casey popped open the Match Me database and searched all of Carrie's details–and noted not once had she clicked on a profile.

Interesting.

Carrie had mentioned long ago she loved the site and was an avid user. Casey looked through a few more databases and turned up empty handed.

Unless…Casey clicked a few more keys, changed her search criteria. She stole a look at the time and scowled when her schedule forced her to pause her search.

"I'll be back," Casey said to herself. Then clicked into her next meeting and left Carrie's and Aimeé's secrets behind.

CHAPTER 4

Travis eyed Luke over the massive cardboard boxes he'd hauled down the stairs for the last hour–by himself.

"No, no. It's okay," Travis grunted as he hoisted yet another box onto a growing pile while Luke sipped coffee while sitting on the island counter, "you sit there. I'll get these boxes by myself." Then he fell onto the couch and leaned his head back and wiped off the sweat.

Luke looked over and grinned, "I suppose I could help some. That is what I told Grace I was coming to do when I left last night." Luke jumped off the counter, ran his hands down his work slacks, and walked over to join Travis on the couch. "But I thought we finished last night before all the beer, pizza, and poker."

"No." Travis looked over and scowled at his need to shower and get ready for work. "I was sick of packing. Speaking of, what are you going to do with all of this?" He motioned to the living and dining room furniture with a lift of his head.

"You want it?" Luke responded with the question, sounding hopeful.

It was Travis' turn to grin. "Grace put you in charge of your own furniture."

"Yup."

"And you don't want to have to deal with it."

"Nope."

Travis laughed low and deep. "Sorry, I'm not getting anything until I know where I'm going to land. I have a couple walkthroughs near here. Haven't liked any of them yet." Travis looked over, "And I'm not stalling. Just want a good investment."

"No rush here. We'll figure out what to do with this place once you're settled." Luke looked over wondering, "I hope you don't, well, that this doesn't…"

"Remind me of Kat? Nah, you told me you and Grace were moving in together. And you didn't change the locks. Or move my things to storage–on my dime. Though right now," he eyed the boxes, "I'd welcome the assistance."

Luke looked relieved Travis seemed to be joking about the matter. It was a different story a year ago. Travis had been irritable. But he figured that had something to do with Casey. His buddy had sworn off relationships but something about Casey was pulling Travis in like honey would a bee.

"Put me to work." Luke swatted Travis' knee. "I'll grab what I can while you shower. Then let's get one of Aimeé's coffees."

"Don't have to tell me twice." Travis accepted Luke's outstretched hand and lifted himself off the couch. "There are a couple boxes left in my bedroom, those can come down. Whatever you don't get I'll finish up later."

—

When Travis and Luke walked into the Bistro they were immediately drawn to the laughter coming from Grace and Rachel. The two were sitting with their heads back and wiping away tears. Travis scanned the room and caught Aimeé floating back and forth behind the espresso bar. He gave a wave and she blew and air kiss in return. When she held up two paper cups Travis exaggerated his nod and added a pleading look that got its intended response.

As he made his way back to the girls' table–that had become just as much *their* table–he looked through the crowd and didn't see Casey.

"She's at the lake." Rachel smiled knowingly.

"Am I that obvious?" Travis asked while he shed his wool coat.

"Yes." Luke and the two girls responded at once.

Travis only nodded and accepted the response.

"What lake?" Travis asked while gratefully taking the latte Aimeé handed him over the table, "Thanks."

"It's not so much a 'what' as it is a…well yeah," Rachel worked it through in her head, "it's a what. But it's not a lake, it's a house. Her house. On a lake."

"Come again." Travis tried to process the information he'd been given. Maybe if he heard it again it would help.

Travis looked to Grace who made eyes at Luke as he kissed her hand before she answered. "Casey has a house on Lake Minnetonka. She goes there when she has work for Match Me. It's easier to monitor everything from her office, it helps when she has to do a lot of video meetings. And it's domestic, they think she–ow!"

Aimee joined them just in time to kick Grace under the table. "She has a certain image to uphold." Aimee finished for Grace then shot wide, dark eyes, in Grace's direction that said it wasn't her story to share.

Travis watched the exchange. Even if Luke wasn't getting married to Grace, and he hadn't found himself infatuated with Casey, he would have liked to know this group of women. They were fun, and they damn sure cared about each other.

"Is there anything else Casey has going on in her life that would be fun to share with the group?"

The women all grinned at him and suddenly he didn't want to know.

"You know what, never mind." Travis sipped his latte and checked his watch. "We should get going."

Luke nodded and looked to Grace. "Another two days without you. Not sure I'll survive."

"How cute are you two?" Rachel admired while sipping from her own cup, watching as if they were her favorite rom com.

"I know," Grace admitted to Luke, "I'll–hey–what if you come?"

Everybody looked to Grace then looked around at each other.

As Luke started to shake his head after wavering on the idea Grace cut him off.

"I'm serious. Casey's house is huge. You can come, we'll have dinner together, then you can head to her basement while we have our night upstairs. There are bedrooms for days so everybody will fit."

Aimee and Rachel were perking up at the idea of a dinner with friends surrounding a big table filled with laughter and lots of drinks.

Luke and Travis exchanged a look that said they weren't opposed to the idea. Luke shrugged and said, "We could get a poker game going?"

"We'd need two more. We could see if Chris could make it? He filled in last time and held his own."

"That'd be three. I bet there's more than one schmuck out there who'd be willing to throw away his money." Luke smiled at the thought and nodded.

Travis joined in the nod. "Yeah, I'm in. Let's do it."

Excitement surrounded the table and made Travis not want to leave. He was genuinely looking forward to the weekend. And he'd get to see Casey's house–second house. After glancing at his watch once more, he looked up and told Luke he was heading up.

"Right behind you." Luke said, then lingered as Travis walked out.

"He's so dreamy." Rachel watched Travis leave. "He's got that lean, messy-haired, nerd thing going on. But dresses way better."

Luke laughed deeply, "You better not say that to his face. He tries hard to look like that. He does that to his hair on purpose and picks out those clothes."

"Whatever it is," Aimeé added, "it is working on the man."

"Agreed. I can't wait to see their babies." Rachel sighed.

"Did you say 'babies?'" Luke choked out the words.

Grace simply rubbed his back and let Rachel detail out her dream.

"Yes. They are going to be adorable. Both of them have that coppery, wavy red hair. And their sloping noses. Can you even imagine that on a sweet little baby?" Rachel kept staring toward the door and took another sip of her latte. "Anyway," she pulled her attention back to the table, "Casey will figure it out in due time."

"Figure what out, exactly?"

"That she's in love with Travis." Aimeé finished Rachel's thought.

"Did this all happen when we were dating?" Luke moved a finger between himself and his soon-to-be wife.

"Absolutely," Grace confirmed. "We know what we're talking about honey."

"Should I tell Travis?"

"No," Grace leaned into Luke and sighed, "I think we should let them figure it out themselves. Besides, we'll have a front row seat. Sometimes that's more fun."

CHAPTER 5

Aside from not actually having a boyfriend to parade in front of her coworkers at their upcoming dinner, everything from a work perspective was going well. The Match Me technology team was performing wonderfully, and based on the conversation she just had with Theresa and Andy, the Thomas and Jane platform conversion would be hitch-free. Damn she was good. Or, her teams were, and that made her more proud yet.

Casey stood at her desk and stretched. She deserved a drink. The girls wouldn't be irritated if she started without them. She glanced at the clock. Besides, they would be there within the half hour anyway.

Moving around her desk, Casey eyed the bottles and Lean Pocket wrappers, wondering–were they still considered 'lean' if you had three of them? She shrugged and left the desk with its smattering of garbage. The girls wouldn't judge her, and they most likely wouldn't be back in her office anyway.

On the way down to the bar and wine cellar Casey felt her phone vibrate in her back pocket. She paused mid-step as she read *Linette Whitley* on the screen.

"Over my dead body," Casey muttered as she declined the call and shoved the phone back into her pocket.

"Now," she said, shaking off the irritation of her mom's third call of the day by wiggling her body, "what shall we have to drink?"

The bar wall was lined with every whiskey, bourbon, tequila, and vodka imaginable. The glass-paneled fridges that sat below the counter provided lemons, limes, juices, and a variety of sodas that would mix up any drink order imaginable.

For tonight she thought, as she slid to her right, positioning herself directly in front of a stone cellar: wine. A nice, heavy red. She was ready for spring, but seeing as her mid-week attitude had changed, she could savor one more bottle of Pinot Noir.

Casey stood over her counter in the kitchen after she moved four bottles up the stairs and savored her first sip. As she did the doorbell rang and a hammering of knocks pounded on the door while excited voices sang out to let them in.

Smiling, she set her glass down and moved toward the door. As she did the voices grew louder and she felt a little bit more in love with her girlfriends. This was going to be a much needed weekend–a relaxing woman retreat.

Casey swung the door open and watched as her friends threw their bottle and bag-filled hands in the air. She grinned slyly, nodded, and was about to join in when she saw them.

It was a line of handsome men, walking up the path to her door like they were walking slow motion in an action movie. All of them sleek and handsome, their chiseled faces talking and laughing at each other as they sauntered up. All of them finding themselves completely hilarious. And all of them completely uninvited.

"No." Casey took a step backward and closed the door leaving everybody on the outside, then stared at the wood panels from the inside.

She heard the pleading begin but the words were muffled by the door and the image of Travis she'd just seen that was now frozen in her mind.

Casey had successfully managed, and carefully dodged every attempt a man had made toward her over the years. When she did allow it, it was on her terms, and usually because she knew after one night–if he even made it until the next morning–she'd never want to see him again.

Travis was different.

Travis was persistent.

Though claiming he had been a victim of a bad breakup he seemed awfully eager to pursue her. Except, he was patient too, and willing to wait for her to come around. That was the hard part. It wasn't easy to stay uninterested in an intelligent, sexy man, who thought you were equally as intelligent, funny, and even more sexy.

"Come on, Case."

Casey listened to Grace's plead from the other side of the door and leaned her forehead on the hard surface.

"I promise it will be fun. And we are banishing them to the basement after dinner. It's still a girls night."

"Men are bad. Bad juju." Casey rolled her head on the door, shaking it without raising it.

"Men are wonderful juju." Aimeé combated her argument.

"There aren't enough rooms, I have more friends coming to stay."

"We are your only friends." Rachel said through a giggle.

"My friends wouldn't bring…" she was going to say Travis but decided that made it a little too personal, *"them."*

Silence bounced back and forth from one side of the door to the other. Then she heard his voice.

"I brought you a 2015 David Ramey." Travis' voice was even with just a hint of dangling a carrot in front of a donkey.

He was going to make her an ass, she thought. But his words forced her head from the door. How did he know the Russian River Valley red was her favorite?

Now she had a decision to make. Did she want the wine more than she *didn't* want the rusty red of Travis' hair and the impossible blue of his eyes in her home? They would undoubtedly try to catch her gaze most of the night. And she had her so-called friends to thank. They must have invited the men, and told Travis how he could win her over. They anticipated her reaction, and they were right.

Stupid.

Casey backed away and opened the door, but didn't move aside. She eyed Travis who was holding up the bottle with "RAMEY" neatly printed across the label.

When she looked to Rachel, then to William, and back to Rachel her eyes narrowed and wondered how they got Rachel to agree to sharing a weekend with William, Grace's brother?

Rachel grinned slyly and William smiled without showing his teeth–something Casey would have to ask about later. Because sure enough, the wine won.

Casey held out her hand for the wine. When Travis released the bottle to her his look was disturbingly charming.

She was going to need this entire bottle to herself, plus finish the one she opened if she was going to make it through the evening. Then she stepped aside and let her friends, and their male counterparts, move in.

The women headed straight to the kitchen to join Casey in her Friday wine, and the men paused to take in the extravagant home.

Having already baffled in the extravagance of the home, the women served as sous chefs to Aimeé, slicing beautiful rounds of vegetables for the Ratatouille that would serve as the main course. It would be served after the soupe à l'oignon. It was the perfect menu to warm their bodies from the outside chill, and just fresh enough to feel like spring.

The men followed William around the house. The tour was his responsibility as the women were drinking and he was the only one of the men who'd been there before.

The upstairs bedroom floors were informal and quickly navigated. It was impressive and appreciated by the large bodies, but they were bedrooms. Mostly people just slept there like they would any other bedroom they'd ever been in.

As William brought the herd back to the main floor he heard Casey yell for him to stop. She ran by the men who stood still and watched her with only the movement of their heads. All of them sending her questioning looks, except for Travis, who's face held a hint of amusement.

Inside her office Casey looked around at the mess. She looked at the garbage can that was already overflowing. Wheeling around the desk she pulled open the drawers, and briefly looked around for any more favorable options. Finding none she swept the empty bottles and Lean Cuisine wrappers into her drawers. She straightened her desk, then herself, just as the guys walked in.

"We aren't interrupting anything," Travis' words laughed as they came out, "are we?"

"No," Casey said, quickly diverting her eyes so she wouldn't have to look at him and hold the lie, "I just had…"

Casey looked at her screens and quickly brought up the screen savers to block the content. She stole a look at Christopher, whose eyes had been locked on them.

"I had to make sure there wasn't any sensitive material laying around." Casey shrugged. "You know, burden of wearing so many hats."

She forced her body to relax to one side as she placed casual hand on her hip for effect. Her left hand found the desk as she attempted to lean, instead finding a piece of paper that slid out from beneath her causing her to catch herself and reposition.

Casey smiled once she regained her balance and strode out between the men, not missing the spiced scent of Travis' cologne.

"Damn it. Damn him. Shit, damn, shit." Casey stalked into the kitchen swearing. Not one of the girls lifted their heads to acknowledge her tantrum. "Hello! I'm irritated here."

Aimee stood over a Dutch oven of buttery, caramelizing onions, and sang, "We know, sweet. We figured you would be."

The steely look Casey shot over the pan held until Grace cut in.

"But," Grace started, looking first to Aimeé trying not to be amused at either woman, then to Casey, "this will be fun. To have a full group for dinner. Everybody having fun, laughing, eating, and drinking together. Why would you have such a long, beautiful table in here, just to have it sit empty?"

Casey considered it a low blow. She was certain Grace thought it was a savvy business move. One point for Grace.

"Why aren't you saying anything?" Casey looked to Rachel. "You do realize William is here? You know, long lost lover who you swore you would never forgive? How come you're fine?"

Rachel tried not to let the sting of Casey's words cut too deeply as she considered the source–who was usually insensitive toward matters of the heart–and the fact that she was forcing herself to learn to live with the fact that she would always love William, they would just never be together. And she had used their history to get a little something out of his coming here for herself.

"I'm fine because I agreed it would be okay for him to come as long as he split his winnings with me." Rachel went back to slicing carrots when the three women smiled.

They knew William would win, and so did Rachel. The poor men who would sit at the poker table with him tonight had no idea.

Casey's mood lifted a bit when she thought about William taking a bit of Travis' hard earned money. It might take the edge off of his overly confident allure. Parting with money was one thing, taking a hit to manly pride and ego was another entirely.

"Okay," Casey conceded, "dinner only. Then they are banished to the basement."

Aimeé's red lips curved as she stirred, and Grace came around to hand Casey her glass of wine and place a kiss on the side of her cheek.

"We knew you'd come around." Grace hugged Casey with one arm then turned at the sound of the tour coming back toward the kitchen.

Casey took a sip of her wine and savored the flavors as she slowly inhaled and swallowed. When the men were out of earshot she asked the question she'd been wondering since her guests arrived. "I want to know who told Travis the 2015 Ramey is my favorite?"

When the three women looked up and stopped what they were doing, they stared. They exchanged looks from one to the other, and not one of them spoke.

"Aimeé?" Casey targeted the French connoisseur first.

"I did not. Grace?" Aimeé continued the inquisition, now curious herself.

Grace shook her head and added, "No, I didn't even think of it. I wish I would have though. Rach must have done it."

"Don't look at me. I was surrounded by hellish children all day. I didn't have time to make sure *Mrs. In Denial* over here got her favorite wine." Rachel sipped away her hectic day, thankful for the weekend and added, "But it is divine."

"You must have told him in passing without realizing it," Grace concluded, using practicality to get Casey to linger on the thought.

"Yeah, probably," Casey added, knowing she hadn't said a word about it.

William walked the men to the basement door without a sound or a notion toward the women who stared back at them. He opened the door, turned and said, "I hope you're ready for this." Then made his way down the stairs and the single-file line followed him.

The basement wasn't so much a basement as it was an adult playground and haven.

"Holy sh–"

"The house used to belong to a Viking's player."

William cut Travis off. Though, the news the house was once lived in by an NFL football player might get the same reaction.

The men's eyes began at the bar and cellar wall Casey had been standing next to only moments earlier. They trailed across the long dark walls that held large framed glass doors that led out to the back patio with a view of the lake.

The lake, Travis thought, as he moved toward the view. As he moved he passed an elegant pool table and a dart board framed by large wooden doors that would hide it away when it wasn't in use. A poker table sat in the middle of the room with a hanging lantern light directly above it. He circled it once, not touching, but staring at the deep wooden tones and suddenly couldn't wait to be sitting at it with a beer or good whiskey.

He kept walking the length of the room and moved around a large couch that was facing the biggest screen he'd ever seen–if you don't count the movie theater. But who would need one of those if you had a place like this in your basement?

Travis walked a bit farther, wondering how much square footage the house actually had, and came upon three doors. The one straight in front of him was a bathroom that was nicer than most of the apartments he'd ever lived in, and on either side of the bathroom were two bedrooms fully outfitted with a bed and a furniture set.

He guessed if he drank himself into oblivion at least he wouldn't have to worry about climbing the stairs again.

"Well I'll be damned."

Travis heard Luke's voice come from a room behind him, then watched Christopher follow the sound.

"Wow." Christopher's word was short appropriately stunned.

Just as long and wide as the lake side of the basement, was the street side of the basement. And it was a complete home gym with monitors lining the walls in front of the cardio equipment, and mirrors lining the walls holding the free weights and strength equipment.

Travis didn't know why the thought crept in, but suddenly he wanted to know how Casey would have found out about the house. Did she *know* the player? Did they have a relationship? Just what kind of a woman was he trying to pursue?

Pursue. Travis almost laughed out loud at himself. That was a poor version of the truth. Ex-pro football player relationships or not, he had fallen for Casey the moment he saw her. It was taking longer than expected to get her to come around, but he'd get her there, he just needed to find the right time to get her to take a chance on him.

William followed the men out of the workout room, all of them silent until he spoke, "If Aimeé wasn't making our dinner, I would stay down here, drink my dinner, and get the game started. I find it's better on my friends when I take their money quickly and swiftly."

The guys laughed and Luke responded, "Is that any way to treat your new brother-in-law?"

"As far as I'm concerned, there's a ring on it. You're not going anywhere so you're fair game. These guys," William motioned to Travis and Christopher, "I'll go easy on them at first, but only to make the loss more painful."

"Who's idea was it to invite him?" Travis asked Christopher, ignoring the other two.

"I don't know. But if he plays like the two of you, I don't even know why I'm here. I should leave my money at the bottom of the stairs and drink with the women."

—

Casey had tried to be irritated but as she and her friends lounged in the living room next to the kitchen, sipping on their wine and listening to the stories of their weeks, she couldn't help but enjoy it.

Everything was as it should be, she thought. Just her and the girls, and the heavenly scents wafting in from the kitchen joining them in their conversation.

When the hearty male laughter had come from the stairs she winced, but tried to curb her cynical nature from taking over. It was just one night, she reminded herself. So she sipped her favorite wine to assist in the reminder until dinner.

When they finally gathered around the table, laughing and enjoying their drinks, she couldn't deny the joyful feeling of having the table surrounded–of being surrounded–by fun and loving people. Her friends, of course, but the guys too.

Luke had settled in as one of their own. It was easy to love him. Anybody who treated a friend with the kind of doting and care he gave to Grace was worth the exception and acceptance in Casey's book. And he had become fast friends with William, which was saying something. It wasn't hard to be liked by Grace's brother, but respect was earned, and so far it seemed as if William had it for Luke.

Casey let her eyes wander the table and smiled when they paused on Christopher. A goofball for sure, but she and Grace had known that since elementary and high school. Maybe that's why it was so easy for her to like him. Typically she didn't trust men or their intentions. But she had known Christopher so long, it somehow seemed okay. That and you'd have to be blind to miss the way he watched over Aimeé, seemingly trying to protect her. That, too, was a relief. Especially after digging into Aimeé's financials. Because she'd have to tread lightly, she was happy Aimeé had somebody like Christopher around.

When Casey's eyes met Rachel's, Rachel tipped her head to the side and offered a sweet smile in return. It was a question if everything was okay. Casey grinned and gave a small nod.

How was it Rachel could sit here, caring for Casey, when it must have been agonizing to be next to the one man she'd ever truly loved, knowing she couldn't ever show it? Never be able to follow through?

But, Casey thought, that's how love was, wasn't it? It was all-consuming and heartbreaking. It willed you and allowed you to give everything and all of yourself to a single person. And in that giving you put all of your hope and faith in another person.

That's where things went wrong.

You started to have expectations. Expectations that they would care for you as you would care for them. And when they failed to do that, disappointment started to set in. And because you are closer to this person than any other person, you aren't afraid of telling them about your disappointment. And they start to believe they are failing. Slowly the feeling of failure is shared between the two. Resentments bubble up and grow, and before you know it two people who were once completely in love are looking for any way to get out and save themselves from the overwhelming hurt of being let down or not being enough.

Rachel was stronger than anybody gave her credit for. She was hurt, but she'd healed herself and wouldn't allow for it to happen again. She tried for love, sure. She was an avid believer in romance and love. She said it was because she wanted the ultimate love, but she always made sure to end every relationship before she got too close.

Finally, unable to ignore the stare she felt burning into her skin, she continued her trail down the table, and locked eyes with Travis.

Casey narrowed her eyes and scowled, as if he was the sole reason the men had ruined her evening and weekend.

When he shot her a calm and handsome, gentle smile, it rocked her. He raised his glass of wine and mouthed *thank you for dinner.*

Holding eye contact but relaxing her face instinctively–definitely not by choice–Casey nodded once in response, and held her gaze. Their locked eyes didn't bother her, but the kind way he looked upon her forced her mind to wander and sent her into unwanted, and uncharted territories.

Casey noticed, when Travis wasn't smiling, the lines that crowed next to his eyes left small lines, matching the long creases caused by a grin. Rusty red stubble made the usually smooth face look rugged, but she'd noticed that before. Every Friday Travis took a break from his polished look and took on a rougher, weekend image.

His face wasn't long and lean like his friend Luke's, but strong and square. Hazel eyes that looked almost amber in the evening dinner glow brightened the face that sat beneath burnt, copper hair. It was styled today, Casey noticed the messy strands leaning to the right and just slightly up. It surprised her to find somebody she so adamantly refused and turned down to be so physically appealing.

Travis felt comfortable with Casey's stare. He figured he'd let her look as long as she wanted. When she was looking, she was thinking–analyzing. It was one of the first things he noticed about her. She held a look, a gaze, and her mind fired. He supposed it's what made her maneuver so quickly around a computer. He wondered what her mind was navigating now.

"I do not want you lovely men to feel I am removing you from the table…" Aimeé paused and thought on her words while swirling the wine in her glass. "No," she corrected, "I am certainly removing you from the table. We have wine to drink and words to share. And you," Aimeé gracefully wanded her finger back and forth from Luke, Travis, and Christopher, "have money to give to William."

The men acted out their defensiveness with agonizing sounds and desperate words, playfully begging Aimeé not to force them to leave to go drink whiskey and smoke cigars over their favorite game. The women simply laughed and shook their heads.

Aimeé's intended words were the truth, not a joke, but that made Casey's laugh and the intrusion to her thoughts welcome. Poor guys, she thought now, they didn't realize William had logged long days and nights of play in the U.S. and overseas when he was a young athlete.

His hockey skills brought him to countries near and far, and in them he not only gained recognition for his skills on the ice, but earned a name for himself as a card shark as well. They would all learn soon enough.

The choice to linger over the table with its crowded comfortableness of scattered plates, half-filled glasses of water, and empty stemmed goblets of wine; or to move to the comfort of the living room and sit next to the fire wasn't easy; but they made the choice to move.

Each woman settled comfortably into a corner of the couch, stretching their tired legs or tucking them in, cocooning into the plush cushions. Aimeé set a tray of cheese and crackers on the coffee table between them and opened a new bottle of wine. Even though they had just met the night before, this was different, this was their weekend, and they were set for another round of much needed gossip.

Rachel sped through the chaos of school winding down as summer inched closer, and Aimeé share her plans for The Bistro as it awaited the first sign of spring. Then the patio doors would open and lure more patrons out from their winter hibernation.

Grace and Luke had talked, negotiated, and efficiently planned the next year of their lives together. Starting with the merging of assets. Grace's brownstone won the argument for where they would live, and Grace won the furniture debate–including the furniture that could stay and that which would find its way out of Luke's inventory. Luke's timeline won the argument for when they would get married–a picturesque January wedding at the Depot in downtown Minneapolis.

Casey had tried not to share, but her friends pushed, pressed, and effectively trapped her between a rock and a hard place.

"I couldn't tell them." Casey slouched into the couch and buried her face with a nearby pillow. "Carrie," Casey whined out her peppy co-workers' name, "is leading the charge with her marketing pets who are running an advertising campaign featuring the company's creator. I just found out today."

Rachel stifled a snort. "Ah, I hate to break it to you, but *you* are the company's creator."

"I know." The flat words drew laughs out of her friends. "It's featuring me *and* my boyfriend."

"I think you still don't have one of those." Grace sipped and grinned.

"Just go onto your internet and match yourself. Or, I can give you the names of men I know." Aimee waved off the difficulty of finding a boyfriend like you would a butterfly from a flower. Her delicate hand wafting the air.

"I'm assuming you've slept with all of them?"

Aimee peered at Casey over the rim of her glass, "Of course. I save their numbers in my phone with a description of what they look like so I can remember them. Would you like to take a look?"

"God no!" Casey shook her head. "For more than one reason do I *not* want to look at your phone. And I can't match myself."

"That is your choice."

"Why can't you match yourself?" Rachel looked confused.

"Because, they'll see it. Or at least there would be the potential for somebody to see it. They'd know it wasn't my boyfriend–or at least not long term. And before you ask, yes, people in technology do that kind of thing. Because they can."

Casey looked up, thought, nodded, "*I* would do that. I would absolutely dig to find the dirt if somebody else were in my predicament." She'd done just that today, trying to find information on Carrie.

"You're all nuts," Rachel shook her head at the endless need for her friend to obtain information. She was happy living in her middle school world where the only thing that changed was the way you taught. Thinking up new, innovative ways to get kids to learn was hard enough. Thank goodness the information usually tended to stay the same.

"So, what will you do?"

Aimee was intrigued, and the feeling was shared between them as they stared at Casey. The one friend who had sworn off men and relationships needed one, and she needed it to appear to be a happy one. In Casey's case, the latter might be the hardest part.

CHAPTER 6

William proudly handed Rachel five-hundred dollars and received a tipsy kiss on his angled jawline. He had been drinking–for six solid hours, he noted as he checked his watch–but there wasn't any amount of drunk he could have been that would have kept his heart from suffocating knowing the kiss meant nothing to Rachel. He saw Casey study his reaction so he quickly perked up to hide the hurt.

"Not a bad night all around, don't you think?" William asked while swinging an arm around Travis' shoulder.

"I don't really think I want to talk about it."

The women laughed as they watched two more fallen heads walk toward the fire pit, both dejected and confused.

Luke's shameful eyes looked at Grace and said nothing.

"That bad, huh?" Grace tried to be sympathetic, though the wine was making it hard.

"After an hour we stopped trying to win and shot for who could last the longest."

"And?" Casey was curious.

"As far as losers go," Travis cut in, "I'm the best."

Casey couldn't help the slow smile that crept across her face. A great dinner, an even better wine and gossip session, and William had taken Travis to the cleaners. This weekend wasn't shaping up to be that bad.

"Well, how about some sore loser s'mores?" Casey offered, gesturing to the tray Aimeé had thrown together. The presentations of the basic grahams, chocolates, and marshmallows cascading throughout the tray could have been featured in the latest Martha Stewart catalog.

"Don't mind if I do." Travis moved to the tray, swiping a stick and a mallow, then stole a spot on the outdoor cushion next to Casey before she could object.

He shifted the faux fur blanket so both of their bodies were tucked beneath it, and Casey's pulled up feet were nestled into his thigh.

It was intentional, his closeness. If she moved her friends would notice. And she wouldn't want to draw the attention.

"Really?" Casey whispered out of the side of her mouth. "The five feet on the other side of you wasn't enough room?"

Casey's eyes zeroed in on Travis' profile and watched his lip twitch in response. The shadows of the night and flame of the fire added a playful flicker in his eye.

Travis turned and held Casey's gaze, surprising her into silence.

"Rather than forcing yourself to be irritated," Travis said as his thumb slowly brushed away a graham cracker crumb from the crease of her lip, "why don't you let yourself enjoy the moment for a change?"

His voice was already a whisper, what came next was softer, but deeper somehow.

"Let yourself *feel*."

Casey stared, unable react to the tenderness of the delicate suggestion. When Travis laid a hand on her feet that were resting at his side it pulled her thoughts away. She watched his hand and felt as the warmth seeped through the blanket. The pressure comforted rather than agitated.

When Travis turned his attention back to the fire and moved his hand to continue roasting his marshmallow, Casey closed her lids and noticed the absence of his hand.

It was so simple, his actions, but it was the first time a man had comforted without pressing or wanting something in return: a drink, a date, a commitment. It was the first time, she realized, she wanted to feel a man's warmth again.

No, she thought, not a man's, *Travis'*.

CHAPTER 7

Casey would have slept in. She would have rolled to a fresh fluff of pillow and cuddled into the cool sheets. The time would have drifted past nine and she would have savored the early morning dreams that often found her while slipping in and out of sleep.

But this weekend her house was filled with friends. Friends who *thought* they were quiet. But since ten minutes to six that morning she'd heard soft voices echoing throughout the halls, the coffee pot gurgling, and coffee mugs clinking.

At seven, Casey reluctantly gave up the fight for more sleep, and threw the covers off while giving a little kick and a stretch in rebellion against the cold. She slid sweatpants over her long underwear, and wrapped a Sherpa robe around her body, holding it close to her chin as she moved out of her room.

A click from the door next to hers had her turning to see who else's sleep was disturbed. When she saw Travis in his own pair of sweats and pulling a t-shirt over his bare torso she stared at the trim body.

He walked by her with his tired eyes drooping, then stopped and turned.

"Huh," Travis huffed out the sleepy sound, "still pretty even under all of that fluff." Then he continued down the stairs toward the morning clatter.

Casey stared after him trying to process his early morning analysis and was still gaping as William came out of another door and walked toward her.

"Hey Case, morning," William said as he wrapped a single arm around her shoulder and planted a peck on her forehead. "Coffee will help."

The exchanges couldn't have been more different.

William offered a touch and a kiss, and she felt the brotherly embrace as she had thousands of times before. Travis hadn't touched or lingered, but his easy words caused her heart to race, then thud as she forced it to slow.

"No," Casey said to herself as she shook her head and fought the idea that had been nagging at her mind since the night before. The terrible thought that lingered as she and her friends surrounded the fire pit late into the night.

As she grew comfortable with Travis nestled close to her on the outdoor sofa, and as they laughed and exchanged jokes and drinks, the idea that she could ask Travis to be her stand-in boyfriend had crossed her mind.

The longer the night went on, the longer she tried to fight the idea. But with every denial, Travis displayed a touch, a mannerism, or a witty remark that drew her in again.

The way he held eye contact with the person he was addressing and didn't look away until they no longer required his attention. The way he thought carefully about the words he chose, but let his laughs come easily. Or the way he would shift the drink in his hands to help with a s'more or to rest his hand on Casey's legs as one or the other led the conversation.

Casey watched him now from the top of the stairs, clearly tired, but interacting with the others with the same care and respect as he had the night before. He handed Rachel a refilled mug of coffee and shook William's hand as he was greeted and welcomed into the brood of morning.

He was easy, she thought. It was almost enviable, the comfortable way he interacted. That would be another huge benefit if she were to ask him to act as her long-time boyfriend.

She watched Travis bite into a chocolate croissant Aimeé had packaged and brought with her for the weekend. His savoring the buttery bite didn't give her time to resist the thought about him being a good stand-in. When Aimeé threw her head back and laughed her eye caught Casey looking on.

"Casey!" Aimeé's French sang up to her, "Come down. We have coffee and pâtisserie."

How could she say no to that invitation? She wouldn't be able to spy, but seeing as she had been studying only Travis, it wasn't a bad idea.

"Seeing as I'm not getting my beauty sleep with all you crazy morning people around, I suppose I deserve coffee and carbs."

"That's my girl." Grace smiled and patted the island chair next to hers.

Casey looked Grace and Luke up and down. "Why are you dressed?"

"Luke and I went for a walk this morning."

For a moment Casey didn't say anything, just stared blankly.

"I should make both of you leave. That's disgusting."

"I'll help." Travis sipped his own mug of steaming coffee and lazily walked to the breakfast nook and fell into a padded chair that had a view of the lake.

"Who would help Aimeé make you brunch if we left?"

Casey didn't want to show interest but her auburn brow arched slightly at the idea of brunch.

"Go on," She said inquisitively while sliding her attention to Aimeé.

"I think we will have a Croque Madam with a parmesan and lemon salad."

"Add breakfast potatoes and I'll let them stay."

"For you," Aimeé glided over and placed a kiss on the side of Casey's cheek–much like the brotherly peck William had offered–and finished, "anything."

—

"Are you still on a sex hiatus?" Casey asked Rachel as she finished the last of her second mimosa.

"It's before eleven on a Saturday. It's only been three full days." Rachel answered with disapproval of the topic so early on in the weekend–and the fact that she had just shared her sex hiatus idea on Thursday.

"And?" Aimeé pressed, knowing how quickly a woman could change her mind, and the right man could help. She wondered if Rachel had ever thought about what it would be like to sleep with William. Their relationship had been full of love, but also young and innocent.

Rachel sighed, "Yes, I am. And I only wavered once Friday afternoon when the kids were driving me to insanity and I was craving a dark place to drink wine." Rachel sipped her own orange juice and champagne. "So naturally my mind drifted to Morello or the Meritage. And with it came blissful memories of sexy dates that led to sexy nights.

But I held strong." Rachel straightened to show her resolve. "Then I drove here instead."

"Well," Grace joked and raised her glass, "we are a close second to sex."

"Coming from the one of us who probably embarked on that journey last night." Rachel's words sounded more like an accusation than a compliment.

"As a matter of fact, I took a *wonderful* journey last night." Grace grinned and received praise from Aimeé.

"Of course you did." Casey grimaced out of jealousy and the ease Grace would have in finding sex for the rest of her life–and from the troubling way her mind drifted to Travis, wondering what it would be like to take that journey with him.

"What is it?" Rachel abruptly stopped Casey's thoughts as her finger pointed directly between her eyes. "You have that look."

"I do not have *that look.*" Casey tried to defend herself. "I don't even know what *that look* is."

"She does!" Aimeé agreed.

"Might as well let it out now." Grace's smile grew beyond her sex-induced happiness at knowing Casey better than she knew herself.

"I don't know what you're talking about."

"You're scowling and staring."

"I always scowl."

"No, you furrow. This is a scowl. And you're thinking." Rachel went on. "Tell us, now."

"Where did the guys go?" Casey asked, wondering if they were within earshot.

"The basement, they can't hear." Grace read her mind.

Casey pouted and leaned back knowing it was either give them what they wanted or never hear the end of it.

"I'm thinking–no, not even thinking–I accidentally let a thought weasel its way into my mind."

"About?" Rachel edged closer to the table, making up for the distance Casey put between them.

"It was the circumstance. And," Casey agreed as her mind raced, "it would have happened with anybody in the moment."

Aimeé refilled Casey's empty glass and encouraged as bubbles nearly toppled over the rim. "You will have to elaborate."

"Last night. At the fire." Casey sipped. "Travis didn't bug me."

"I *knew* it was about Travis!" Rachel cheered.

"Okay, see, this is why I can't tell you things."

"Come *on,*" Rachel pleaded, "just keep going. You're doing so well."

Casey felt like a spectacle.

"So I let the idea of Travis being my stand-in boyfriend jump into my head. But it left just as quickly." The last part might have been a lie but they would already bombard her with questions.

Casey sat and waited.

When nothing happened and silence filled the room, she looked from one pretty staring face to another.

"What?" she asked blandly, irked when she didn't get the whooping, irrational response she expected.

Aimeé, Grace, and Rachel shared looks before they nodded in agreement that Aimeé would take the lead. Rachel was too much of a romantic, and Grace was mushy in love with Luke while she prepared for wedded bliss. Aimeé would get straight to the point and not sugarcoat it.

"We are surprised you would consider Travis."

"Why?" Casey asked, sounding less stern and more aggravated.

"Because you like him."

"Isn't that the idea?" Casey rolled her eyes.

Grace cut in, "Case, you don't usually date or do anything like it with anybody you actually *like.* Why Travis?"

"It's not real. I would be using him for a limited amount of time. And it would be easier to hide the fact that we aren't actually together if I was pretending to be in love with a man who I don't mind. And I already know a little about him."

"Whoa." Rachel took a gulp.

"Okay, this is over," Casey said while pushing herself away from the table, "no more Travis talk. Let's go shopping."

"Shopping!" Rachel sang as she backed away from the table and left the room to change.

"Clever girl." Aimeé winked at Casey as she began clearing the food and dishes away from the table.

Casey offered a sly smile. "It gets her every time. And you two," she moved a finger back and forth between Grace and Aimeé, "no more talk of this. I have things to think about and can't have you softies muddling my brain. It's taken years to become this cynical and I won't have you ruining it."

Grace and Aimeé watched Casey follow Rachel up the stairs to do her own version of getting ready for the day.

"She will do it," Aimeé said without looking at Grace.

"She's desperate."

"She's in love."

The two shared a look and said together, "But she doesn't want to be."

CHAPTER 8

The Bistro could have been crawling with people or completely empty, Casey wouldn't have noticed. Given it was Monday morning and everybody was treating themselves to a coffee to start their week, she scrolled through the next four months of her life on her laptop calendar–from March straight through June–without even the slightest idea she wasn't alone.

In one month she would need to flaunt her boyfriend while she hosted her collogues for dinner.

"This is a terrible idea," Casey muttered to herself as she scrolled up again, "nobody in their right mind would do this."

Nobody in their right mind.

She had to be crazy to even *consider* doing this. But there was just no time. And, she admitted, there was nobody from her past that she would want to call because like the girls said, she had never been with anybody she liked. It was easier to not commit.

"Has it changed?" Aimeé asked when she brought Casey a lavender latte to go.

"No," Casey tugged at the paper cup, "it's still going to be roughly eighty days of hell."

"And, have you decided what to do?"

Casey stared at the dwindling March days.

"I'm going to need another latte to go."

CHAPTER 9

Travis Mavens was a lot of things, and smart topped the list. On the rare occasion he found somebody he thought could hold their own in a room with him, he jumped at the chance to collaborate. So when Casey walked into Travis' office and stared, it was no surprise to her that Travis and Seth had their heads down working on the Thomas and Jane acquisition. Probably reviewing budget reports, and how the actuals were doing compared to what they forecasted.

Casey stood in the doorway as the two talked, pointed, nodded, and smiled when their brilliancy aligned.

She was already uncomfortable seeing as she thought she would dress up and wear heels with her pretty camel colored blouse and curve-accentuating straight trousers. When she shifted to alleviate the discomfort the two men looked up and stared. That's when the discomfort peaked.

"Not a good idea," Casey said, and turned to walk back out the door with both lattes in hand.

"Weird," Seth said, not thinking anything of it until he glanced over and saw Travis' ambitious grin. Then he shook his head, "I can pretty much guarantee that's not a good idea."

"Yeah," Travis said as he pushed up from his desk to follow Casey, "probably not."

Seth watched Travis slowly meander toward the open door of Casey's office where she retreated after her awkward departure. He supposed for Casey it wasn't that awkward considering she never seemed to mind what people thought of her. But that still didn't mean Travis following her was a good idea. Office romances–at least in his case–didn't work out. They were humiliating, actually.

Travis heard Casey mumbling to herself as he peered around the opening of her office and was pleased with the view. He noticed the heels that made a rare appearance and the cute way she wobbled in them, unfamiliar with the height and pointy edge.

She made an effort today, he thought, but nothing would make her stray from the perfected round mound that sat on top of her head, causing him to smile even wider.

Glancing at her desk he noticed the two coffee cups still steaming and wondered, "I don't suppose that one is for me?"

Casey turned, then followed Travis' eyes to the cups on her desk. Without commenting she picked up one of the lattes and shoved it in Travis' direction. He casually took the offering.

"What's this for?" he asked, then took a sip. When he did his amused brows rose. "Dark chocolate. Extra shot. My favorite. It must be important."

"What must be important?" Casey was irritated her plan hadn't gone according to...plan. And something told her the edge in her voice wasn't from Seth's untimely meeting with Travis. She didn't anticipate she would lose her resolve from the elevator to Travis' door.

"Whatever it is you want."

Casey let the whirlwind of thoughts race through her head: How attractive Travis was in his fitted navy blue suit. The smug way he knew she needed something from him. The consequences of not just getting it over with and asking him to be her short term boyfriend the first time around.

"Bribery," Casey said, receiving an inquisitive look in response.

"I'm listening."

Casey turned a circle on her toes to face Travis head-on, and was thankful when the onset of a cramp eased itself out of her calf.

"I need you to be my boyfriend for a few months."

The surprise that showed on Travis' face cut into the embarrassment slightly. But when she noticed the commotion in the doorway and saw Luke and Seth looking on, experiencing the same shock as Travis, it was too much.

Casey let out a groan that matched her eyeroll and said, "Oh, come on."

"Why?"

Travis' question surprised her.

"Because you like me."

"How do you know that?"

"You hired me."

"No."

"You knowingly paid me too much to get me here."

"Not as much as you're worth."

It was Casey's turn to be surprised. The pause allowed their audience to give their swinging heads a rest from ping-ponging back and forth between the two.

"Just, never mind." Casey held up her hands.

"What's it for?"

Travis stole a look a look at the door and saw Luke nodding with a grin and Seth shaking his head in warning.

"It's for work."

Casey's voice brought Travis' attention back to her. When he just stared in response, her frustration grew.

"Yeah, bad idea. Just get out." Casey unsteadily walked toward them shooing them back into the hall, all of them bumping into one another. "Out, out. All of you."

When they were out Casey closed the door and leaned against it, relishing the quiet and the solitude. It was bad, she thought, but not altogether the worst it could have gone. She supposed the irritating way he knew what she was doing allowed her to get irked rather than embarrassed.

Casey pulled off the heels where she stood and flung them toward her bag, then walked around her desk to pick up her coffee and turn on her laptop. She needed to work up another plan.

—

"You like her," Luke said as he followed Travis back into his office.

"Obviously." Travis had since he hired her, and though he wasn't paying Casey enough for all the improvements and the work she'd done so far, he did pay her more than they budgeted to get her to commit.

"Then why not agree to it?"

"Not like this." Travis looked up.

"What could it hurt to spend a little time with her?"

Luke was never one to back down from an opportunity. Usually they worked. He and Grace had even hit a rocky road, but eventually that worked itself out too.

"Not as a favor, or a job."

"Then make it seem like you're getting something out of it, too–aside from getting the chance to make her see how much she likes you." Luke leaned against the door jam, not willing to give up.

"I don't like where this is going." Travis folded his arms in defense.

Luke smiled, "She needs a boyfriend, and you need a place to stay. Seems to me this could be a little business deal that benefits both of you."

"That's something you would do, not me."

"Things seemed to work out pretty well for me."

"You're obnoxious." Travis was still objecting but he hadn't sat down at his desk yet.

"I'd get a timeline."

"Out." Travis pointed toward the door.

"You're starting to sound more like each other already." Luke grinned and took a step backward to ward off another verbal instruction. He held up his hands as Travis started to speak and slid behind the wall and out of sight.

Slowly walking toward his door, Travis didn't intend to mimic the actions of the woman who had intrigued him from the moment he saw her, but he closed his door. He stood behind it and shoved his hands in his pockets and thought, this *is* a really bad idea.

CHAPTER 10

Like he would analyze anything else, Travis spent the night weighing the pros and cons of accepting Casey's proposal.

The pros: he would get to spend more time with Casey outside of work–they'd be forced to. He would learn more about her and why she was adamant about avoiding relationships and marriage. He would, if he got his part of the bargain, get to live in one of two awesome properties.

The bad? Travis stopped at an intersection and sipped the black coffee out of his steaming travel mug and adjusted the strap on his leather workbag. The bad would be he would fall for her more than he already had and she...well, she wouldn't.

He slowly crept up the stairs at his new temporary home in the Thomas and Jane building. Grinning, he recalled their interaction from the day before. Casey in her heels, worn for confidence, and prepared for battle. She probably hated that she'd slid them on that morning.

When he pulled the door open he heard the ragged and comforting voice of Maggie–the second woman he'd fallen in love with since the acquisition.

"I've seen that smile twice before." She waddled around her desk with her back to him then turned and took her seat. "Once when I fell in love with my Fred, and the second time when Grace walked in after bumping into Luke. Want to tell me what yours is for?"

Travis kept walking but let Maggie see his grin. "Not particularly."

He felt Maggie's eyes follow him to his office. Before he walked in he heard, "Casey will be in at nine. She has another matter at eight she needs to tend to before work today."

The chuckle Travis gave as he walked into his office was low and throaty. Yup, he thought, he loved her. Any woman who knew him that well was worth it.

The hour went by quickly. Most would have felt like it dragged on, but Travis preferred keeping his mind engaged and occupied with work while he waited for the tell-tale sound of Casey's thick, square-heeled shoes. When he heard them, he looked up from a spreadsheet that most wouldn't have been able to navigate, and stood.

As he exited his office he let his eyes drift to Maggie who only offered a wrinkled brow as acknowledgement that she saw him—without actually looking up, he noted.

The first thing Travis noticed when he stood watching Casey was the tiny earbuds poking out from behind a stray curl that had fallen from her bun. She walked in, he thought, so she must be staying downtown this week. And she was on a call. Her face was hard, thinking, and her head was slightly nodding as whoever was on the phone spoke. Rather than pick up stray bottles from her desk, he watched her lean over the top and move all of them to the edge with the long swipe of her arm.

Travis had to smother a laugh with his hand to ensure he could continue his study without Casey noticing, and without disturbing her call. He watched as she docked her laptop and powered it on, then typed ferociously with her fingers flying over the keys. New windows sprung to life on her monitors and black screens with white text he would never understand scrolled upwards at a rapid pace, Casey obviously keeping up with their meaning.

She was fascinating. Her manicured brows furrowed only slightly as she concentrated, leaving the rest of her freckled, pale skin unblemished. It forced him to wonder what her morning routine consisted of. As he looked on, it didn't seem as though she required one. Her cheeks were lightly blushed and her lashes darkened slightly. He mused at the soft way her favorite Chapstick glossed her lips and thought, if somebody were to look at the soft, clean face, and the pretty twisted bun, they would have no idea Casey was a hard-nosed, combative pessimist, with a clever wit that could make even the most stubborn lift their lip.

There was one thing, though, he knew other men hadn't seen. Beneath the hard mind, and the simple, fresh exterior, there was a beautiful woman who loved harder than anybody he'd known. How could a woman who gained the support and love of three clever, smart, and funny women, not love? It wasn't possible.

Where her family lacked–or so he'd heard–she'd built unbreakable friendships in its place. Where honesty and commitment were missing in her life, she created a website dedicated to matching potential lovers together using an algorithm that essentially promised people they wouldn't be hurt. That, he thought, wasn't the work of somebody who didn't believe in love.

Casey's sign off from her call brought Travis back from his survey of the pretty red head. He stepped into view as Casey closed her eyes and leaned her head back on her chair, obviously tired from a call that seemed like it was long and exhausting. This could be interesting he thought.

"I'll do it."

Casey lifter her head, opened her eyes, and stared. Her usually quick mind stuttered, "You'll–what?"

Ignoring her question, knowing she was already catching on, Travis continued with the business at hand. "What's the timeline?"

"Three events. A dinner with my executives in April. A conference in May. A gala in June." Her words came out as though they'd been recited.

When Travis didn't respond and only offered a smug look in return she asked, "What?"

"So much love surrounding somebody with so much cynicism."

"It's good money." Casey relaxed and stated the rebuttal reserved for people's questions to why she developed the match making company at all.

"Mm hmm."

"You know what, I'll find somebody else." Casey turned to her monitor, ending her side of the conversation.

"I'll make a deal with you."

The typing stopped and her fingers hovered over the keyboard.

"This isn't a one-sided venture."

Casey folded her arms and returned her look to Travis, a silent allowance for him to continue.

"I need a place to live while I search for a new apartment. It shouldn't take longer than three months, so by the end of the gala I'd be out. You'll get what you want, and I'll get what I want. Then we go our separate ways." Travis added the last bit before Casey could make argument.

The idea that it was a two-sided business deal did make it more intriguing. Casey continued to think as she held eye contact. It was only three months. And, she thought, she needed it. Apparently so did he.

Casey felt a sense of relief settle over her and agreed with her body's reaction that it must be the right decision if it immediately alleviated the stress she'd been carrying around for days.

"Okay. You can have access to the lake house and my loft. We should coordinate schedules."

Travis hid his excitement well, as Casey's look didn't waver after he heard the news. She certainly would have called attention to it if he had.

"Perfect. Let's discuss the details Friday over dinner."

Travis walked out of the room and left Casey's objection unsaid and her mouth gaping.

As Casey's stare held the doorway she saw Maggie's body fill the empty space. She coolly carried a pile of folders in, set them on Casey's desk, and said, "I find sometimes it's best just to go with it."

Then Maggie waddled out and left Casey baffled and dumbfounded.

CHAPTER 11

"We're discussing the details tomorrow, over dinner." Casey finished her uninterrupted recount of the agreement she and Travis had come to while sipping the pretty pink drink Aimeé had placed in front of her. "This is…"

"A French Kiss," Aimeé sang, "a beautiful drink for spring."

Casey, Grace, and Rachel all turned to look outside at the snow.

"Spring, right," Rachel mumbled, defeated by yet another day of schooling and dreamed of summer.

"At least the snow looks like its melting!" Grace jumped on the spring bandwagon with Aimeé.

Casey looked to Rachel and addressed her alone, *"They* are both getting laid."

"Ah, yes. That makes sense." Rachel nodded, understanding their optimism. "Hey! *You* could get laid!" The words salivated in Rachel's mouth.

Casey took another sip of the raspberry, pineapple, and vodka concoction wondering if it was just the thing to take the edge off, or if she should be prepping for a momentous hangover.

Sitting quietly for a moment Casey tried to place her feelings. Nervous wasn't the word she would have used to describe them. It definitely wasn't excited. But surprisingly, it wasn't dread either. What did that leave? Anxiety maybe? And you know what relieves anxiety?

"No. No sex." Casey answered her own question and stomped out the flame in Rachel's eyes. "Your sex moratorium is not my responsibility."

Rachel huffed back into her chair. "It was worth a shot."

"I bet she does it." Grace lifted her glass and winked at Aimeé.

"Hmm." Aimeé studied Casey with her glinting dark brown eyes. "I don't know. She's stubborn. But yes, I think she and Travis will have sex."

"Oh, this is *good,*" Rachel said examining Casey's reaction. "She doesn't seem fazed." Rachel tipped her head from left to right trying to read Casey's blank expression. "Yes, she's thinking about it. I think you two are right. She's going to do it."

"You got all of that by looking at this?" Casey pointed to her stone face.

"Yes." Her friends agreed in unison.

"Absolutely," Grace added while they continued to nod and smile, happy with their conclusions.

Sex *was* just a natural, evolutionary response to finding an appropriate mate.

Casey let the facts flood her mind. It did have a lot of benefits; sex was good exercise and a good stress reliever, but it also released oxytocin–that's where things went wrong. It tricked you into thinking you were in love. There were plenty of other things she could do to get the same effect. She could pet a dog, laugh, call a friend, give money away, go for a run. Okay, she probably wouldn't exercise, but she could have a little fun, that would do the trick.

Her smile was slow and as hers grew her friends' lips leveled out.

"How about a little wager?" Casey began. "I'll pay each of you one thousand dollars if I sleep with Travis."

That would ensure even if things got a little spicy between she and Travis, she'd have extra incentive to resist. "You know what, make it two. Two-thousand if I give in."

"I'm in!" Rachel agreed willing. She'd take the extra income.

"Me too."

"I also accept."

The women clinked their glasses in the middle of the table and Casey laughed, "It's lovely doing business with you."

"Well, I'm satisfied with the night, but I want more. More of this drink and more details about your date tomorrow." Rachel pried, not ashamed of her obsession with anything involving romance.

"It's not a date."

"If he pays, it's a date." Grace helped argue Rachel's case.

"Why would *he* pay for dinner? Compared to me, he's poor."

"Everybody is poor compared to you. And I'm not just saying that because I'm a teacher, it's a fact."

"We are going to the new restaurant on fourth." Casey ignored the recent fact and decided to give in–it would be the easiest way to end the conversation.

"Great food, good drinks. I've been. I like the choice." Aimeé approved of the classy, sophisticated, slightly rustic, farm-to-table establishment.

"Ditto on the good drinks," Grace nonchalantly agreed, then let a lazy smile come over her.

Rachel laughed, "I'm guessing Grace has experienced a little more than good drinks after a night out at the new establishment."

"Good drinks lead to really good-"

"Yeah," Casey cut Grace off, "we get the idea."

The three women laughed again. Casey was beginning to feel like this night was going nowhere fast.

"What will you wear?"

"I don't know?"

"You mean you haven't thought about it?" Grace sounded concerned, recalling how much effort she'd put into choosing an outfit when she and Luke had first met. Of course at the time she thought she was meeting somebody else. Either way, she'd been prepared.

"I think you are forgetting," Casey leaned forward and rested her elbows on the table then used her hand to chop her point onto the table, "this is *not* a real relationship. I am not trying to flaunt or impress my way into a relationship. This is a business deal. I get a boyfriend, Travis gets a place to live. Nothing more, nothing less."

Casey watched her friends stare in silence once more, then it was Rachel's turn to lean forward.

"So, what are you going to wear?"

Laughter filled the Bistro, and kept on late into the night. They were pushy, but God did she love them.

CHAPTER 12

Maybe she should have planned her outfit.

Casey stared at her closet, then eyed the alarm clock in her downtown loft. It told her she only had twenty minutes to put herself together before she'd be late. Later than the fashionable ten minutes she'd allotted herself. It wouldn't take her long to get there, and she'd insisted she get there of her own accord, so she decided it gave her a little wiggle room.

Casey looked at the options she'd already messily laid out on her bed. Two dresses were immediately disqualified as the razor sat unused on her legs during her shower. One outfit, with a sleeveless sequined top, was also voted out. So that left the deep plum jumpsuit. The satin sleeves cuffed at the wrists, and flowing pants mimicked the cuff around the ankles. The loose material cinched appealingly at the waist, but would be infinitely more comfortable than a tight-fitting alternative. And, she'd be able to wear the glittery, silver booties Grace had bought her for Christmas.

Casey did a quick outfit check in the sliding glass door that led to her deck—why invest in a mirror when this worked just as well? She turned, front then back. Satisfied the deep-V of the neckline was doing its job to make her boobs look smaller, she added one more detail by swooping her long copper waves over one shoulder and adding a clip so at least one side of her face wouldn't be agitated by the loose strands. And, she supposed, it looked damn sexy too.

Casey's phone buzzed to life as she pulled a barely used clutch from her closet.

"I'm already out the door." She cringed at the lie but hurried out as she heard Rachel's disbelief.

"Sure you are. You just don't want to take a picture of your outfit and send it to me."

"Maybe, but this time I'm not lying. My car is waiting downstairs. I might lose you in the elevator."

Rachel sighed. "Fine, but we better get a text later letting us know how it went."

Casey pressed the button to open the door and let a small smile form on her nude lips as she held it open to keep the call. Maybe she didn't get as excited as her friends about dating or going out, and maybe the nuance of dressing up wasn't her style, but she did love her friends and couldn't deny how much they cared. And they were nosy. But she loved that, too.

"Okay, promise," Casey agreed, "Now I'm letting the door close."

Casey waited a beat then said, "Love you, Rach."

Rachel's smile sounded through the phone, "Love you, too. Knock him dead."

———

The atmosphere was lighter than she thought it would be. She had imagined something that looked like a cave, where the lights were low and the amber glow of a candle would barely make the menus legible.

"Hi, welcome." The hostess at the greeting stand smiled pleasantly. "How many in your party?"

"Hi, thank you. Ah, two."

"Wonderful, do you have a reservation?"

Casey wasn't ashamed that she had done some harmless snooping earlier that day using Travis' phone number as her target. She knew he'd made a reservation.

"Yes, it's under Mavens, Travis Mavens."

The dark-eyed waitress brightened and blushed.

For goodness sakes, Casey thought. Well at least she knew he'd beaten her there.

"Of course, Ms. Saunders, your date has already arrived. Please follow me."

Ms. Saunders, she thought, and *date.* Nice touch, *Mr. Mavens.*

Casey didn't see Travis until he was already motioning to stand. When he faced her, the way he looked at her stopped her movement forward. His hand paused as it smoothed the tie on his shirt, and his face held hers. Serious, captivating. Different than any of the playful looks she'd seen before.

Thousands of times–like she would see him a thousand more. She'd seen his hair styled with the same rusty waves, his trim suit fitted perfectly. But seeing him in this setting, and standing before her like a gentleman would while doing his best to impress a woman with his manners, he took her aback.

Travis thought this would be easy. No different than the fun way he would wittily banter with Casey at work or while out with friends at the Bistro. He would fluster her and try to cause her intelligent mind to trip and idle, hoping one day it would slow enough to get her to notice he was always there. Always consistent. Good days and bad, he was hoping to prove it would always be him. But today, tonight, when she walked in, he was the one who was flustered.

This was a side of Casey he thought he'd only ever imagine. She looked like a porcelain model. And her hair, it was longer than he thought it would be. He was thankful she paused feet away, as the urge to twist the strands between his fingers would have had him giving in to the impulse. Her creamy lips didn't move as he stared, just held the rested look as he analyzed everything about her.

"Have a wonderful meal, Ms. Saunders." The waitress grinned and departed, leaving them both motioning thanks toward the young woman before returning their interest back to each other.

Casey forced the burn in her belly away and made herself move forward.

Get a grip, she thought, this is not the first time you've seen Travis. He's *always* been attractive. This is simply a different setting. And you're feeling this way because you're dressed up, you're excited to eat after inhaling these savory aromas, and the atmosphere is altering your normally sane judgement.

"Travis." Casey nodded as she closed the gap between them.

Travis took her hand and led her toward the chair he pulled out. He kissed her cheek before she lowered herself and he swore he felt a burn where he'd placed it.

"You look beautiful."

"You don't look too bad yourself," Casey agreed, not ashamed to admit the truth. It had nothing to do with her feelings, it was a simple fact.

"I hope you don't mind–I waited to order wine." Travis moved into the chair next to Casey's. He favored a round table and being next to the person he wanted to have a conversation with. They would hopefully cover a lot of ground tonight. It wasn't his intention to learn only the details that would get him by in front of a crowd of her colleagues, he wanted more. He wanted to learn about the incredible woman sitting next to him.

"Thank you," Casey said, surprised he didn't try and impress her with his choice. She eyed him, wondering if she should tell him she enjoyed looking over the menu and deciding if she was in the mood for a wine from Italy, or favored one from France.

"I thought you would like to analyze the selection and filter through more details than anybody should possibly consider before selecting a bottle."

Casey lifted her gaze from the menu wondering if he read her mind. She nodded slowly, agreeing, as she wanted to do just that.

The wine arrived, was sampled, and poured. Travis took care sipping the light red Casey had chosen. "I'm always satisfied with a decision well-made."

"I'm glad you approve." Casey mused.

"No, not you. My decision to let you choose."

Casey couldn't help the grin that played at her lips. Of course he was satisfied with himself. Her shoulders lifted and fell as she relaxed slightly into the beginning of their evening. It wouldn't be hard if she didn't let it be, she thought. Why not enjoy the time. It's not like it was long term. And they'd have to pretend to be effortlessly comfortable with each other. Like any other couple would be in a long term relationship.

"Can I give you a compliment?" Travis asked after placing his stemmed glass back on the table.

"We are in a relationship, you're supposed to give me compliments."

Travis smirked and tilted his head forward in acknowledgement. When he looked up, he said, "Your smile is beautiful. You keep it hidden–when you're not around the girls–but when you share it with the rest of us, it's spectacular."

The way he said it, as if it was a fact rather than a ploy or obligatory conversation, had her cheeks blushing pink. Her natural response was defense, "I don't think-"

"Please," he paused, waiting just long enough to let the quiet linger when she stopped her argument, "just let me give that to you. I promise I won't say any more...tonight." Travis grinned. "Besides," he tried for more humor, hoping to encourage her to relax again, "we're in a relationship, I'm supposed to give you compliments."

Casey exaggerated her eye roll and gave in. "Fine. But no more. This dinner was specifically designed to go over the details of our arrangement and to make sure we know enough about each other to have you pass as my boyfriend."

Whatever you say, he thought, satisfied that he won the first round. "I think the duck sounds good, what are you leaning towards?"

———

"Oh my God, it's just too good," Casey moaned out the words as she savored a mouth full of braised lamb.

Travis leaned his head to the right and lifted a brow, impressed by her appreciation. He decided to try and ignore the moaning sounds coming from the woman he had more desire for than he knew what to do with. Save that for later, he thought.

"What?" Casey asked. "You don't think I can appreciate good food?"

"It's not neon green and it doesn't come in a bottle, I thought there might be a chance you'd hate it."

"Funny, coming from you," Casey quipped. "I'm half surprised you didn't order a traditional crust with pepperoni, mushrooms, garlic, and extra cheese."

"Touché."

He thought it best not to mention she knew his favorite pizza order. She'd prefer business.

"So, should we cover the basics?" he asked, his desire for Casey safely stowed away with the shock of realizing she paid more attention than he'd given her credit for.

"Now is as good a time as any."

"How long have we been dating?"

Casey swallowed and shot him a side-eyed glance. "Three years."

Travis nearly spit up his wine as he choked down the sip he took.

"Three years?" The surprise in his question caused her lips to press together. He supposed her silence was enough of an answer. "Ah, don't get me wrong, but if this," he moved a finger between the two of them, "was a real relationship, I would like to think we'd be married by now, not meeting the co-workers for the first time. How did you avoid bringing me around for so long?"

Casey cleared her throat. "You were working."

"Work is usually between the hours of eight to five."

"You were on call…"

"Doing what exactly?"

Casey squished her nose and cringed a little. "Saving people's lives."

Travis' laugh reached the ends of the room. "I'm a doctor?"

"You might be."

"And nobody ever questioned my not being around?"

Casey looked at him and leaned toward him. "My boyfriend, not *you* in particular. But sure, some people asked questions. Most just understood that surgeons don't have a choice."

Leaning in, mirroring her movements, he brought their faces together. When the waitress came to check on them, Travis didn't break eye contact when he made another order.

"Whiskey on the rocks please."

"Do you have a preference?"

"Whatever the bartender suggests."

Casey's eyes searched his, seeking out what he might be thinking. When she found nothing but his continued stare, she asked, "Losing interest?"

"I'll manage. I'll have to brush up on my anatomy."

"Brain. Brush up on the brain."

"Right. This just keeps getting better. Anything for you, darling."

It was slim, Casey thought, but it was an opening. "Speaking of darlings. I noticed you had a profile on matchme.com." Their bodies moved away from each other to rest back in their chairs. "And that you matched a while back. What happened?"

"Typically I'd avoid past relationships on a first date, but considering we've been dating for three years and I'd never try and hide anything from you, I'll give.

"I matched with a woman named Kat in a couple categories I thought were important: faith, family expectations, income expectations. Turns out she and I had a little bit of a different idea of what those meant as she was unfaithful, decided after a while she didn't want a family at all, and–though I do very well and would have been happy if she'd chosen stay home–I didn't expect her to go out and spend my money like it was unlimited, ultimately cleaning out my bank account."

Casey looked for any sign of regret or remorse. She found none, but did feel badly that her site wouldn't have caught this woman's true intentions. Her algorithm and the questions asked were meant to do just that. "I'm sorry."

The apology sounded like she was taking responsibility for what happened. "It's nobody's fault but hers. Nobody could have known what she was really like."

"I could have," Casey said, feeling protective of…Travis? Or her company? Science? "That's precisely why the questions are specific and laid out in the order that they are."

Travis left his napkin on his lap and moved his hand to cover Casey's and said, "No, you couldn't have. She was good at lying and saying the things she needed to say to get what she wanted. Trust me."

"How did it end?" Casey was too curious to notice she'd let his hand linger over hers.

"That's the best part. She made the decision for me. Obviously at the time it wasn't the best, but she changed the locks and moved all of my things to storage. Or, I should say, all of the things she didn't want to keep."

Casey couldn't help the laugh that bubbled up. "I'm really sorry," she said, moving her hand only to cover the laughter.

"Don't be." Travis shook his head and joined her. "It is pretty funny. And I can't complain. I had a great friend who let me stay with him for a while, I met some pretty great people because of it." Travis lifted his glass in a toast. "And now I get to play pretend boyfriend to one of the most intriguing women I know. That's not half bad."

Still feeling badly about what her site had put him through, Casey let the compliment slide and raised her glass. As she clinked hers to his, she thought: a lot of people would have handled the situation differently. Not Travis. He was composed. Always seemed to find the good in things. God, that must be terrible.

"Now, I told you mine, you tell me yours."

"What do you want to know?"

Travis noticed the conversation had become natural. It would get a little bumpy with what he was about to ask of her, but she was comfortable. No, he thought on it a bit more, she might not have been comfortable, but she felt safe. He knew, no matter how much she tried to deny it, she trusted him. That was the first step, he thought. Trust.

"Tell me about your mom and dad."

Her face snapped to his. "Why would you need to know about them?"

"I don't need to, I want to."

"That answer seems selfish."

"Maybe it is. It doesn't make it less true or make me bad for wanting to know. And whether you like it or not, knowing something about you that only your closest friends know–something your boyfriend *should* know–will make what we are trying to do seem more authentic."

Casey's mind would have usually raced to find the answers, to weigh the pros and cons, but he had laid out what she would have considered. It would only be normal for her boyfriend of three years to know about her family and their estranged dynamic. And as much as she hated to admit it, she knew Travis wouldn't use the information against her.

"Would you like more wine, Miss?"

Like an answer to her prayers. Casey nodded to the waitress and waited for her to leave before taking a sip. For a moment, she stared at the red circling her glass. Just the facts, she thought.

"My dad is Ian Saunders. He's an engineer and does well for himself. My mom, Linette Whitely–her new married name–is a nurse." Casey paused. "Do you want to write this down so you remember?"

"No."

His response was simple and easy, so she nodded and continued.

"My parents married when they were twenty-four. They were happy and loving. Then they had me, and from as early as I can remember, they fought."

Casey closed her eyes and vividly remembered the countless nights of yelling. "God, if they could have heard themselves shouting. Each trying to be heard. One practically begging the other to try, and the other begging to leave. Neither willing to state exactly what they wanted, and neither wanting to be the bad guy. Dad felt sorry for himself and Mom tried to make it his fault.

"Anyway," Casey shook her head and looked at Travis who was listening intently and emotionless. "Mom had an affair and Dad found out. It was the one thing she could have done to escape. And for him, it was the one thing he couldn't forgive.

"She ended up marrying the man she had the affair with and created a new family. Including three daughters. She decided to raise these ones this time around."

Travis didn't react to the information, but couldn't help but notice Casey's numbed recount of her mother's new life.

"Dad met a woman named Pamela. They never married but have been sharing their life together, well, since my mom was unfaithful."

"Your parents," Travis started, "they're the reason you don't believe people can fall in love and stay that way?"

"My parents. Your parents. More than half of our friends' parents."

Travis lifted an eyebrow, "I'm going to pretend you learned my parents are divorced from Luke or Grace."

Casey smiled sweetly. A visual admittance to having scoured every virtual component of his life. He did have an excellent credit score and responsible retirement investment accounts.

"What about the people that make it? Grace and Luke. Do you think that will end badly?" Travis' suggestion brought a slight smile to Casey's lips.

"No," she began, "Grace and Luke will make it." It wasn't hard to admit her best friend would be successful in a relationship. She had seen the way they fought for each other, even with their greatest loves and pride at stake. They were the exceptions to the rule.

"Then why not you?"

Casey looked at Travis and didn't know what to say. She thought about how she had scored when she entered her personal information into her own Match Me algorithm. What the questions she had answered said about her as a person and as a partner.

For the first time Casey wondered what would happen if she matched her information with Travis'. Would they be compatible?

"Maybe," she began, not quite believing what she was about to say to Travis. "I'm not worried about me."

CHAPTER 13

Casey stomped into the Bistro the next morning and halted when she walked through the threshold. She peered at their table, then sneered at the laughing trio of Grace, Luke, and Rachel for putting fanciful and terrible thoughts in her head.

Casey narrowed her round eyes and turned to see Aimeé cheerfully taking orders from the line ahead of her. Not ready to greet her obnoxious friends, she slid into the back of the line and waited.

After five slow steps she stood facing Aimeé and her creamy French skin and crop of wavy black hair.

"Why don't you believe in marriage?" Casey asked, rather than placing an order, ignoring the waiting line of people who had come in behind her.

"Lightly sweetened latte?" Aimeé asked in response while she judged Casey's ragged sideways bun.

At Casey's nod, Aimeé entered the order and began to answer while gracefully maneuvering receipts to order clips and lining crisp white mugs on the counter to be filled.

"I do believe in marriage," Aimeé spoke nonchalantly and went on before Casey could forge another question, "I happen to also believe you can love more than one person. It is up to the individual, and the relationship to determine how they would like to move forward with their love."

"You think it's an agreement?"

"I think it's more of an art." Aimeé smiled and leaned around Casey to take the order of a nice old woman standing in line.

Casey rolled her eyes and moved to the left so the woman could move forward.

"It's all up to the couple in the relationship." The woman's crackly old voice piped in. "I was faithful to my husband for fifty-eight years, and he to me. Then he died."

"Ah, I'm sorry." Casey did a double take wondering how this woman slid her way into the conversation.

"Don't be! I've lived an exciting and promiscuous life after Allan passed." The woman leaned in between Casey and Aimeé and offered what she thought was a whisper, "I fraternized with every eligible man on my wing of our senior living center. And one who wasn't!"

Casey watched the woman pay and slowly step to an open table in the middle of the room, place her bags in one chair, and sit in the other. When she looked back to Aimeé she was greeted with a satisfied, I-told-you-so smirk.

"And I did not even pay her to say such things." The quip was quick. "But I believe what you can take away from this is you have to be willing to commit to whatever kind of love you choose to have. Paint your own picture, so to speak."

Casey swiped the mug as belligerently as she could without spilling the precious contents, scowled and turned toward the table.

"Good morning, sunshine." Rachel's eyes gleamed as Casey was given the second look-over of the day.

"No, it's not." Casey took a seat next to Luke.

"Bad date?"

"I suppose that depends on your idea of a good one," Casey snapped in his direction.

"Ah," Grace responded knowingly, "it *was* good and now you're upset about it."

The night replayed in excruciating detail in her mind. Never had Casey wished she didn't remember everything in her life more than now.

"This is how it starts, you know?" She looked from friend to friend. "First you date, you share intimate details of your life, you get tricked into thinking they care–worse, that *you* care–then before you know it you're spending more time together, and suddenly you're wishing that person was there when they're gone."

Luke bobbed his head as he followed Casey's logic. He looked admiringly at Grace and smiled, "Yup, that basically sums it up."

Grace laughed and Rachel swooned at his charm.

"You disgust me. You and your friend," Casey muttered.

"So the deal is off?" Luke questioned, and noted Grace and Rachel didn't seem to share the same worry about the situation as he did. In fact, they looked more satisfied than anything.

"No." Casey's response was flat.

"No?"

"No."

"I'm confused," Luke admitted.

Casey brought the mug to her lips and moved it away before sipping.

"No! It went really well. He was kind, fun, serious, rational–I *hate* it when they are rational–and cute. And handsome." Casey looked at Luke. "Yes, you can be both things."

She tried for another sip but the words kept forcing her lifted hands back to the table. Each time Luke leaned forward to see if the latte would finally make it all the way.

"He tricked me into making a terrible admission. *Then* he had the audacity to do the lingering bullseye kiss."

"The nerve!" Rachel mocked.

"He should know better," Grace added, unable to hide her delight.

"He kissed you?" Luke was the only one at the table who shared in Casey's shock.

"No."

Defeated, Luke dropped his shoulders and admitted, "I give up."

Grace comforted with a hand on his as Rachel guided him through the concept.

"The bullseye isn't a kiss on the lips. It's a tactical *almost* lip kiss where the guy leans in and kisses you right here." Rachel pointed to the soft spot of her face just to the right of her lips. "Then he lingers there just long enough to make you *wish* he was kissing you on the lips."

Casey relived the moment as Rachel described the worst–and best–part of her night. Okay, not *the best,* but when a kiss that innocent sends her body and brain into a tailspin, it's bound to mess with logic. What a jerk, she thought. He knew *exactly* what he was doing.

"Come on," Grace coaxed. "Let it out."

"It's like he knew my emotional and physical state were precisely aligned to get the proper reaction from *the bullseye.*"

Luke stared, unable to find words that would show just how far the conversation was ahead of him.

"Luke, this is Casey–the *real* Casey. Casey, this is Luke." Rachel exaggerated the unnecessary introduction, then turned to Casey, "You're going to have to assume the newest member of our friend family doesn't know you're not only a brilliant tech whiz, but that you basically had your choice of careers because you are in fact, brilliant."

Exasperated, Casey acknowledged Luke. "Arousal, for a woman, can only happen when her hormones, physical, and mental state are aligned and in agreement that sexual stimulation is an appropriate course of action. And no two women are the same. He caused this in me with a simple kiss to my cheek."

Luke gulped and blushed, wishing he hadn't received the lesson.

"I hate it when they move too fast," Rachel joked.

"Well, they have been dating for three years." Grace grinned over the top of her own mug.

"Seems to me he moves quite slow." Aimeé joined the conversation as she walked up to check on the table. "I've slept with a man after only three minutes. Another round?"

"This is why men shouldn't come to things like this." Luke looked at Aimeé. "I'll get mine to go."

"Where are you going? I just got here." Travis' bright tone received different reactions from everybody at the table as he strode up and winked at Casey.

"No." She stood and pointed a finger at Travis. "I need a day away from you."

Casey gathered her things and walked out without a salutation, leaving everybody's eyes following her through the door.

Travis moved to the now vacant seat. "Anybody going to drink this?" he asked, pointing to the untouched latte Casey left behind.

"It's all yours." Rachel beamed, feeling like Travis might be the one, perfect person for Casey. He was completely unfazed by her logic and cynical view of love.

Luke wavered slightly before asking Travis how the night went, but took a chance. "Well, how did it go last night?"

Travis closed his eyes as he sipped and enjoyed the warm latte. "Great! Couldn't have gone better."

He looked to Luke who seemed relieved with his response, then to the women. "I'm assuming that's why she left?"

The wide smiles he received were all the answers he needed.

CHAPTER 14

The week hadn't gone as badly as Casey would have expected it to. Aside from declining calls from her mother all week–if Linette Whitley wanted to relay a message, she could leave a voicemail–she had relaxed nicely into the normalness of work.

By Tuesday she was no longer completely irritated with Travis and how nice he had been at dinner. She figured the way her body reacted to his kiss was exactly as she had described to her friends–just a hormonal response.

And *he* was acting as he always did, popping in every once in a while to talk over some work logistics, and only briefly discussed a plan to move some of his things to the lake house for use over the next three months.

Casey rolled over to look at the time by tipping her phone sideways on her nightstand. Ten to nine. A perfect night of blissful sleep. And she still had a couple hours before everybody would arrive to help move Travis' things in.

"Let's shoot for one."

She recalled the way Travis had smoothly delivered the suggestion, then added that it would give everybody a chance to sleep in and have the morning to themselves. He knew *she* would be better if she had time to herself and didn't feel rushed.

Not bad, Mr. Mavens, she thought, grinning as she remembered how the waitress had addressed both of them during their dinner a week earlier.

When her phone lit up and she saw her mother's name scrawled across the screen, her grin dropped and agitation at her mom's persistence was the only driving force behind sliding her finger to answer.

"Hello." Casey's voice sounded like steel.

"Casey!" Linette's greeting sang out as if she hadn't registered Casey's unwelcome tone. "I've been trying like crazy to get a hold of you. How are you, dear?"

"Dear?" Casey asked, exaggerating the question. "I'm surprised you remember you have another child to offer the endearment."

"Oh now, don't be so grumpy with me."

Casey could hear Linette try and cover the slight anger in her voice with even more sugar.

"I am calling–and *have been* calling–because I would like to take you out to lunch. Just you and me. To have some much needed one-on-one time to catch up. What do you think?"

The offer stunned Casey. She had expected anything but an offer for lunch. She had come up with every sarcastic remark and rebuttal to her mother's usual passive aggressive comments. But she had nothing for a proposed lunch with her mother without the presence of her new herd of children or husband. She had no idea what they would talk about or what she would tell her mom if she went.

If she went?

There's no way. Why was she even considering this?

"Hello? Casey, are you there?" Linette questioned.

"Yeah. I'll have to think about it. When were you thinking?"

"Thinking? Oh, I-I hadn't thought that far in advance."

Clearly her mother thought she would immediately get turned down just as much as Casey thought she'd deliver the rejection.

"What if we tried for two or three weeks from now? I can come to you, somewhere by the lake. That would be nice for spring, don't you think?"

Casey breathed deeply a couple of times to see if she could slow her mind from all of the negative thoughts that raced through it as they usually did when she talked to her mother.

Finally she said, "I'll let you know."

"Do that. I think–"

"I have to go. I have something I need to do this morning."

Linette hated being cut off and Casey heard the edge in her sign off. But she didn't think she could listen to more flighty conversation that morning.

"Right. I'll wait for your call."

"Okay, bye, Linette."

"I'm your *mother,* Casey. Goodbye for now."

After the click, Casey threw the phone at her plush covers then pulled them back over her head and growled out a muffled scream of frustration. Then closed her eyes and forced her mind to close and willed a new round of sleep to come over her.

—

"Casey! Case? Are you in here?"

The click from the latch on her door woke her again. She pushed the blanket away from her head and stared at the ceiling.

"Case," Rachel's voice was clear as day, "what are you doing in bed? It's nearly one."

Three bodies bounced on her bed causing her body to roll slightly in each direction.

"Linette."

"Your mom was *here?*"

"No." Casey closed her eyes again and started flopping her hand around her bedspread. When she found her phone she lifted it and said, "Phone call."

"You answered?"

She shared in her friends' surprise.

"It was my frustrated response to her incessant barrage of calls over the past two weeks."

Grace leaned over and smashed a pillow down to see Casey's face, "What did she want?"

"Lunch."

The room went silent for a few seconds as each of the women waited for more explanation. When it didn't come, Rachel pressed.

"With *the herd?*"

It was the affectionate name given to Linette and her precious children. Under normal circumstances it would have made Casey smile, or at the very least roll her eyes, but today she was still registering.

"No, just…us."

"Oh."

Rachel didn't know what to think either; that made Casey feel a little better.

"Wow."

"Wow, exactly."

"Will you go?" Aimeé was curious. She understood the tangled web of emotions that haunted every decision when family dynamics weren't healthy. The idea that a simple request for lunch might be just that, or it might be something entirely different. You could be walking into a new and terrible round of heartbreak. Then you'd have to live with the fact that it was your own fault for putting yourself in that situation. And, as much as you told yourself you were fine, a little part of you would have to heal all over again and you'd have to accept that no matter how much you wanted it, needed it, or craved it, your family would not be able to give you the type of love you wanted.

"I don't know."

A loud thud, a deep grunt, and the sound of Luke's voice letting off a string of strained profanity drew the attention of the women toward the door.

Grace grinned. "We told the guys to get started and figured we would hang out up here, at least until they finished the big stuff. That way we didn't have to do any of the heavy lifting."

"You are great friends." Casey let a small smile play across her face. "And because I don't have to carry anything, I'm going to ignore the fact that you told Travis he could have a room up here on my floor and not in the basement."

"We also figured since you were sleeping, and we had some money on the line, you forfeited your chance to dictate what room he took."

Casey nodded, letting her curls rub against the pillow as she remembered their bet, and accepted. She would have done exactly the same thing.

"That's fair. And it doesn't matter anyway. I have the willpower of...well," Casey searched and found a dead end, "something with god-like will power."

She pushed herself up and looked at her three friends who were dressed and made up for the day. All in yoga pants and cute sweaters or sweatshirts–just in case they had to help with the move. But mostly, they were dressed for a spring walk outside on the paths around the lake, where the snow had finally melted–followed, as usual, by pizza delivery and lounging. Casey had no choice but to follow suit, really. There was no need for her to throw on jeans when stretchy pizza pants would do.

The women adjusted themselves on the bed so they could see Casey as she walked to the sprawling en suite bathroom to get herself ready.

With her mouth filled with foaming paste and a toothbrush, she looked over as her friends talked and waited. They were wonderful people, and even more amazing friends. Some wouldn't have understood her need to shut down for a bit after a call from Linette, and others would be irritated she was still in bed, or frustrated that they had to wait for her to get ready.

But not them. They were the best friends she felt she didn't deserve–but would do anything to keep close.

Casey grinned as she twisted the hair on top of her head and wound a black elastic binder around it. Rather than pin up the stray, curly wisps she let the red strands fall around her face.

"Are you thinking about Travis?" Rachel dragged out his name as though she were referring to a middle school crush.

"Not specifically, but he would be a part of the pizza quorum. I thought I would spring for dinner and drinks tonight to celebrate my best friends, and–as ashamed I am to admit it–Travis. For stepping in and saving my ass. Sure, he thinks he's benefiting from all of this, but really, my stakes are high. My career–my company–is on the line."

Casey looked over and folded her arms across her chest. "It was the right move to go public. It was risky, and I knew that. They could, at any time, oust me. I have a feeling that's what Carrie is trying to do. She's secretive, a little too happy, and as much as I hate to admit it, she's good at her job. People would respect her decision to consider tossing me out."

"They would never," Rachel argued.

"They would."

It was that simple. They would. It was business.

"Then you can buy, but I'm handing Travis his first beer." Rachel smiled proudly as Casey walked out with forest green leggings and a cream-colored crew neck sweater.

"So cute." Grace agreed with Casey's choice in outfit.

"Should we go down? Do you think they are done by now?"

"Probably," Grace started, "he didn't have much. The biggest thing was a leather recliner. Apparently he likes to stretch out with a book before bed. Why anybody wouldn't want to do that when they could just be *in* bed is beyond me. The rest was just boxes and suitcases full of clothes and shoes."

"Why anybody would want to *read* is beyond me." Casey smirked.

"Coming from the woman with the huge library."

"You know that's *your* library, Grace. And I have the added benefit of it making me look smart."

"You're already smart."

"Yeah, you're right."

Grace and Rachel filed out. As Casey reached the door Aimeé wrapped her arms around Casey and held her for a moment. Casey gave in and squeezed Aimeé in return, savoring the warm feeling.

Aimeé leaned her head on Casey's and whispered, "We are not our families. I am proud of the strong, beautiful, and generous woman you are. Do not let your mother sway your thoughts."

Casey listened and let her eyelids fall closed as Aimeé held her up. They stayed wrapped for a moment longer before Casey began to look up. She didn't see Travis looking on when she smiled genuinely at Aimeé, and with more sincerity than she knew she could muster, she said, "Thank you."

———

Casey handed Travis another beer as she joined him by the fire pit. They were the only two left after a day of moving, walking around the thawing lake, and laughing themselves through a dinner of pizza and beer–where Rachel had handed Travis his first of the day.

Aimeé had gotten a car to drive her back into the city so she could get a brief night sleep before waking early to open the Bistro. Rachel had hopped a ride with Grace and Luke on their way home. And Travis was now effectively in his new temporary home.

"I don't think I got my own beer all night." Travis eyed the open bottle that was just handed to him. "It's nice, but I can't help but feel I'm being bribed."

Casey let the grin come easy. "I wouldn't call it 'bribed.' It's more of a 'thanks.'"

"What for?" he wondered, knowing he had an idea, but he wasn't feeling put out in any sort of way.

"The girls know how important my job is to me. And I think they realize the pressure I am under to provide a living, breathing, stand-in boyfriend. You're saving me, and my job."

"That seems like a stretch," Travis admitted, thinking there was no way a company could hold a person accountable for being in love.

"It's not a stretch when they want to feature the creator of the most successful match-making company of all time in their upcoming advertisement. Apparently it's a big deal to lead by example. Sort of a *'Hey look, I'm the vision of love and happiness here with my boyfriend, and you can do it, too!'*"

Casey's tone was mocking as she tried to be humorous, but knew her words held a touch of acidity. Especially since she knew if she declined, it would make their decision to give her the boot that much easier.

"The business of love is more cutthroat than I thought." Travis sighed and ran a hand through his auburn hair.

"Tell me about it."

Casey settled into a cushion and leaned her head back to stare at the flickering fire before her. It was comfortable, she thought. Sitting here with Travis. He didn't press for conversation, just simply let things trickle out if they came to him, or sat quietly when he didn't feel the need to talk.

But, she realized, he was like her. It only took one look to know when he was deep in thought. It was the unblinking eyes and the face that was free of its usual satisfied grin. He stared emotionless at the fire and Casey found herself wanting to know what was going on in his mind.

"What are you thinking about?" Casey asked, holding her gaze on Travis' profile. This time, rather than irritate her, his slow smile forced a grin on her lips.

"I'm wondering how many people know that deep down you're a softie?"

"A softie?" Casey laughed at his assessment. "That's not a label I have *ever* been given. By anybody. I'm curious as to how you stumbled upon that observation?"

"Really?" This time Travis looked surprised. "That's one of the first things I thought when I saw you with *'the girls'* for the first time." His fingers quoted the affectionate name given to them by Luke, Christopher, and now him. Come to think of it, he had heard William refer to the four women with the same words.

Casey stared at Travis with a bit of wonder.

"You can lift your jaw, it's not like I'm the first person that cares about you enough to see you'd do pretty much anything for your friends." Travis side-eyed Casey in time to see her close her mouth. Then he took a satisfied sip of beer.

"Are you always like this?" Casey's arms folded over her chest. "You know," she began at his questioning brow, "calm. Sure of yourself. Borderline irritating."

Travis' laugh was quick and easy. "It's good to know the effect I have on people."

"Me," Casey corrected, "just me. It seems others don't get irritated by you."

"I think it's because you like me."

"Sure, I mean, I don't hate you." Casey shifted and pulled her feet up on the outdoor sofa.

"No," Travis started, stopping her movements, "you like me. And it makes you uncomfortable and defensive."

It took all of Casey's willpower not to show she was uncomfortable, and her initial words would have been defensive. She tried to freeze her facial expression to hide the eyes that wanted to narrow and the lips that wanted to purse and argue.

"That's very good." Travis pointed with his beer-hand to Casey's face. "Constipated is a much better look for you than anger."

Laughter was the last response she expected from herself, but at his words it easily flowed out of her. Travis joined in at the contagious sound.

"I can't help it," Casey admitted through long breaths as she tried to calm herself, "I just *know* the odds, and natural human responses, and I've seen two people destroy each other. People might call it cynical, but for me it's simply fact. It's science and years of study."

"I understand that, but I wonder, who was your good example?"

"What do you mean?"

"Your company. Your algorithm. The questions. You wouldn't have been able to so accurately match people together with just what your parents *didn't* do."

Casey knew what he meant, she had just never had to answer beyond her standard sentence or two. People accepted without question she learned everything based on watching two people who didn't love each other anymore, interact. Travis saw, and wanted more.

"Grace's parents, Raymond and Lydia. And Rachel's parents. We weren't at their house much, but when we were at Stacy and Dennis' it was a different dynamic."

Casey looked from Travis to the fire and smiled at the memories, how she'd sat down and analyzed her friends' parents. How she used human nature, psychology, personality, and individual needs and wants to create her initial match concept when starting Match Me all those years ago.

"Lydia didn't have to work, so I watched how she handled herself at home and with Raymond. Both of them completely understanding and willing to execute the roles they chose for their lives and lifestyles. Both appreciating what the other provided.

"Stacy and Dennis both had to work. Their relationship seemed to be more about communication and navigating situations. Things I would say most people have to think about—who picks up the kids from school and takes them to activities, who makes dinner, who cleans, who manages the money."

Casey took a sip of her beer and returned her gaze to Travis, who was looking only at her. Listening intently.

"Would Stacy ever be unfaithful to Dennis?"

"What? No, why would you even ask that?"

"I wanted to see how quickly you came to the defense of somebody you cared about. And how quickly the logic and odds of knowing marriages fail were disregarded."

"For every marriage that fails, one succeeds." The defensive words slipped out. "Stacy and Dennis are wonderful together."

"Ah, there we go. Not just a pessimist. You *are* a softie."

"I am not."

"Just a big old pile of mush."

"You're ridiculous."

Casey didn't know what else to say so she sat and listened to the fire crackle and watched it begin to flicker out.

It was nice, she decided after a while, not being alone tonight. She peered out of the side of her eye at Travis who was doing the same as she—quietly relaxing next to the fire, not needing conversation, just enjoying the warm ambiance as it dulled the chilly spring air. Or maybe simply relishing in an amicable evening in each other's company.

Then she admitted to herself, it wasn't nice simply not being alone, it was nice having Travis there. For as irritating as she wanted him to be, he was probably the one man she wouldn't mind sharing her home with for the next three months.

They would most likely share meals, mornings, and evenings. They might share rides into the city for work, and probably lunch and coffee breaks as they prepped for her events.

It was interesting to think he would know more about her than any man ever would. He probably already did. He would see her before bed at night and early in the morning. He would see her pre-coffee and pre-makeup. He would see her before she put her bra on in the morning and when she immediately took it off after walking into her home at night—because that is *one thing* she was *not* giving up.

Casey shifted and swung her feet to tuck them in on the other side and continued her thoughts. Because her mind had gone there, she wondered if he would find her attractive. Would he find her flannel pajamas, sweatpants, and sweatshirts attractive? Would he wonder what was beneath them? Or, would he not think twice? Did he prefer satin and lace?

Sleep was such an intimate, relaxed, and unkempt act, she wondered if he'd imagined lying next to her at night. Would he try? Would she let him?

"What are you thinking?" It was Travis' turn to ask the question.

"I'm deciding if I'm going to sleep with you or not."

The amused surprise on his face was apparent. "I didn't know that was an option."

"It might be." Casey stood and looked down. "But for now, I'm going to bed. Alone."

Travis smiled and lifted himself from the couch. "Have a good night, Casey."

Before Casey could register what was happening, Travis pulled her lips to his.

The way his fingers lightly grazed the side of her face felt delicate. But they felt as though they were locking her into the moment. Her head screamed to stop, but her hammering heart distracted her thoughts, pumping blood to her face where his hand was resting.

Without having time to process the feeling of the kiss, Travis pulled away and left her wanting more. She wished she would have focused on that tender sensation rather than the thousands of other emotions and feelings that rushed through her body.

"Sweet dreams," he said.

Travis turned and walked up the path toward the house before her, leaving Casey staring after him.

CHAPTER 15

Casey watched Grace and Rachel apply sweet farewell kisses on each of Aimeé's cheeks in the sprawling kitchen, then laugh at her own expression of amazement as they walked toward the front doorway where she was standing.

It had only taken Casey mentioning how overwhelmed she felt by the task of preparing the lake house for the work event for her friends to show up and help. While Aimeé manned the kitchen, the other two had cleaned–even the dreaded bathrooms–lit candles, diced and chopped as if they were professional sous chefs; all while cracking jokes and poking fun at each other about their scrubbing and knife techniques.

The house looked sparkling clean and even more inviting than usual. Blankets were draped casually but neatly over couches, and pillows were puffed. Between the trays of food and Ray Lamontagne crooning happily from the surround speakers, it struck exactly the right ambience. Casey grinned, relieved and touched at her friends' handiwork.

"I don't know what I would do without you," Casey said, dropping her work bag and kicking off her shoes as the two women opened their arms and pulled Casey into a three-way embrace.

"Yeah," Rachel joked, "us either."

Casey laughed and said, "It's true," through quick breaths.

Grace pulled back and held Casey at arm's length. "You would do just fine." Grace motioned to the top of the stairs where Travis appeared. "And this time, you're not going to be alone."

Casey would have issued a snarky comment or told Grace to knock the slick grin off her face if she'd been able to pull her eyes away from Travis. Something about the way he was unbuttoning his shirtsleeves and rolling them up just so, captured her attention. He looked every bit the classy and comfortable boyfriend–he'd present nicely and was sure to please the crowd. But what she couldn't quite ignore, was that he looked every bit himself.

"Casey?" Rachel questioned when both she and Grace realized they hadn't gotten the expected sarcastic response.

"Right," Casey said, as her eyes drew back to the girls.

"Right?"

Casey quickly modified her tone with a little edge and a hint of sarcasm. "Right. I won't be alone. Let's just pray that *he* isn't the reason I get fired. I probably would have been better off just telling the truth."

"There's our girl." Rachel squeezed Casey one last time and gave her a farewell peck on the cheek and skipped out.

Grace intentionally mirrored Rachel's actions and added an exaggerated bounce in her own skip to get a smile out of Casey as she mocked their overly energetic friend.

Casey shook her head as she closed the door. When she turned she saw Travis' head bent over a tray of pan-fried slices of French bread. He was carefully placing marinated tomatoes and Kalamata olives on a thin layer of goat cheese that would serve as finger food for their *mingling hour*.

Casey felt her eyes roll as she thought of the term coined at their last hosts dinner by Carrie.

'Oh, a *mingling hour!* How fabulous!' Casey remembered the exhausting and overly energetic words that had purred out of Carrie's mouth a mere twenty seconds after she walked in.

Casey wiggled her body and shook out her hands to rid herself of the memory and the feeling of dread that was inching up to the pit of her stomach.

Just one night, she thought. All you have to do is pretend for one night. Then you'll figure it out.

Travis watched Casey hold her eyes closed and roll her head over her shoulders. He wondered what was going on inside the fascinating brain. Was she trying not to worry? Giving herself a pep talk? Telling herself she just had to get through dinner?

He figured things would be easy enough to navigate while standing. If you were standing you could walk out of an uncomfortable situation. But dinner? When you were stuck around a table with everyone listening with at least one ear, things could get…interesting.

Crossing to Casey, Travis threw the towel Aimeé had handed him over his shoulder, wiped his hands, and moved behind her. He slowly began to knead her shoulders. He figured she would have tried to resist, but when he felt the tension in her muscles and applied a bit more pressure she relented and let him continue.

"I find it's easiest to settle into a night by playing hostess."

"Hmm?" Casey questioned listlessly as she let Travis' hands work the anxiety out of her neck and shoulders.

"Just greet people, walk around, offer drinks and appetizers, and work yourself into the night slowly." Travis peeked around Casey's back to see if she was listening. When he saw her slow nod he continued. "And don't forget to enjoy sips of a drink for yourself. You created something pretty remarkable, why not just enjoy it?"

Travis felt the deep inhale and slow exhale Casey, her final attempt to relax. When she opened her eyes, she turned, nodded, and walked away rolling her head from side to side and shaking out her arms.

Pep-talk success, he thought as he breathed in his own short laugh and shook his head. He mused at the way Casey was taking on the evening: like an athlete mentally preparing for a game. And physically, he thought with an amused grin as she poured herself a glass of wine and took a slow sip.

Aimeé elegantly maneuvered on the other side of kitchen island. As she did, Travis watched her add a bit of small talk to her routine and directed it toward Casey. Without drawing attention to her intentions, she slowly pulled ingredients together for a cream cheese, dill, and fresh salmon crostini, then slid them effortlessly in front of an island stool. An unspoken request, followed by unthinking acceptance, Casey sat and busied herself with the task of putting one ingredient on top of the other until a pretty little appetizer tray came together.

Nicely done, Aimeé. Travis walked back to the kitchen to join the women and to continue his delegated task of dropping the salty tomato and olive concoction.

Trays filled with buttery toasted breads and their toppings, simple stuffed mushrooms, beautiful cheese boards, and savory spreads with crackers stretched across a long buffet. While people gathered to select and eat their snacks, they would have a front-row view of the beautiful lake. Candles were lit on the table and throughout the main floor, and the savory smell of roasted chicken climbed the stairs to Casey's room where she had departed to change and ready her hair and makeup for the evening.

Upon walking into her room she narrowed her eyes and said, "You sly, sly women."

Casey found flowy white pants and a matching deep-necked blazer hanging on a pretty hook. And, she grinned, a thin gold lariat necklace draped on her bed next to a note that read:

Hair down and pinned back on one side. Maroon lips. This necklace. And no shirt beneath the blazer! Knock them dead.

Love,

Grace and Rach

Eying the blazer once more, Casey lifted a brow. *No shirt beneath.* That's business and the party *all* up front. She shrugged, accepted her orders, then made her way to the bathroom to start on task number one–hair down.

The next time Casey took a good look at herself in the mirror, she did a double take. Everything about the outfit was confident and sexy. She would take on dinner and her coworkers like the hard-ass she was. And maybe she'd switch to white wine to keep the edge off with less potential staining.

Leaving the heels that were also generously left by her bed, Casey walked to the top of the stairs barefoot. There were some things that were just nonnegotiable. The outfit was a great idea. The shoes, not so good. She would be comfortable in her own home.

At the edge of the stairs she saw the kitchen had been cleaned, and Aimeé had changed into black ankle slacks and a black chef's apron. Her crop of hair had been slightly curled and her lips painted her signature red. She looked every bit the part of the French chef she was. Casey wondered why anybody would ever choose anybody but Aimeé when they required a caterer or chef. She was worth every penny.

Aimeé poured herself her first glass of wine then topped off Travis' glass. When he lifted his head from his phone–where he was probably catching up on work–he took a sip and caught Casey out of the corner of his eye. His glass nearly slipped out of his hand and he ended the spectacle with a little choke and a cough. Then he stood and stared.

Casey couldn't deny the satisfaction of watching Travis try and regain his composure, knowing it was lost after taking her in. But she needed him on his A-game and she had successfully prepped her look and her mind for the night. She didn't need a mushy bumbler, she needed the witty and confident man he was.

Oh shit. Did she really just think that? *Witty and confident?* No, no. Not right now. Game face.

"You-ah-you look…"

"Pull yourself together, Mavens." It was the best she could do with the limited time her mind allowed after the uncomfortable thoughts. "It's almost go-time."

"Ah-right. Yeah." Travis tried to reign in his own not so innocent thoughts. "Right. Ready. As I'll ever be."

Casey shot him a look at his comment. "As you'll ever be?"

"Casey," he visibly calmed, "I'm ready. And so are you."

His words only gave her a moment to join his calm. At the chime of the doorbell, Casey closed her eyes and took a final deep breath that did little to ease her nerves. She looked at Travis, wondering and worrying, if he was ready for the task he signed up for.

"You get the door," he said, and before she could object he added, "because it will be nice for you to greet everybody and you won't have to stand here awkwardly waiting for them to walk in."

Surprisingly, it made sense. And in the middle of all of her thoughts about it not working and Travis not being ready, his words cut through the racing in her mind.

Casey looked at Travis, nodded, and said, "Thank you."

With every step toward the door Casey felt a little better. When she inched closer and finally looked up, she saw a large, dark body outlined on the other side and smiled. She was genuinely excited–and relieved–knowing Sasha Mosely and her husband Zeb were the first to arrive.

"Sasha!" Casey said as she opened the door and was welcomed by the comfort of a familiar, safe and happy face that was beaming back at her.

Match Me's long time general counsel, and her athlete husband, offered hugs rather than handshakes.

"I'm happy to see you. How was your drive over?" Casey asked, stepping aside allowing both beautiful people to walk in.

They had been there before. But as everybody else did, they had to linger, eyes wide, to appreciate the home.

"We are so, so good. And Casey," Sasha began with just a trace of a southern accent that had faded over the years, but refused to go away completely, "I know I say it every time, but this home is beautiful."

"Thanks, I do love it." The ease and honesty of her agreement caught Casey by surprise. She really did love it. "Please, come in." Casey looked up. "There is somebody I'd like for you both to meet."

"Well, I'll be damned." Sasha followed Casey's eyes and let them widen with approval. "If it isn't the doctor himself."

"Former." Travis strolled up with the casual confidence of a lion leading his own little pride, and offered his hand and a smile that would have put a room full of anxiety-ridden people at ease.

As Sasha and Zeb softened and returned Travis' smile and handshake, Casey's eyes burned into him. *Former?* What was he thinking?

"It's really nice to finally meet you," Sasha said, then moved aside for her husband to offer his own greeting. "We had no idea you were thinking about a career change."

Casey watched the exchange: Sasha and Zeb were genuinely intrigued and Travis was twisting what was once a lie into a half-truth.

"I love analytics, and at the end of the day that's what I wanted to do. A buddy of mine offered me a shot." Travis included Casey into the conversation by glancing in her direction between eye contact with their guests, and she couldn't believe it. "So I took it."

The hearty nods showed Casey they didn't judge or find anything wrong with what Travis was saying. Just simple admiration.

"That's really inspirational." Zeb gave Travis a pat on the shoulder as he followed the offered hand toward the kitchen. "I appreciate people who really feel like they are doing what they love. That's what made me quit the game."

Travis nodded and led Zeb to a drink table to continue the conversation. "That's right, Casey mentioned you quit the game. Wasn't that a tough transition?"

He remembered. Casey didn't give herself time to identify the feeling that came over her as she watched Travis. A part of her wanted to believe it was a fluke. That he'd remembered just this one bit of information about her coworkers that would make the night easy and seamless. But she knew that wasn't it. She knew he would remember everything.

"Oh, I remember that feeling."

Casey pulled her attention away from Travis to acknowledge Sasha. "Sorry?"

"You know, that feeling before you're married. My mom called it *admiration.* She said I was filled with it when Zeb and I first met. Everything he did was so impressive and brilliant and smart to me."

Sasha's laugh at the innocence of their young relationship gave Casey a bit of time to recover.

Admiration.

Was *that* what she was feeling?

"Isn't it amazing that after three years together you still feel that way about him? How lucky that we've found men we can look at like that."

"Right."

Casey's words were quiet as Zeb held a drink high toward his wife. She passionately agreed and made her way to him, her own arms wide. They clinked their glasses together and laughed, and Casey felt their energy vibrating throughout the floor. They were excited about the night out and the fun they could have. And they *were* fun.

Shaking her head at their youthfulness, Casey grinned and nodded when Travis held up a bottle of white in an attempt to lure her over.

"Okay." Her voice was low, relenting, and happy. And somehow he knew she'd prefer the crisp white, but this time, it wasn't as much as a surprise as it was appreciation that he took care in the details–her details.

The four settled into relaxing conversation, and when Witford Lewis, the Chief Financial Officer, and his wife, Tara, arrived, they joined the laidback start to the evening.

Travis watched Casey and the way she settled in with this group. He wondered why she was nervous at all as he took in the small exchanges and the quick laughter as they all shared details of their lives. She seemed satisfied with his portrayal of her long-time boyfriend, or she'd forgotten all about it.

When he rested a hand on the small of her back as they stood before taking comfortable seats in the living room, she didn't flinch. When he offered her another drink she took it graciously and smiled at him in a way that seemed more natural than he'd ever seen.

Was it an act? He wondered, as Casey leaned her back into him in a playful bump as he told a childhood story about his glory days of running around and getting into trouble with his best friend Luke.

Then the doorbell rang, and he understood.

Travis watched Casey try to hide the shift, but her demeanor and breath inched closer to a sharp edge. Her back straightened and tightened slightly, and the up and down of her chest increased with every inhale and exhale.

"Our last guest has finally arrived. I'll grab the door," Travis said to the crowd as though they could now get the festivities started. Then he leaned down to place a slow kiss to Casey's temple and whispered, "You're doing great, don't worry about a thing."

The enthusiastic inflection of Carrie's voice unfolded as it crept down the entryway hall to meet the rest of the crowd in the living area.

"Well," Witford began, "I think there's one person that might be even more satisfied about your relationship than you are, and she just walked in."

The comment had Casey's mind fighting nerves in a barrage of questions and doting that would inevitably follow Carrie's arrival, and the idea that Witford–and apparently all of her guests–thought she was *satisfied* in her relationship.

"Satisfied?" Casey tried to mask the question with a cloak of humor.

"Girl, you don't have to try and play it cool with us, we see the way he looks at you and the way you get that spark with his touch. He's your guy. We see it."

Sasha had a way of speaking that allowed your mind to visualize her comments. At her words Casey felt Travis' stare once more and the feeling of his lips innocently pressing against her, but causing slightly suggestive thoughts to dance into her already busy mind.

"And she's blushing!" It was Tara's turn to get excited.

Now Casey felt like her co-workers and their significant others were starting to embrace the ideals of her girlfriends. She needed to get out.

"Yeah, yeah." Casey stood. "I need to go greet our guest."

"You can leave," Sasha laughed as she leaned across the couch to follow Casey's movements to the front of the house, "but that blush on your face is matching your pretty lips!"

Casey waved away Sasha's comment and the humor it caused in the rest of the crowd. Then followed her actions with a drink of wine, less a dainty sip and more of a gulp.

In what world would she retreat the safety of Sasha and Witford and their wonderful plus ones, to go *toward* Carrie? That was just ridiculous.

The sight of Carrie's arms wrapped around Travis shouldn't have bothered her. And shouldn't have for more reasons than she could quickly file through: they had hugged all of their guests that arrived that night, Travis wasn't *really* her boyfriend, it was Carrie's nature to be outgoing and friendly, and Travis was doing exactly what he was supposed to do in welcoming people he had theoretically known for three years into what could be assumed was *their* home.

But something hit Casey in the pit of her stomach as she watched Carrie squeeze the last bit of their hug to an end, then pull back and gaze at Travis from arm's length.

Jealousy? Mistrust?

What was that feeling?

Travis felt her presence, and when he turned, saw the pallor in her face. The smile he'd used for the greeting turned immediately to concern. He needed to go to Casey, but couldn't cause a scene–especially in front of the woman who caused most of Casey's anxiety. Dote and care, he thought.

"Here she is." Travis easily broke away from Carrie's arms, smiled, and walked to Casey with an outstretched hand.

Without thinking, and wanting nothing more than to comfort and draw Casey back to him and away from her worry, he did the only thing he could think of–and wanted nothing more than to do since the first time their lips met.

Travis reached down to link his fingers with Casey's, then lightly pressed his lips to hers. With all of the tenderness he could, he let the moment linger; and the breath from the slow closeness of their faces innocently, but intimately, pulled them into a world all their own.

When he felt her lips relax and her fingertips gently grip his, he opened his eyes to see Casey's lazily do the same. He tried for a small grin and then saw the most beautiful thing in the world. Casey's lids became bashful, a rosy hue flushed her cheeks, and a laugh escaped her lips.

It was beautiful, he thought, because it was unbridled, unblemished happiness.

If Carrie hadn't squealed at their display of affection, Casey would have forgotten she had been there at all. She felt Travis wrap his arm around her back and rest his hand on the delicate curve of her waist so they could open up to their final guest. And because Casey couldn't think of much else, she simply lifted a slacken arm and said, "Welcome!"

—

Cioppino might have been created by Italian immigrants on the San Franciscan coast, but the raven-haired French chef in Casey's kitchen had mastered the herby tomato sauce, and the salt-water fish was cooked to buttery perfection. The stew decorated large earthy stone bowls and was served with slices of toasted bread soaking in the broth. A light lemon and parmesan arugula salad accompanied the dish. The only thing more impressive than the flavorful feast in front of them was the flowing conversation that only paused due to the occasional moan of a satisfied bite, or agreeable silence, as nobody felt words should interrupt the extraordinary quiet that was deserved while devouring the indulgent meal.

When Casey leaned back contentedly, the only thing that could have ruined the moment was the sound of Carrie's voice—or more specifically, the sound of Carrie's voice turning the conversation toward her and Travis' relationship.

"Casey, I have to tell you," Carrie started, placing the last bit of crusty toast on her bread plate and daintily wiping the crumbs off her fingers, "I had an idea of what you two would be like together, or the type of man you would be with, but," she stole a pretty little look toward Travis and Casey couldn't help but follow her eyes, "Travis seems perfect for you in every way."

Casey felt her internal temperature rise and wasn't sure if it was due to the offense taken at Carrie's words or the fact that she felt the urge to defend their lie.

Folding her napkin and deliberately placing it on the table, Casey couldn't stop the pointed question from coming. "What do you mean *the type of man I would be with* exactly?"

Travis' hand came to her thigh and rested for a moment before she pulled it out of his reach.

"Oh you *know!*" Carrie sang, flipping a blond tendril behind her shoulder, looking around the table knowingly.

"I don't." The words were a short and sharp opposite to Carrie's fun and exaggerated. Casey felt Aimeé's eyes on her from the kitchen, where her competent movements were quietly replacing dirty dishes with new dessert plates. Even with the silent calm Aimeé was trying to send her, anger flared.

Carrie was too confident and strong to let tone scare her away. She was hard-nosed in a kind and tactful way, always responding to the words that were said, rather than the way they were given—or in this case, thrown.

The table of guests weren't as unsettled as they could have been with Casey's snap of words. Perhaps they've known her too long. Carrie smiled to assure them she wasn't concerned at the question, and relaxed her face before responding.

"I mean, Travis," this time Carrie nodded in his direction rather than looking on adoringly, "complements you in every way. He seems smart enough to keep up with you–which isn't easy. He's funny enough to match your wit. He's your rock and you are his light, and," Carrie looked around the table and wriggled her eyebrows before gathering her glass of wine and raising it in a faux toast, "he's gorgeous, just like you."

The toast coaxed cheers from the rest of the table. Casey circled the table with her blank gaze. She didn't want to, as the comments were supposed to be a compliment, but she saw through Carrie's words and their secret affection for Travis, and raised her glass anyway. Casey joined in clinking her glass with the other smiling faces. When she finally touched hers to Travis', who was either playing along nicely, or sincerely liked the attention, he winked and offered her a killer grin.

Obviously not learning her lesson, or simply satisfied that she'd gotten the rest of the table on board with the discussion, Carrie dove into the marketing campaign that would feature Casey and Travis.

"It's going to be fun and full of life!" Carrie said, her energy rising with every word. "Just like Casey!"

Travis choked back a sip of wine at the comment. He played it off by giving Casey a hard time about being "fun," just as any other couple would do, earning laughter all around. But, as he sat and watched Carrie, he wondered if this woman knew Casey better than Casey realized.

The way Casey was around the girls and the way her busy life kept her moving, the way she indulged for herself and gave to her friends. He would have used similar words to describe her if he had been tasked with marketing the pretty red-head to his left. Now *that* was interesting.

"The way you both play off of each other and the stunning image you will make photographed together–I just–there are no words." Carrie covered her heart and shook her head in awe.

Giving herself a couple points for restraint and not commenting on Carrie actually not having words for something, Casey tried for sarcasm but landed somewhere between amicable and funny: "Well, we are just, so, *so* attractive."

"I just can't believe we didn't do this sooner. Casey, had you flaunted Travis before this night we could have done this years ago."

"Yeah, well," Casey widened her eyes, "I guess I just wanted to keep him all to myself."

"And I suppose his need to save lives played a part, too."

"It's a shame the medical industry is losing you, but we'll love having you around more." Witford joined the game, and at his words it was Casey's turn to cough on the liquid she'd just sipped.

Casey watched the information register with Carrie and saw it add a twinkle to her eye as if it were exclusive gossip about the royal family.

Shit.

Casey wouldn't have used the word *panic* to describe one of her common reactions; distress and fear weren't in her wheelhouse. But the way the wheels were turning in Carrie's brain were evident and it nearly sparked just that.

"I had *no* idea you were stepping away from the medical field." Carry spoke to Travis and shot a shaming look at Casey for not divulging such critical, and life-affecting news. "That must be difficult." Carrie's eyes smoothed and offered concern. "Casey, how do you feel about this?"

As if somebody's profession was her choice. Casey had to try and take Carrie's stupid question seriously. In what world would she ever tell somebody, especially the man that was supposed to be her boyfriend, what they could or couldn't do with their life?

"I'm surprised at your question, Carrie."

Travis' words caused Casey and the rest of the table's attention to turn in his direction.

"If anybody understands that a person should be able to do what they want in life and have the freedom to find their own happiness, it's Casey. She herself has created a work palate that yes," Travis grinned in her direction, "sometimes causes her personal life to run on a thin line, but it works perfectly with the ambitious and intelligent–beautiful–woman she is."

Carrie smiled knowingly, as if she knew Casey was exactly as Travis had described, but found additional appreciation that Travis had been the one to defend his choice on Casey's behalf. That saved her from doing something that she would have never done–speak highly of herself regardless of the situation.

Zeb cleared this throat from the end of the table before adding his two-cents. "I think when a man gets to a certain point in his relationship and life, he begins to reevaluate his priorities." He looked at Sasha, "Sometimes being closer to home, and the woman in it, becomes what you want most."

Sasha leaned a head on Zeb's shoulder and smiled like a woman who was still madly in love. Everybody watched and agreed, except Casey. She stared at Travis and couldn't help but think the words he and Zeb said were what they truly believed.

Casey watched Carrie nod appreciatively, seeming to know exactly what Zeb was talking about.

—

"Interesting night so far, no?"

Casey looked up from the bathroom sink and found Aimeé's reflection in her mirror.

"I don't want to hear it."

"What do you mean? I'm making conversation." Aimeé waved a hand before folding her arms across her chest.

Narrowing her eyes, Casey wiped her hands on the towel then folded it back into the neat rectangle Grace and Rachel had made hours earlier. "You," she said, pointing toward the mirror, "know *exactly* what you're doing."

"And that is?"

"You're trying to get me to make a comment about Travis and how well he is doing. And how he's stepped in exactly when needed. And that he has successfully dodged any of Carrie's irritating advances and comments."

Aimeé smirked. "Well, I wasn't going to say *that,* but since you brought it up…" Aimeé waited for Casey's annoyance to settle. "It seems to me the night, thanks to Travis and to your obvious affection for him, has gone better than you expected. Possibly, it has even gone well."

Aimeé reached forward to hand Casey the maroon lipstick that had been assigned to her when Grace and Rachel left. She was to help Casey reapply when needed. The deep hue boosted confidence and desirability. Aimeé couldn't turn down the task with those added benefits on the line.

Swiping the gold stick, Casey applied the fresh color while sneaking disapproving looks at Aimeé. When she finished, she handed the stick back to Aimeé, who placed it neatly back into her apron pocket, and floated out of the room.

Casey's eyes trailed Aimeé as she sauntered out of the door and leaned against the counter when she made it to the kitchen. The moment had her assessing the night and the time. She still had a couple hours left before everybody would finally pack up and head out, but she felt the hard part was over. Now they could add more drinks and talk about the upcoming work that would pile their plates high with meetings, travel, and unfortunately, love.

CHAPTER 16

The tables and counters on the main floor no longer held plates and trays of appetizers, dinner, or dessert. Dishes had been cleared and loaded into the industrial dishwasher. The candles were burning down to small mounds of lightly scented wax, and lights where people could have wandered when the meetings were finished had been dimmed. Everything was quiet.

Casey cherished the silence as she stood under the single amber light that hung above the sink and dried the remaining glasses that needed a gentler wash and wipe.

Aimeé had retreated to a bedroom on the far end of the house, rightfully exhausted at the undeniably exquisite cuisine she'd prepared for the evening. Casey hadn't seen Travis since he finished running a rag over the dining table and counters, and wandered down to the basement, most likely to view and sample the whiskey collection.

Casey closed her eyes as if the action could erase the image of Carrie and Travis sharing a welcome hug when she first arrived. It was innocent, but the idea that it was bothering Casey was an issue enough. She didn't want to let Travis affect her in a way that would cause her to feel jealousy. It wasn't something she wasn't familiar with. And it definitely wasn't something she had anticipated would make her a bit nauseated.

Travis had immediately come to her when she had appeared in the foyer. He'd comforted. Had done all of the right things. Then, and throughout the rest of the night. Never in her lifetime did she think she would be grateful for a man. But she had to admit, having him there with her, even with the questions they'd had to answer about their fictitious relationship, was better than having to go through the evening alone.

The last of the glasses were gently placed in a large hutch, and Casey turned to weigh her options. Upstairs to change into her baggiest sweatpants, or, she eyed one of the glasses she just put away, pour herself some wine, stretch out on the sofa, and let the blur of a final glass help ease her into relaxation.

"Always choose wine."

Casey's eyes traveled to the door where Travis had climbed the stairs from the basement, standing and grinning at her with one hand in a pocket and the other holding whiskey over ice.

"Especially when you're wearing *that.*" Travis let his eyes travel the length of Casey's body.

As his eyes moved, Casey felt a cool air tickle her bare skin, traveling down the deep-V of her white blazer.

For the first time that evening she realized with the undoing of a single button, Travis could explore far more of her body, and with more than just his eyes. The thought caused a warm ache that challenged her cool exposed skin.

No. Casey fought the feeling and her thoughts. Don't go there, or let yourself *feel* those feelings.

"You have an irritating way of reading my mind," Casey said as she reached for a glass.

Travis shrugged, lifted himself from the door frame, then casually walked to the living room where Casey had planned to take her rest. She watched him out of the corner of her eye as she poured. When she corked the bottle, she turned. "Thank you."

The words were simpler than she thought they would be. But she wanted to say them before she became more irritated with him and the feelings he was causing.

Casey waited the length of the room for Travis to make a witty remark about his charm and classy display of character he'd had that evening. When nothing came she sat on the opposite end of the L-shaped couch, stretched her feet toward the middle, and rested her head on the large pillow cushion behind her. Casey sighed and thought–like many times before–*this* is the best feeling in the world. Feet up after a long day, after a nice dinner, savoring a glass of wine.

"I couldn't have said it better myself." Travis mimicked Casey's sigh. "And, you're welcome," he continued, responding to her earlier thanks, "for the evening."

There was no cocky remark, or polite conversation that she would have been just fine on her own. Casey watched Travis swirl the whiskey around the block of ice and thought, no, there wouldn't be, would there? There was a place and time for his charismatic humor, but here, with her, he didn't feel it was needed. And it wasn't, she agreed with him, though she didn't need to. It seemed how she saw him now was exactly how he *was*.

Sipping the last of his whiskey, Travis looked at Casey and held her stare.

It was either his look or her wine, but one of them sent a slow burn into the pit of her stomach.

Then she heard his voice.

"Well, there's nothing I want more than my sweats and a good book. I think I'm heading up for the night."

Casey's mouth gaped. He was *leaving?* Going to *bed? What?*

Travis hid the smirk that was trying to break his even tone. He stood, and walked toward Casey and her terrible poker face. She could lose all of her money with a look like that. But nothing could have made him happier. He bent down as Casey lifted her jaw and brought her lips back together.

"You are stronger than you give yourself credit for, and have too much love not to share it. You did good tonight."

Travis kissed her cheek then walked away.

Baffled, Casey watched him drop his glass at the sink, then turn to walk up the stairs. When he was out of sight Casey returned her head to its forward position and thought, *the worst has happened.* Worse even than realizing his words were true.

Casey realized she wanted nothing more in that moment than to sleep with Travis Mavens.

CHAPTER 17

Grace and Rachel had beat Casey to the Bistro, and they noticed–which to Casey's mind was worse than being late and not getting a head start on whatever adult beverage Aimeé would be serving them for their weekly girls night.

Typically, she wouldn't have driven in from the lake house. She would have been downtown already, either working from her loft or upstairs at Thomas and Jane. And she would have had time to get a couple sips of alcohol before her friends would start drilling her about Travis. But today, she and Travis had carpooled into work together because when he offered, her logical brain had, now regretfully, agreed.

"Well, hello."

Casey didn't like the way Rachel's words dripped with knowledge. The two words felt like she'd said, *'I know you're having thoughts of sleeping with Travis, and I can't wait to receive my payout. Thank you. Oh, and hello.'*

"Don't cash your check before it's written." Casey walked in without her usual backpack of laptops. A perk, she supposed, of going home before her night out. "I'm not, and will not be, sleeping with Travis."

Though, she was quite certain that had Travis so much as *started* to ask for just that Saturday night, she would have given in. At least then she could have blamed the wine.

Rachel just smiled and tilted an eyebrow.

"Come on now, Rach," Grace said as she set four martini glasses on the table, "go easy on her. This is new territory for Casey."

"I'm right here. And how do you know I haven't done it yet and I'm just not telling you?"

The women spared a questioning look at each other, then turned to study Casey. Grace squinted her eyes for effect and Rachel leaned obnoxiously too far across the table as if to get a closer look.

"Because you look," Aimeé paused when she got to the table and gave herself another couple seconds of examination, then settled for, "stuffy."

"Stuffy?" Casey questioned as she held out her glass to accept any form of alcohol Aimeé was offering in the pitcher she'd brought from the kitchen.

"Yeah, I can see it," Rachel agreed.

"Yes, stuffy." Aimeé nodded. "Like you want to sleep with Travis because you like him. But you don't let yourself. So you stuff it all inside."

"Well, I'll tell you what's *not* going to be stuffed inside."

"That's crude." Grace laughed with the rest of the girls. "Even for you."

Even Casey joined in, against her usually solid self-control. Why not have a little fun, she thought. But she didn't have to try to let go because Grace started talking about her wedding and spared her.

"I've made a couple of *big* decisions about the wedding. Do you want to know what they are?" Grace lifted the world's largest three-ring binder onto the table and opened to a middle tab with precision.

"Ah, *yes*," Rachel said, clearly unable to reach beyond two-word sentences today, leaving the intonation to do the job for her. This tone meaning, 'Of course we want to know. Why would you ask such a ridiculous question.'

"I've determined colors, and," the pause had everybody leaning in, "my maid of honor."

Cheers erupted around the table.

They all knew they would be a part of the special day–whatever role they played. Casey hoped it wasn't hard for Grace to make the decision and hoped she knew hard feelings wouldn't be felt. The choice, to Casey's mind, between Aimeé and Rachel would have come down to availability and money.

Rachel would be available, but it would be easier to ask Aimeé to front some of the cost–because let's face it, being a maid of honor was time consuming and expensive. Casey would help the best she could and understood the role she would play. She would be proud to stand up as a bridesmaid with Grace and do whatever she could to help plan the day.

And, she was *not* maid of honor material, which made Grace's choice a heck of a lot easier.

Leaning back, Casey took a sip of her drink. Hmm, lemon, and was that lavender? She lifted the skinny glass to look inside. Not only did it taste like spring, it looked like it too.

Taking another sip she looked to Rachel and Aimeé who were waiting expectantly. They obviously had come to the same conclusion she had. By the looks on their faces Casey half expected a repeat of the 1700's, round two of the French-American war.

Aimeé politely crossed her long leg over the other and Rachel tried to fold her hands neatly on her lap. Both smiling as courteously as they could.

"Casey," Grace said.

Everybody waited for Grace to continue, assuming she had a quick question or comment before moving forward with her decision.

Casey looked over and waited for her to continue, and when Grace said nothing, Casey pressed, "Well? Are you going to tell us?"

"I just did. Casey. I choose Casey."

"What?" It wasn't unanimous surprise, it was unified confusion.

"You mean like," Casey began, "like, you're picking *me?* To be your maid of honor?"

"Exactly like that." Grace beamed.

It took a second for Rachel and Aimeé to register what had just happened, but as the realization set in, their eyebrows shot up, and they whole-heartedly agreed it was the perfect choice.

"It's Casey!" Rachel couldn't hide her excitement.

"I cheers to that," Aimeé agreed with a lift of her drink.

"Wait, wait. I'm not–I mean, that's not–I can't." Casey stared at her three friends' faces.

"Of course you can. You're perfect for the job."

Casey blinked at Grace. "Why would you ever think that?"

"You are organized, good at making decisions, people know you, and the most important of them all," Grace's smile turned genuine, "you love me."

Oh, she was good. Casey felt the inside of her body soften, and she realized, with those three little words Grace plopped right at the end of her argument, she was hooked. Her head dropped, and she shook it but couldn't keep the smile from forming–or the tears from welling in her eyes.

"So, will you do it?" Grace asked, leaning down to try and see Casey's reaction.

When Casey looked up, tiny water droplets fell from her eyes, and she couldn't believe that her emotions were letting her down. But she couldn't help them any more than she could help the overwhelming sense of happiness she had for Grace.

"Yes, I'll do it."

Aimeé was the first to wrap her arms around Casey because she was sitting right next to her. Grace and Rachel launched out of their chairs and rounded the table before Casey could tell them to sit their asses back down. And before she knew it, Casey was in the middle of warm hugs and more tears.

"Okay, okay," she huffed out a chuckle, "get off me already. Sit down and tell us all the colors and whatever else it is that goes along with making that decision."

"Fine," Grace agreed, but none of them let go.

"Off! Now!" Casey laughed again and finally felt her friends unfold one by one. She pulled out her phone and opened a new notes page and looked up. "Ready when you are."

"Oh, you really are going to be good." Rachel smiled as her bum found the bottom of her chair.

"Might as well be the best."

The women waited patiently after Aimeé announced she had pesto flatbreads warming in the oven for their dinner, and excused herself to take them out. When she returned they were all once again patiently waiting on Grace, this time through scalding bites of cheesy garlic and herbs on thin, fresh dough.

"Cream," Grace said through a heavy breath as she tried to keep her mouth from burning. "Everything will be cream. Your dresses, the flowers, the dinner plates, the linens. The only thing that won't be cream will be the leaf fillers for the vases, which will be deep, pretty greens."

"Elegant and beautiful," Aimeé said as she rested her chin on her hand and daydreamed Grace's vision. Everything about it reminded her of her grandmother. Whenever she thought of the French countryside she thought of creamy whites and ivories. Everything from the walls, to the sheets her grandmother hung on the lines, to the cookware that sat on the light stone countertops. Yes, she thought, Grace's day would be beautiful, just like her Grandmother's memory.

"I hope so," Grace admitted. "I went through every possible color option but every time I came back to a beautiful light cream."

"Just like your love," Rachel smiled. "Pure."

"It makes sense."

Three faces turned toward Casey ready for her explanation. She couldn't help the rush of information that flooded her mind any more than she could help explaining it. And they knew it.

"You have a psychological tendency for order and symmetry. You are organized as a person and with your thoughts. It's a clean color that lends well to those traits. But," Casey said, not wanting it to be all about the A-type personality of her friend, "it also displays an appreciation for life, family, and friends. It's a welcoming and helpful color. And yes," now Casey looked to Rachel, "it is also pure, like your love."

"I believe you have just confirmed your color." Aimeé smiled and rested a hand on Casey's, silently letting her know that she did wonderfully, and would continue to do just that until Grace and Luke's wedding.

The knock on the Bistro door surprised everybody but Aimeé. Casey watched Aimeé excuse herself, then smile and wave before unlocking the door to let Christopher in.

When he turned and saw the smirks on their faces he gave in. If you can't beat 'em, join 'em.

"Hey, girls." The words dragged out as if he was a fifteen year old Los Angeles socialite, earning a laugh around the table.

"Don't 'hey girl' me," Casey joked with a straight face, "I'm a maid of honor. Much more sophisticated than your greeting."

Christopher stood at attention. "I had no idea I was in the presence of such…such, yeah, I have nothing. What are you ladies up to?" he asked through the laughs.

"Typical Thursday night, drinking our sorrows away."

"School's that bad, huh?" Christopher asked Rachel.

"They are all exactly like *you* were as a child. Rambunctious and they all *think* they are hilarious."

"Hey now, I *was* hilarious," he said, remembering the many classes he, Rachel, Casey, and Grace shared as kids. He might have disrupted a class or two, but he would have been better if he'd had a teacher like Rachel.

"I'll give you that."

"What brings you around?" Grace asked.

Casey didn't have to. Her mind floated instantly to the afternoon she had viewed the Bistro's suspicious finances.

"I'm checking on some things for Aimeé in my spare time."

"That's nice of you, nothing too serious I hope."

Christopher looked at Grace wondering why Aimeé hadn't let them in on what was going on at the Bistro. "Nothing we can't figure out." He shot a look at Casey who stared long enough for him to nod. A silent agreement. He knew she could–and would–help in an instant if needed.

Everybody but Christopher noted the change in the way he stood, and just about every other detail, when Aimeé walked in. His body got a little straighter, his smile a little wider, and his eyes a little brighter.

Aimeé saw it too. Which is why when she handed him the manila envelope, when she would normally have let her hand linger and flirt, she pulled it away, smiled nicely, then let her eyes drift from his.

Interesting, Casey thought. One man Aimeé wasn't willing to flirt with. She shook her head to shake the thought away but it held firm: she, Casey, *wanted* to have sex, and Aimeé *didn't*. What was this world coming to?

When the door was securely locked behind Christopher, Casey needed a new topic to get her mind to focus on something else. She waited for Aimeé to sit, then asked.

"What's going on?"

It wasn't a light question, and it wasn't a request. She, and the girls had seen the quiet and the secrecy, and now they wanted to know.

Aimeé refilled their glasses, crossed her long legs once more, then pushed a stray, piece of short black hair behind her ear.

"Somebody is stealing from me. Not physically at the store. Somehow they are making small transfers from my Bistro accounts and making them look like normal expenses."

Casey figured it was exactly that.

"Christopher is helping me investigate my employees first. My bank is tracking my payments and helping me verify what is a good–" Aimeé paused, searching for the word.

"Transaction?" Casey offered, having seen the emails come and go from Aimeé and her bankers.

Aimeé figured Casey knew as much, but this time welcomed the intrusion.

"Yes, transaction."

"Has it been a lot of money?" Grace wondered aloud.

Aimeé looked to Casey then down, knowing Casey would know if she lied.

"Yes, it has been. I foolishly did not pay close enough attention over the years. It is almost two hundred thousand dollars."

"Two hundred *thousand*?" Rachel's surprise matched only Grace's.

Casey was surprised it wasn't more. It was an effective way to swindle money. Especially when the bank accounts were scattered throughout the world. It would take a while to trace them back to a single source.

She thought of Jimmy–Aimeé's best employee, and his business degree. She hadn't looked into him for the simple fact that she didn't want it to be him. But with Christopher unable to find anything as of yet, she might have to do just that.

"I am lucky I do well. It hasn't impacted my business operations."

"But it's a big deal," Rachel insisted.

"Christopher is helping me." Aimeé brushed it off. "I don't want the night to be about this. Let's move on."

The room was silent for only a moment until Rachel grinned and nodded, "I'm perfectly willing to talk about Christopher instead."

"There is nothing to talk about." Aimeé coolly dismissed the topic.

Casey smirked, "You mean *nothing* because you don't let yourself stare at him, smile at him, touch him, or flirt with him?"

"Precisely," Aimeé said, looking pointedly at Casey. Her dark eyes squinting and her lips resting in a challenge.

Grace and Rachel shared a glance that told them they could sit back and watch the show if the two held their ground long enough.

Then Aimeé's dainty features relaxed and Casey knew what was coming.

"I will sleep with Christopher, when *you* sleep with Travis."

Casey and Aimeé held their stare.

"This is the best day of my life." Rachel looked on as if she were watching the latest reality TV show.

"Look at the time," Casey said, the first to break eye contact. Normally she would have gone down with a fight, but she felt the need to let herself and Aimeé off the hook. "I still have to drive to the lake. All my crap for work's there."

"Boo." Grace lamented her early departure.

"I know. But I also have to do some early morning organization for some crazy wedding I'm now the maid of honor for."

"Well played." Grace slanted her eyes at Casey. "Very well played. You may leave at your leisure."

Casey moved around the table, placing her first kiss on Aimeé's cheek and lingered whispering, "I'm always here to help." Then rounded to Rachel, and lastly Grace and moved to the door.

"Love you all. Night."

"Drive safe, love you."

The girls watched her leave, then Grace and Rachel focused on Aimeé.

"What?" Aimeé said innocently.

"You *know* she wants to sleep with Travis," Rachel said.

"Of course."

"Then why did you say-"

"To give her a bit more to think about."

The sly smile played across Aimeé's pretty face and her two friends grinned with her.

"You think she'll do it," Rachel said. It wasn't a question but an interpretation of Aimeé's thoughts.

"I do."

"It's dangerous," Grace chimed in.

"It's just sex."

"But it's not. It's not just sex when you're in love. It is far more."

"It's dangerous," Grace repeated.

"For her, yes. Probably the most dangerous thing she feels she'll ever do."

CHAPTER 18

"What are you up to this weekend?"

Casey looked up from her screens to see Travis standing in the doorway of her home office. She checked the time and saw it was already five-thirty. He must have commuted home already.

He was wearing his Friday stubble and she saw the same tired look he usually carried at the end of a stressful week of work. The Thomas and Jane acquisition was a great move, and many of the parts were integrating smoothly, but it didn't mean it wasn't hard work. And she had watched Travis work harder than most.

The only thing she noticed more than Travis' appearance was her stomach rumbling in protest at missing lunch. She had only been feet away from the kitchen all day, yet her work had consumed her–mind and body.

Dinner. She wanted dinner.

"How do you feel about grabbing dinner? I think a couple patios are open along the lake. A Friday night on the water?"

"As long as you agree to an appetizer and dessert."

"You read my mind." Casey mindlessly let her fingers close down her applications. She always made a point to back out of everything she was working on. After making a mistake in college, she'll never do it again. It started with an innocent game she played while watching TV, but she forgot to shut down before going out for the night, and found herself with a police escort back to her dorm, where her IP address had been traced due to her latest hack.

"I just need five minutes to change and I'll be ready. If you want to call ahead, get a table for two we might be able to get in right away."

"But I didn't tell you where."

"You pick the place."

"I'm not sure the *places* hold tab-"

"Tell them you're calling on behalf of Casey," she said, her voice trailing behind her as she climbed the stairs.

"Right."

Travis pulled out his phone to look up a couple restaurants, chose, dialed, and was stonewalled. Until he told them he was calling on behalf of Casey. Then he heard, "Of course, we'll have a table for Ms. Saunders ready. Would you like the patio?"

After rolling his eyes he agreed, "Yes, that would be great. Thanks."

The only thing Casey had changed, he noted, was her jeans. But something about the flowy buttoned shirt tucked into the skinny jeans, with her collar sitting tall, and her hair swirled on the top of her head, had him doing a double take. She had added thin gold hoops to her ears that dangled just above her shoulders. And when she reached the bottom of the stairs she grabbed a jean jacket that would assist the outdoor heating lamps in keeping her warm.

A slow smile worked its way to his face and he suddenly knew there was no way he could exist in this world without Casey in his life. No other woman he would ever want to see walking down the stairs. He wanted nights in sweatpants while they watched their favorite shows. He wanted easy breakfasts together, and dinners out on patios when they were too tired to cook for themselves. And more than he wanted to be intimate with Casey–which was a hell of a lot–he wanted to lay with her at night, their arms wrapped around one another as they drifted to sleep.

"Ready?" Casey asked, snapping Travis out of his daydream.

"More than ever." And he wasn't just talking about dinner.

———

Casey read the text message from her mother in the dim glow of the fancy lakeside bathroom. Seeing Linette's name scrolled across the front of her phone made her regret hauling her bag in with her. But her lipstick was in the bag. Travis didn't need to know she was multitasking.

It was a nudge. Her mother was great at nudging. The best, actually. Eventually her nudges broke you down until you felt compelled to make a decision–often the one you wouldn't have made in the first place. This particular nudge was passively, but aggressively, asking if Casey had given more thought to joining her for lunch. Which to Casey, read a little like, *'Are you joining me for lunch, or not?'*

Casey took a long, slow breath and stared at her reflection as she washed her hands. She applied the subtle plum to her lips as women came and went in groups to the restroom. Smiling, then becoming oblivious to the other women, she wondered what Travis would do in her situation.

Weaving in and out of tables, back to the patio where Travis was waiting, Casey hurried so her body could move faster than her mind–though it never worked.

"What would you do?" she asked as she sat and leaned over the table anxious for an answer.

"Ah, like, in general? About anything?"

She held her phone out, hovering it over her drink, waiting for him to take it from her. Without breaking eye contact he reached for the phone and let his stare linger a few seconds more.

Travis scrolled through the barrage of messages from Casey's mom and noted the ratio of texts; Linette, twelve, to Casey's one. His eyes widened, an unspoken judgement. Feeling as though if this were his phone he would be irritated. He analyzed while wondering how one person could be so persistently annoying.

"What would you get out of it? The lunch, I mean." Travis handed the phone back to Casey and watched her wheels start turning. When he saw her first thoughts form on her lips he stopped her, "Not the first thing that comes to your mind; really think. What would you get?"

Closing her mouth, Casey sat back, surprised he'd stopped her. But she did think–what *would* she get out of it?

Immediately her mind took her back to her childhood, when she as a young girl wanted nothing more than her mom to show her how to apply lipstick, to curl her hair, or to have a girls day–mom and daughter–all to themselves. Instead, her dad was the caretaker, and her friends had taught her how to be a woman.

"Time," she said, looking and feeling more vulnerable than she'd ever been. "I would get time. Maybe it wouldn't be the unlimited amount that I wanted as a kid, but for those two hours, I would have time."

Travis nodded, then reached across the table and held out his hand. He didn't know if she would take it, but he hoped.

When Casey lifted hers and let it rest in what he offered as comfort and strength, he felt confident to add, "That's what you *want*. What would you get?"

While Casey searched for an answer, Travis intertwined his fingers with hers.

"I would get heartbreak, and I would be let down."

"Knowing that, are you willing to risk what you want, for what you think you'll get?"

Nobody had asked the question in quite that way before. Her friends would warn, or support, depending on the day and what she needed. But this, this was logical *and* emotional. Travis combined what she wanted and what she knew to be true, and asked the ultimate question: knowing she would most likely be disappointed, was it worth the risk?

Finally, she answered with words that had only come out of her mouth a handful of times in her years of knowing the answers to everything. "I don't know."

—

Three and a half hours, to Casey, was an eternity–especially when it clocked the amount of time spent out to dinner with a man. And yet, when the waiter arrived with the offering of another drink and the dessert menu, she didn't hesitate. She also noted Travis' relaxed nature didn't seem to mind her decision to stay–and he let it be her decision.

Along with the perfect evening of feeling like they had nowhere to be and all night to get there, she noted her sore abs as she reached for the menu. A result of laughing through dinner. Travis shared childhood stories about Luke and the *many* times they nearly lost a business deal or lost control in an executive meeting because of their inside jokes or quoting their favorite movies mid-presentation. She enjoyed listening to him talk about poker nights and how he acknowledged William and Christopher as he spoke. It was interesting hearing him describe who they were when the women weren't around. She found herself enamored with how close they'd all gotten so quickly–though, she wasn't surprised.

By now the spring sun was setting behind them, causing the far side of the lake to shimmer, and turning the water just in front of them into a cloudy London blue. It was beautiful, she realized. She'd never lingered long enough or even bothered to notice before tonight.

"Beautiful."

Casey heard Travis read her mind.

"It is, isn't it," Casey agreed softly without pulling her eyes away from the view.

"Not the lake, Casey. You." Travis watched her pull away from the evening scene and look at him. *"You* are beautiful."

It wasn't a trick. It wasn't a gimmick. He wasn't asking for anything in return. And wasn't bargaining or pleading for her to let the compliment stick. He didn't wager with her not to argue–because he didn't leave her a choice, and he didn't need to.

His words were kind and sincere. And there was so much truth in them Casey felt no desire or compulsion to resist. She didn't have to force the pleasant satisfaction that rested on her face, but she didn't smile. Just let it settle peacefully into the moment as she held his eyes.

"Spend the weekend with me."

This comment did make her smile.

"We live together; that's kind of a given."

"No." Travis lifted his glass of white wine. "Spend the weekend *with* me. Let's take walks, drink coffees, make lunches, have happy hours, eat dinners, watch movies. Spend the weekend with me," he said again.

You could get lost in his easy confidence. If this moment was the first way a person experienced Travis Mavens they could easily mistake him for boastful or conceited. But if they lingered for even a second more, or took enough care to notice the kind, playful smile that always tugged at the corner of his lip, or the soft way his eyes rested on the object of his attention–or in this case, affection–they would see he was simply at ease.

Casey measured his words and determined they fit the man. He wanted an easy, kind, playful weekend with just her. Doing things that most overlooked.

Had he not suggested they spend the weekend together, they would have done all of the things he'd offered, but in passing. It would have lacked attention. It wouldn't have been *together.*

"Okay," Casey agreed.

It was the first time she had ever accepted an offer from a man she liked. And, she realized, he asked for nothing more than her time.

CHAPTER 19

It was a sunny and springy seventy degrees. By far the most pleasant April day Casey had experienced in a long time. It lent well to the morning walk around the lake and coffees on the deck, both they and the coffees warmed by the morning sun. She was even up and dressed by eight-thirty. It's funny what your mind can do to you when you're excited about what lies ahead.

There was no doubt her cortical functioning and conscious control was low. Lying in bed she had been rested but could feel the physical agitation growing as thoughts of Travis, and the day ahead of them, stimulated her adrenaline glands. Her oxygen and glucose increased and her pupils dilated–never a good sign for a woman who wasn't looking for love, or a woman simply trying to sleep in.

The feeling was only temporary, as all science-backed excitement is, but it was enough to make falling back asleep impossible, and enough to keep her going until the endorphins from their walk took over.

They passed a local market where they bought fresh tomatoes, lettuce, avocado, and bread to make BLTs with avocado for lunch. And as the sun shifted, moving morning into afternoon, Travis read a book he pulled from the library and Casey thumbed through a magazine until the sun streaming through the windows helped her doze off for an afternoon nap.

Happy hour began when Casey woke to the sound of Travis pouring a mixed drink over ice. When he saw Casey turn to look at him over the couch, he poured another for her. They sipped and talked while music crooned in the background. They casually moved throughout the kitchen as they rolled and flattened hamburgers to grill for dinner, and munched on veggies before they were folded into foil for roasting.

After dinner they took another stroll down the street, commenting on the houses they passed and the people who lived in them if the gossip was good enough to share.

Now, as Casey looked at the fire, she couldn't believe how long, but how short, the day felt. She wanted to do it again. And wouldn't it be nice to do it with everybody?

"We should invite," Casey wanted to say *'the girls'* but realized they were no longer just *them,* "everybody?"

Travis laughed as he watched her try and process how to define their new friendships.

"I was boring, wasn't I?"

Casey returned the laugh. "No. I was just thinking about how great today was and thought it would be fun to share it with friends." She looked at Travis. "I didn't realize I needed a day like this. Something that was full, but relaxing."

"I feel the same way. And yeah," Travis sent his satisfied smile toward the lake, "it would be fun to have everybody out."

He hoped it didn't sound like he was referring to the house as if it was his own. The last thing he wanted to do was make Casey feel like he was invading her space. He knew that was a big deal for her. She wanted people to stay there, but at the end of the day, it was hers to make the offer–or to take it away.

Travis relaxed when he saw his words seemed to have little effect. She would have shown it if they had.

"I'll send a message to the girls. Want to reach out to the guys?"

She asked the question, but mostly so she could process how she felt about Travis speaking as though he was providing the invitation. '…it would be fun to have everybody out.' *'Out'* as in, where *they lived.* It didn't bother her, she realized. She also realized had it been anybody else, it probably would have.

Casey would never have noticed the song that came on the radio, but she did notice the shadow of a smile that flickered on Travis' face when it did.

"What are you smiling at?"

"It's the song my mom and dad danced to at their wedding." He looked over and the smile grew as Bryan Adams began his serenade. "Oh to be children of the eighties," he said, starting to make his move.

"What are you doing?" Casey asked with a sideways eye as Travis stretched to place his drink on the outdoor coffee table and extended a hand in her direction.

"No way, I'm not dancing with you."

Travis' deep laugh had her own words breathy with laughter as she finished her rejection.

"Come on, one dance. Humor me."

Casey looked up shaking her head. "This is ridiculous." But she put a hand in his and let him lift her from the cushion. He placed her drink next to his and led her to an open area between the house and the lake.

Pulling her close, Travis placed her hand over his shoulder, then wrapped his around her waist. The hand that pulled her to their dance floor held hers up, but intimately close to their bodies as they swayed.

"Doesn't this make you sad?"

"The song? Why would it?"

"It was your parents wedding song. They ended up getting divorced. It's sad."

Travis thought about what she said.

With his long silence, Casey worried she might have said the wrong thing and wished she could take the question back. Rather than press, she leaned her head on his shoulder and allowed him to move her.

"It isn't sad," he finally said, "because in that moment they were in love."

The song slowed and their movements with it. Travis placed a kiss on Casey's forehead. And began to pull away. As he did, just as he was about to let their fingers fall away, Casey's held firm and he paused, looking back.

"Follow me."

———

Their dance was enough to punish him. The desire he felt as her body pressed to his and the smell of her hair breathed through him as she rested her head on his shoulder nearly killed him.

Now, as Casey led him into the house, he wanted everything from her. So much so, he was afraid he wouldn't know where to start–if they started anything at all. For all he knew she was walking him in for another drink. Though he prayed that wasn't the case.

The house was lit only by the light of the moon and a stray amber glow coming from a forgotten library lamp.

Casey said nothing as her mind raced with what would happen when they crossed the threshold of her room. That's where she decided they'd go. That was a decision that came easily while they were dancing.

Now the thoughts and feelings of desire that were tugging and aching, causing her body to shudder with lust, were clouded by questions she hadn't had to consider for a long time.

Had she showered today? Did she shave? Was she ready *for a night filled with passion? Was this passion? Would he mind if she opted for her regular pajamas rather than uncomfortable, stringy lace when they were finished with…whatever they were about to do?*

With the next step her momentum and mind lost their purpose. Travis turned her, pressed her back to the wall, and took her mouth in a rapturous kiss.

Casey tried to think but the irresistible heat and cavernous need she felt radiating through his hungry lips as they consumed hers, left her mind blank.

All she could feel was longing. Longing and an intensifying urge to pull him closer, to feel his hard body press against the tingling ache coursing through her.

A low, growling moan, escaped as the pressure intensified where his pants detained his arousal.

"Casey."

The staggered, urgent sound of her name barely registered. Casey pressed to her tiptoes and wrapped her arms around him. Her fingers combed through his tousled hair.

As her body moved, Travis feared the friction might put him over the edge.

"Let me," his words escaped, frantic through desperate kisses, "take you to my bed."

"Mine." It was all Casey was allowed before her mind plunged into a dangerous, sensual world of no return. When they crossed the threshold of her room, there would be no turning back.

Travis had every intention of being able to pull himself away from her damp, silky mouth, but with every thought telling him to move back, his body fought like a man fighting for his last breath to continue. He had wanted Casey–all of Casey–for too long. Now that he could have her his heart wasn't letting her go.

His arms slid down her back, over the curve of her bottom, and lifted her around him.

Their lips continued their hunt for pleasure as Travis tried with all of his might to find a soft place to lay the most beautiful woman he'd ever known, so he carried her into the shadows beyond the door.

Travis placed Casey gently on her feet at the edge of the bed and stepped away.

"No," he said, when she tried to move toward him. He wanted to see her. And what he saw was the most miraculous vision he'd ever seen.

"My God, you're beautiful."

The moonlight streamed through the wall of windows, tinting the dark room a deep blue. The reflection of the moon off the water danced little white lights across the walls and the pale of her curves. Then, as if reading his mind, Casey slowly began to undress herself, so he could watch the light shimmer on her smooth skin.

As the sheer material of her shirt slid to the floor, Travis marveled at the sight.

Taking a step toward her, Travis lifted a hand to her face. He stroked the smooth, delicate line of her jaw, and felt her head lean into the caress. He watched her eyes close in pleasure as he traced his fingers down the length of her neck, memorizing every angle, every moonlit freckle. He marveled at her exquisite breasts as the tips of his fingers outlined her beauty. He listened as her breathy moan approved as he slid over the peaks of her nipples.

Without a word he knelt before her and continued the excruciating study of her body. The only thing stopping Casey from exploding was her selfish need to feel him continue. To let the volcano burning inside build toward the crest of a fearless eruption.

Every warm touch of his hand lit her skin on fire, and every light trace of his fingertips sent her into a tailspin of desire, leaving cool bumps in their place. The combination was like a dangerous trip through heaven and hell.

Casey felt her pulse quicken as her stomach quivered instinctively when his hands drew a line from the tender under of her breasts to her pelvis, arching out from her hips. He outlined the delicate line of her arching hip with his fingers. He slowly slid his hands around her and cupped the mounds of her buttocks, dangerously close to her moistened center, then traveled the same trail a second time with his lips.

"Travis," Casey pleaded, first with herself to hold on; then to him, because she couldn't–and didn't want to–wait any longer.

Travis looked up at Casey, her hair a glorious tangle of red curls, and even in the pale blue of night, the flushed rouge staining her cheeks. There he found something he knew was true from the moment he laid his eyes on her. He was in love. Whether she knew it or not, in this moment, she had let him in, and that was all he needed to admit it to himself. And then she spoke, and he was lost in her.

"I need you," she said, "now."

CHAPTER 20

"Holy shit, you sly son of a-"

"Good morning to you too," Travis said, cutting Luke off before Maggie could scold the profanity. There was a time and a place, and his office at Thomas and Jane was not it. Besides, he got in enough trouble there on his own.

Luke dropped into a plastic chair across from Travis and let the goofy grin linger until Travis was forced to laugh.

"I don't know why you're so amused, I'm sly nearly one-hundred percent of the time." Travis leaned back and deliberately folded his arms, his legs stretching out and crossing at the ankles out of habit.

"You have it perfected," Luke said, not needing to state he was implying Travis was being just that right now. "So are you going to make me ask?"

"I don't know what you mean."

Luke chuckled and glanced out the door to see if anybody was within earshot of their shit-shooting session.

"You're cockier than normal, and you haven't said anything to me today. You're wearing your face like you've hit the jackpot. And," Luke looked Travis up and down, "you beat me in this morning."

"I was up early," Travis said with a shrug.

"I bet you were."

Luke stared at Travis and his annoying grin and shook his head. "You really are going to make me ask. Now I know why Casey finds you so fucking irritating."

Travis' grin turned into a satisfied smile. "I'm not making you ask anything. Seems to me you're after information all your own."

"You slept with her."

Travis continued his smug stare.

"Holy shit."

Luke's change of pace and tone got the better of Travis.

"What?" Travis asked, giving in.

"Holy. Shit. I can't believe it."

"Now who's annoying?" Travis rolled his eyes, irritated that he'd given in to the barrage.

"You *actually* fell in love with her."

"Don't know why you'd be so surprised at that," Maggie said as she strolled in and plopped a pile of folders on Travis' desk. "She's about as good a catch as you can get. And Travis," she called behind her as she waddled out of the office, "get some real chairs."

The men blinked from the doorway, to the crappy chairs, then to each other. Where in the hell did she come from?

Travis watched Luke tap the plastic arm of the chair with a fingernail and shrugged at the cheap click it made.

"It's not like I haven't been busy," he said defensively.

Suddenly the smirk was back and Luke said, "Don't I know it."

Luke stood, satisfied he'd learned the truth and stumped Travis' cool façade, even if it took a bit of extra work.

"Shit-eater," Travis said to Luke's back as he stood in the doorway and put his hands in his pockets.

"I'll send you a link to the chairs I got. I know you have a *lot* on your mind."

Travis scowled at the whistle he heard until he knew Luke was out of sight and earshot, then let the grin that had been there since Saturday ease its way back to his face.

CHAPTER 21

Casey was early to the Bistro Saturday morning. It had been a week since she and Travis had slept together, and she had successfully avoided him and her friends since.

She was busy. It made perfect sense for her to stay in her downtown apartment before heading back for the weekend. She had early morning implementations, and meetings late into the evening. Missing Thursday's girls night would have been tough to get out of, but luckily an update had been scheduled at work for weeks. As far as Travis was concerned, with all that was going on it didn't make sense to drive back and forth when she could walk the couple blocks to and from work. It's something she would have done had she and Travis *not* slept together.

At least that's what she was telling herself.

She sat with her laptop open, but Casey had one eye on Aimeé who began a slow saunter over to their table, holding a wicked, *knowing,* gleam in her eyes.

Casey finished typing up the last line of an email as Aimeé slid onto the chair next to Casey and propped her head on a lazy arm and stared.

"What?" Casey's exaggerated annoyance would have worked on anybody else.

Aimeé said nothing and turned up two corners of a red-painted mouth, waiting.

The two stared until Casey's battle with impatience lost out.

"Fine, what do you want?"

"My money," Aimeé said, as confident in the statement as she was in her French baking.

"I haven't talked to you all week, you would have no idea if Travis and I-"

"Exactly. You haven't been here in a week. After you invited all of us to your house today for grilling and the night. You came in *today* so you could tell us–as if we didn't already know–before we see you and Travis dance your way into the sheets together once more."

Casey squinted, wondering how to respond. Unfortunately, she wouldn't be able to lie, and as it seemed, Aimeé already knew the truth.

"Oh, I can see it in her face!" Rachel's excited words sparked like fireworks, then her raised brows turned to Casey and asked, "Did you pay her yet? When's my payday?"

Rachel hopped into the chair across from Casey, eagerly awaiting her reply.

Apparently, they all knew, Casey thought.

"Where's our pre-wedded friend?" Might as well tell them all together and get it over with in one go.

"She's ten behind me. She was walking over when I pulled up–I called to make sure she was on time. I didn't want to wait for this."

Ignoring Rachel's rush, Casey looked at Aimeé, "In that case, I'll have a latte. Lightly sweetened, extra shot. I'm going to need it."

"Lucky." Aimeé pushed away from the table. "I'll make four." She winked at Rachel who giggled and declared her agreement for the coffee with a nod.

A burst of spring morning air rushed in as Jimmy walked four mugs to the table and bobbed a head toward their fourth.

"Looks like you're on the hook now," Jimmy said to Casey as their eyes followed Grace and the blonde curls floating behind her. She raced to the table, nearly tipping the chair as she slid in.

"Does *everybody* know?"

"Oh, look! Coffee! Thanks, Jimmy." Grace inhaled the rich espresso scent, then sent expectant eyes over her mug at Casey.

"Come on, really? Has this been an ongoing topic all week?"

Grace cradled her mug in front of her and leaned forward. "Technically it hasn't been a full week yet, since the first time we," Grace waved a finger between herself and the two that weren't Casey, "discussed your scenario was Monday."

"Cute," Casey growled, earning a sweet-as-pie smile.

"So," Aimeé began as she walked back to the table with a plate of fresh fruit and yogurt, "are we to understand you've avoided Travis as well?"

All of the heads turned and Casey could feel the heat moving to her cheeks. She shouldn't be embarrassed, so why was she feeling humiliated?

"I had a lot of work to do this week and couldn't deal with distractions."

"Bedtime distraction, or full distraction?" Rachel prodded.

"Full for sure," Grace added.

"I agree," Aimeé chimed in.

Casey couldn't help herself, "Can you explain to me what the difference is? A distraction is a distraction."

"Not all distractions are equal." Grace took the lead. "A bedtime distraction isn't emotional. It's used to distract from things like work, family, *men.*"

"Full distraction means…" Grace paused wondering if she should finish what she started.

"You're in love." Aimeé's words were matter of fact.

Casey's head snapped to her right. "What did you say?"

"Don't fuss. I'm simply stating what you feel. It is not my fault you won't admit it."

Casey let the anger wash over her. She said nothing while she packed her computer and the rest of the equipment she'd scattered on the table into her bag. She was quiet because she didn't know why she was so angry.

When she stood her friends simply watched. There weren't smirks or knowing grins. They just let her be.

Casey took a deep breath after she hoisted her backpack to her shoulder. "I'll be finished being angry with you all by the time I see you this afternoon. Don't forget the wine."

Then she turned and walked toward the door. She wanted to keep being angry but she already had millions of thoughts running through her head.

Just before the door closed behind her, Casey heard Rachel's voice flutter out the door. "Don't forget our money! An angry check cashes the same way a happy one does!"

CHAPTER 22

The worst thing about driving was the uninterrupted time to think. Casey's mind rarely quieted, so when faced with an open road she usually enjoyed as she headed to the lake, it was torture. Usually her thoughts lingered around work or irritation with her family. But today, confused and wondering thoughts about Travis–and how he would act toward her after sharing her bed, then finding her absent the rest of the week–consumed her.

Would he be distant? Put-off? Crack a joke to ease his own tension or at whatever irritation she would show toward him? Would he act like they hadn't slept together at all?

She couldn't lie to herself and wish they'd never found themselves in each other's arms, because what she felt that night was more *feeling* than she'd ever allowed herself before. Emotionally and physically. Which was exactly why she had to avoid him.

But, with her stomach in knots, what she could wish for was for things to go back to the way they were the day before they'd crossed that line. Back to the great day they'd shared, enjoying the company of one another. When things were strictly business.

Casey stared at her home, inhaled deeply and puffed out her cheeks for an exaggerated exhale.

Here goes nothing.

Confusion set in when she walked through the door, but not the kind she anticipated. The smell of bacon drifted toward the front door as she inched through it, and she wondered what Travis was up to.

"Hello?" Casey's tentative voice questioned through the entry.

"Hey! Welcome back."

Travis' voice sounded normal, happy even.

"I'm making breakfast. Want any?"

Dropping her bags at her feet, Casey walked into the open expanse of the kitchen and found Travis in sweatpants and bare feet, a pan in one hand and a spatula in another.

At Casey's stare, he continued.

"Bacon, scrambled eggs, and toast in butter on the stove." He turned to tend to what must have been the toast and commented as he worked. "Mom wasn't stellar at cooking, but she did understand the basics. At one point she watched Julia Child and learned the only way to toast bread was on the stove in a vat full of butter."

Casey couldn't stop the twitch of her lip at his story and the ease of him telling it. If he thought anything about her being gone that week, bad or good, he wasn't showing it. He was just being–Travis.

As her stomach grumbled from skipping out on breakfast with the girls, she thought a little bacon, eggs, and toast might be nice. Casey pulled out a stool and sat comfortably at the island and watched Travis flip, stir, burn the side of his arm on the toast pan, and swear his way to the fridge where he revealed a peppery looking bloody Mary with bushy celery sticks poking out of the top.

Casey nodded at his gestured offering and wondered aloud, "Were you expecting a crowd this morning?"

He eyed the pitcher and smiled like a third grader who was too small for his teeth. "I have an affinity for tomato juice, and I happen to know if I didn't drink it all myself, I had you and eventually a bucket load of friends who enjoy a good morning cocktail."

"Who am I to argue with that logic?"

Casey took the offered glass and held it up to meet his in an appreciative toast. Leaning back, she sipped and watched Travis finish making their breakfast in silence. She liked that there didn't need to be small talk. She liked watching his easy movements and the calculated way he'd timed cooking the eggs slowly to finish just as he pulled the bacon out of the oven. She liked the easy way he set the pans in front of her on the island, then walked around it to take a seat next to her. It wasn't fussy, it was perfect.

It was just like him.

—

"Are you going to tell us, or not?"

Hours later, Rachel's question sounded less like an *are you, or aren't you* and more like a *start talking*. She didn't even take the time to turn around or stop setting the outdoor dining table as the accusation flew out.

"Tell you what?" Casey rolled her eyes once for Rachel, then back the other direction to roll them away from Aimeé and Grace who were waiting, arms folded leaning against one set of the French doors leading back inside the lake house.

When none of her friends' gave an inch, Casey balked. "I mean it. Tell you what? Sex or the aftermath?"

"Both." It wasn't unusual for her friends to speak unanimously, in fact the sound of their combined voices was distinct and utterly annoying given the circumstances they were usually heard in.

As she worked up her excuse, Grace cut her off.

"The guys are fishing. Nobody here but us. Better get started."

Rachel stood satisfied over the finished table-scape of denim napkins, deep blue and white checkered plates, and bright green foliage in a tall pitcher as a centerpiece. Nodding once, she turned and linked arms with Casey on her way back into the house and led her to the couch where she handed out glasses filled with wine. Then sat patiently, waiting for Casey to start talking.

"Start with whatever's easiest," Aimeé encouraged, knowing Casey would either start talking and spill it all, or start talking, then get angry, and get up and leave. Either way she'd start talking–and in her own house she couldn't go far.

"He was completely normal today." Casey led with what was easiest to talk about, but less easy to digest. His normal had led her to some uncomfortable feelings she didn't want to have. But, he was normal, so he made it easy.

"Normal is great." Rachel guided her on.

"It is. He wasn't mad, upset, and didn't require us to 'talk about it.' And he didn't act like now, since we slept together, it was expected that we do it again."

Casey stared at nothing in particular as she thought back to the morning they'd shared. Breakfast, then a walk along the lake, parting ways for a bit without the need of explanation, then slowly making their way back to the kitchen for lunch and agreeing to easy salads and BBQ potato chips.

Tilting her head and focusing her eyes, "He didn't try to kiss me or hold my hand. Just was kind of…around."

"Does that bother you?" Grace asked, curious to understand how Casey was processing the normalcy of the day.

Casey looked to Grace with a bit of surprise, then to Rachel and Aimeé and couldn't believe the word forming.

"No."

Nobody dared push the subject since all but Casey were thinking the same thing–that she loved him and had no idea what it was or how to handle it. Which meant, after a reasonable sixty seconds they could transition.

"Great!" Aimeé chirped with a little too much cheer. "Then you can tell us about the sex."

Casey could have recounted every exhilarating detail of the evening she and Travis shared. It was her gift and curse that she had the ability to remember everything. It came to her mind as if it was happening for a second time. But, she wondered, as the memories of that night scrolled through, if she would be able to forget that night even if she tried.

Forgetting the time, and getting lost in her story, Casey–with zero help from her friends–didn't realize Travis had walked in through the back door they had left open. When she gave the description of his fingers gliding over her skin and calling it *sensual,* Travis was quick to jump in.

"You think?" He walked over and plopped next to Casey on the couch and propped his feet up. "I would have gone with something like *magical,* or *extraordinary,* or," Travis looked Casey in the eye, *"breathtaking."*

He held her stare long enough to let her know he was talking about her. The way he had seen her that night. Then pushed up. "But," he turned to the other girls, "that's just me. I better go fire up the grill."

There wasn't anything to say, so Casey sat and stared at the cushion where his body had been before he walked away. She didn't need to look around to know her friends would be hiding their smiles behind their wine glasses or giving her the *oh yeah, you've got it bad* look.

Her wine glass leaned back with her as she slowly inched down to the couch and took a sip, letting both of her eyelids fall. After minutes, without hearing a word from her friends, she begrudgingly lifted one lid to peek out.

"Oh yeah, we're still here," Rachel joked.

Each of her girlfriends sat patiently, as if they had nothing but time to wait for her to spill. The thing was, she didn't think she was ready to admit to what her friends were already thinking. Casey knew they wanted her to be in love. Or, if not love, she knew they wanted her to admit feelings for Travis.

If she were being honest with them–and herself–at this point she *did* have feelings for Travis. But that didn't mean she would have the same feelings in a week, a month, a year, or even ten years from now. And even if she did, there was no way of knowing if Travis would. If she admitted her feelings now, it could be the start of a lie. Feelings change in people. Why would she, or Travis for that matter, be any different?

"Just stop."

Casey looked up at Grace's icy tone.

"Stop it. You're over thinking. What do you feel right now, this moment?"

Were her thoughts *that* transparent?

"How do you even know–"

"Because we know you," Aimeé said softly.

"We know your history, we know the way you think, *we* know the way you can love." Rachel anticipated an argument, so she pushed on as Casey's mouth began to open. "Because you love us. And all you need to say, at this very moment in time, without making promises about the future–because nobody knows what the future holds–is what you feel right now."

Casey sighed, thought of the consequences of admitting her feelings. Shook her head and said, "I won't."

———

Travis listened to the exchange from the kitchen. It wasn't hard to hear. He could practically feel the struggle inside of Casey as her friends pressed. He knew they meant well. And, he'd be lying to himself if it didn't sting a little when Casey wouldn't easily give away how she felt about him.

That wasn't Casey though.

That wasn't the closely guarded heart he'd fallen in love with. She wouldn't say anything she didn't absolutely mean. Sure, she'd fib to avoid an absolute truth, but she wouldn't commit to a feeling–or anything for that matter–if she didn't believe it.

He squeezed another burger between the big metal press as his mind drifted unintentionally to what it was going to take for Casey to admit her feelings for him. He knew they were there.

He'd felt it in her touch when they made love, heard it in her voice when she'd said his name, saw it in her eyes as confusion cleared and nothing but the two of them remained. He would do anything to share moments like that one with Casey for the rest of their lives.

Stopping his movements, he stared, resigned to what he was going to have to do. Lucky for him he was a patient man, because he was going to have to give her time. And not just any time. Time for Casey to realize he wasn't going anywhere. And since he had marriage on the brain, Travis leaned his head back in a rare bout of exasperation, *that* was going to have to be Casey's idea.

"It's just hamburgers," Christopher said, smirking through his words as he walked into the kitchen, on the hunt for more beer. He swung the fridge open and took inventory, talking into the vast selection in front of him, "I'd just tell her how you feel, straight out."

Travis let his head fall to the left where his new friend contemplated his next beverage, "Same goes."

Christopher paused, "Point taken."

Travis heard the phone ringing as he grinned away his latest exchange and washed the last of the meat from his hands. His eyes scanned the counter and paused as he saw who was calling.

Casey stopped as she entered the room, hunting the sound of her ringtone when she saw his face.

"Who is it?" she asked, already knowing the answer.

"Your mom."

Casey moved to the phone, picked it up, but before she slid her thumb across the screen to answer, she said, "Come with me."

He didn't know where they were going, though he had a hunch. And since he was willing to do anything to be with her–anything for her– his answer was simple. "Okay."

CHAPTER 23

Dinner on the deck was casual, filled with laughter, and the mood was electric. It must have been exactly what everybody needed at the end of their busy weeks. Food and witty comments were exchanged; drinks, jokes, and heartfelt compliments were consumed.

Silence filled the table only once, as Casey swirled a glass of red while taking in the scene. It might have been the mood, the setting sun, or the complete comfort that her friends made her feel, but she suddenly heard herself say, "I'm meeting my mother for lunch next week."

The crickets weren't a metaphor, as they were the only audible sound in the background.

"You…you're what?"

It wasn't a surprise Aimeé was the first to question. Aimeé and Casey shared a bond over family drama. Each with their own version, but at the end of the day, it all hurt the same.

"She's been consistently reaching out. She did again today. Today I said 'yes.'"

The way she said it was matter-of-fact. Which made it hard for the girls to question why she would make the attempt after years of getting her heart broken when agreeing to similar situations.

"I know what you're thinking." Casey looked to Aimeé first, then to Rachel and Grace. "This time will be different."

"How?" It was all Grace could manage.

Casey sipped and didn't look at Travis as he answered, "I'm going with."

—

Waves of light reflected off of her walls in the dark of night. When the moon sat just right above the lake it was all the water needed to show off its calm ripples.

Casey watched them and thought about the evening as she listened to Travis finish his shower in her master bath. He wouldn't have followed her in had she not led him there herself. He would have, she imagined as her lips turned up in a wistful smile, planted a kiss on her that would have left her reeling and yearning for him while walking the opposite direction for his bedroom.

The smile lingered as she listened to the soothing spray of his shower, letting her eyes drift to sleep with her thoughts.

Travis had a different idea of what would happen when they made the walk up to her room, hand in hand, leaving her with a kiss before he left her to shower.

"I should go shower," he'd said to her between lazy kisses as he wrapped her in his arms and slowly swayed her across the bedroom floor.

"Do it here. Stay with me."

Casey's response had been like a drug that coursed through him causing his heart to race, but he'd held the easy dance. He left her with a final embrace and a kiss to her neck as he breathed her in before stepping away. He felt as if the bathroom was in another country rather than mere feet away, not wanting to part with her, but hold her for eternity.

Now, he stood over her, wondering if she always looked this peaceful as she slept.

Contemplating, Travis wondered if he should leave her be. Let her continue to dream in her sanctuary. He wondered if he climbed in with her, would she wake and regret leading him there to join her?

Rather than resist, he let his hand graze her cheek then gently smooth a stray curl away from her face.

Casey didn't open her eyes, but breathed deep in sleep, then lifted her hand to his before pulling it close to her heart. If he didn't already feel as though he was completely hers, this moment would have drawn him in. He knew, as he quietly climbed in next to her and as she shifted to nestle into the crook of his arm, using his body as her pillow, he would never love another woman.

When his eyes opened again the sun was turning the dark night into a purple gray. The only thing he could see was the black outline of the trees outside, but night had left and early morning had replaced it.

Travis didn't need to look down to see Casey in the same position, the weight of her body warmed his in the cool morning. Rather than move, he simply lifted his free arm behind his head and watched the world outside awaken.

From time to time he let his eyes fall closed and he drifted in and out of quick dreams that light sleep often provided. When his last dream was of Casey, pressing a soft trail of kisses along his jaw, he tried with all of his power to hold the fantasy. But as need flooded through him in sleep, and her hands trailed feathery lines down his torso, he gave in and opened his eyes.

His waking might as well have been a dream as Casey took his mouth with hers and let the warm kiss and a dance of their tongues seduce him in a way he hadn't known was possible.

Travis begged Casey's fingertips to continue their trail down to where his need craved friction and release. When he tried to turn to her, her wandering hand held him firm and pushed him back, forcing his body to lay open. He felt her smile as she inched closer to him. Relished the surprise of her naked body as her nipples grazed his sensitive skin.

She had undressed, anticipating release, and he was on the verge of explosion.

When Casey found him, he was hard and throbbing, arching with the need for her to hold firm and offer the satisfying movements that would electrify the mounting pressure.

She wanted to be satisfied at what she was able to do to his body. She wanted to gratify only in the natural, sexual act. To make it something less than it was.

But as Travis brought both hands to her face and looked into her eyes, she saw, through his agonizing need, she was all he cared about. It forced the thoughts of natural desire out of her mind, and instead filled her heart until she had no choice but to admit she couldn't have been experiencing any other feeling than love.

The realization stunned her, but it was lost in an instant as Travis brought her mouth crashing down to his. Rather than scare her, Casey let the feelings surge through her and fuel her need for his body, his touch.

Her mouth scorched his body, and her hands scoured as they searched every inch, finding every intricate detail.

"Casey," Travis managed breathlessly as her reckless desire flooded him in haste. He wanted to touch her, to bring her the same erotic rush she was causing inside of him. Instead, she mounted him and in a crash of moist, hot wet, she took him in and gloriously rode him until he could do nothing but take in her beauty in dizzying satisfaction. He tried to feel her when he touched, but all he could feel was the edge of release as his body rose to meet her hard, battling thrusts. Every movement heightening arousal as he found himself deeper inside of her.

All he could do was hold on until he felt her erupt around him like warm lava and take him over the edge, unable to hold in his own rupture.

When she fell to him, his arms absorbed her body and he couldn't remember a time when he'd held on so tight.

Forever, he thought. *I need this woman forever.*

CHAPTER 24

Five days.

They had shared the same schedule, the same meals, and the same bed for five days.

Casey stared over her mug of coffee after a quick refill at the office as she tried to analyze the situation. What she found as she weaved and sorted her thoughts, searching for something that was off, or amiss, was…nothing.

Confused, she tilted her head and wondered, was the feeling that kept popping up *enjoyment? Comfort?* The strangest part of all of this was, though she'd spent nearly every waking moment with Travis, she was looking forward to their ride home together. Now *that* was interesting.

"Normally I would tell you to stop all that thinking," Maggie sang as she bustled into the breakroom, "but something tells me I should let what's going on in that head of yours to keep right on going." Maggie thwittled a finger in circles at Casey's forehead, causing the smile she was looking for.

"I don't know what you mean." Casey tried for coy, knowing it wasn't one of her strong suits, but channeled her best Grace in the process.

"Ah, that was very good. But you don't fool me. That one," Maggie brushed a hand in the direction of Grace's office, "tries without success as well. Now, would you like to share, or would you like me to take a crack at it?"

Casey playfully rolled her eyes and deadpanned, "When have I ever wanted to share?"

"That's what I thought." Maggie waited for the hot espresso to fill her cup before she turned and looked Casey in the eyes. Her look softened, a rare but effective quality Maggie used when she felt it was needed.

"My sweet, Casey," she led off, while a grandmotherly hand found Casey's cheek, "you are the smartest, most intelligent woman I know. I don't share your brilliance, but I'm smart enough to spot it, appreciate it. And I also have a lot of time on my side. Many years of loving the same man, and many years of seeing other people love. Sometimes, yes," Maggie continued, not allowing for Casey to add any dubious comments, "it might not work out. But that doesn't make the love that was shared any less. I see a light and an acceptance in you I don't know that I've ever seen before. It's quite stunning."

Maggie turned to leave, but stopped short of the opening and said, "Let yourself love. Openly and willingly. I've seen the way that man looks at you. His eyes show more care and more compassion than I think I've ever seen in a single glance. That too, is something beautiful. You deserve that."

Casey was left alone with her cooling coffee and wondered if it was her thoughts or Maggie's comments that had her moving toward Travis' office. The sudden urgency to go to him combined with her swift steps didn't allow for a change of mind.

Travis saw her coming and stood, concerned at her pace and the unsmiling, determined face.

"Casey." Worry drenched her name. "Are you okay?"

He didn't extend his arms as she grew closer. He wasn't quite sure if he'd done something to make her angry and was prepared to do anything from defend with words or block a fist. But when her arms wrapped around him and her mouth melted into his, his arms instinctively wrapped around her.

He kissed her back with all of the love he could pour into the single act.

The world around them stopped moving and nothing else mattered. They were consumed with each other, in a moment that was theirs alone.

Casey didn't pull away, she let herself feel as long as she could, as long as he was willing to let her. Because right then, that moment was what they had, and things were perfect.

Neither knew how long they had held on. But it was Travis who pulled back and held Casey at arm's length to study her without letting go. He squinted at her easy grin as if to examine an underlying motive. He pulled her in for a quick second kiss, and to his astonishment the brief meeting of lips had all of the emotion as the first. Her expression didn't change.

When his eyebrows lifted, finally welcoming her surprise show of affection, Casey simply said, "See you after work." And left him staring after her.

As his vision cleared and with Casey out of sight, Travis was able to focus on Seth who was standing in the hall. Who had apparently witnessed the whole thing.

"Well, shit," Seth said as his body slumped and he skimmed a shoe on the floor as if he'd missed yet another chance at love.

Travis laughed at the poor guy who hunched away. "Don't worry buddy, your time will come." He tried to keep the humor out of his voice but feared his mood was a little too good for that. He watched Seth wave a hand behind him and he was gone.

—

"I've transferred your funds," Casey said lightheartedly as she bit into her sandwich. "Mm, oh my God. It's baguette, ham, and butter. How is this so good?"

When she looked up after she realized her words were met with silence, she found a mixture of humored and baffled faces.

"What?"

"It's just–you ah," Rachel stumbled before her thoughts found their footing, "transferred the money?"

"I did." The words were slow and cautious as she eyed her friends.

"I love money! I love that you slept with Travis. I mean, we knew that, but I love that you're *admitting* you slept with Travis." Obviously recovered, Rachel tried for more. "So, did you pay us for each time you slept together or…"

"Don't push your luck." The words were no-nonsense, but the smile reached Casey's eyes from behind another large bite of sandwich.

"I'm so proud of you." Grace offered. "Just, for everything. But especially for following through on your financial obligation."

"Ha-ha."

"You are saying you transferred the money?"

It didn't go unnoticed that Aimeé's question lacked the same playfulness the others' comments had had.

"Yeah. I didn't have any checks. Thought it was faster and easier for everybody."

"No complaining here!" Rachel beamed as she took down a slurpy spoonful of lobster bisque.

"But, how did you get our account information?" Aimeé asked. She attempted to make it light but her dark, cloudy eyes gave away the concern she was trying to hide.

Grace grinned, but carefully as she didn't want to hurt any feelings. She also didn't want to make Casey feel badly for the actions she'd taken. She did just send them each two thousand dollars, after all. "I don't know that any of us really want to know *how* Casey does anything on that computer of hers."

"I'm in the don't care club," Rachel added, "I've already moved on to deciding if I should be responsible and save it, or pencil in a trip to the mall."

"The mall," Aimeé and Grace said in unison.

Rachel sighed, "See, that's why I keep you. You're such great friends."

When Aimeé stood to check on things at the counter, Casey stood to follow her. Before she got all the way there, making sure she was out of earshot from the staff and customers, she didn't say much, only offered what she could.

"Aimeé." Casey gently reached for her friend's hand to halt her progress, and was met with concern and a furrowed brow. "I won't get into it, and I won't keep looking if you don't want me to. Just know that I can help. You just have to ask. That's all."

Aimeé nodded and leaned into Casey and kissed her once on her cheek as a loving sister would. "Thank you." Then turned and continued on to her work.

"Well? What did she say?" Grace asked when Casey rejoined the table.

"Nothing. Still won't tell me any more about what's going on. And she definitely isn't looking for help."

"This is so frustrating. She *has* to know we can help her." Rachel took a sip of water. "And by *we,* I mean *you.*"

"I shouldn't say anything…"

"But you're going to." Rachel finished Casey's thought without giving her the chance to be noble.

Sighing, she looked from friend to friend, both eagerly waiting to finally hear what was causing the anxiety."

"I did look. At her accounts."

"We figured." Grace's words weren't an accusation, but to hurry the story along.

Casey looked around to make sure she wouldn't be overheard, then leaned in and whispered, "We know Aimeé has lost a lot of money, but I couldn't place how. It's not in large amounts at one time, and strangely not in a hard place to find. But it took me a long time to piece it together. I'm not bragging about finding it; it just means they're good."

"How are they doing it?" Rachel asked the question both she and Grace wanted to know.

"It's really smart actually. They aren't taking money directly from Aimeé's or the Bistro's accounts per sé. They are intercepting charges for purchases made for all Bistro expenses, but only the ones that wouldn't be noticed. They aren't doing it to lease payments or anything that would routinely stay the same. It's only happening to supplies, food, those types of inconsistent charges."

"How is that possible?" Grace's business mind was curious.

"The vendor–let's just use that name since it's universal–sends the charge and requests the funds, the charge is intercepted and a random percentage is added to the amount. Aimeé's bank or card sees the increased number and pays that amount. Whoever is doing this then intercepts the payment funds but only takes the increased amount and routes the payment for the original charge to the vendor who is none-the-wiser."

"Obviously, eventually it was easy to find after matching vendor receipts to her accounts, but at first glance you'd never know by simply looking at her statements because they just look like regular old charges."

Grace wasn't on board. "That doesn't make sense. She'd see on the receipts right away that her account didn't match up with the charges."

"If she looked right away. And by right away, I'm talking the first one to five minutes."

"What?" Grace couldn't believe what she was hearing. And didn't want to believe somebody could be doing what Casey was describing.

Then they adjusted the individual charge so what Aimeé was looking at, wasn't the actual bank reconciliation. I'm telling you, they're good."

"So it still looked like she had the same ending balance." Grace was following along.

"Until you want to go in and withdraw a large amount of money, and the bank catches the discrepancy. She's lucky The Bistro does well; and that she hasn't gotten into more trouble. I'm sure that's why there's an investigation. To prove it's not Aimeé herself."

They sat in silence, unable to eat, letting the situation penetrate.

"Wow," Rachel said after a moment, disgusted, "Not only could I never think of doing something like that, I wouldn't even know how to start." She pondered her thoughts over the next spoonful of soup. "I guess I'd have to start by upgrading my ten-year-old computer."

Casey cringed at the thought of using a machine that was so outdated, but figured it wouldn't do her any good to comment. Maybe she could just donate her one-year-old computer to Rachel the next time she upgraded. It probably wouldn't be too long now anyway.

"What are you going to do?"

Grace's question lingered in Casey's mind. The intrigue to investigate was so strong it had her pulling up Aimeé's accounts countless times throughout the week. But one thing was stronger than her urge to search, learn, and find the truth–Aimeé's friendship.

CHAPTER 25

"What would you do?"

The next day Casey sat at her kitchen island sipping coffee as Travis scrambled eggs with sautéed mushrooms, onions, and green peppers. He didn't stop his movements and didn't speak, but she knew it was because he was thinking about his answer.

She had just shared with him everything she'd let the girls know the day before. She loved her friends, but like her, they too agreed they needed to honor Aimeé's request to stay out of it.

Because of that, Casey needed somebody's opinion she trusted, and somebody that would be honest with her. She hadn't hesitated or changed her mind since she'd made the decision to ask Travis. And she'd throroughly thought through the scenario in the shower that morning after he'd gotten out to start breakfast.

When Travis turned with the pan of eggs, he emptied them onto their plates then placed the hot pan back on the stove. He refilled their coffees, still quiet, but still considering.

Casey appreciated the attention he was giving his thoughts. Rather than add more detail she let him think.

When he finally sat next to her and picked up his fork, he began to shovel eggs into his mouth and stopped. He turned his head toward Casey while lowering his fork and said, "I'd have to investigate."

Casey nodded, knowing that's what he'd say, but she wanted to know why.

Reading her mind, or the facial expression showing her curiosity he began without her prompting after finishing his first bite.

"Something–or someone–is hurting my friend. I would do whatever I could to help."

"But she's requested I *not* help."

He nodded, considering as he bobbed his head back and forth. "Let's think about the different scenarios that might be causing that sort of response in her?"

"Okay." Casey didn't want to appear excited but the idea of talking this through with Travis, an emotionally intelligent man, did give her a little kick. Usually she had to work through things by herself, then hope to eventually find the right answer. Many times she just bruited her way through whatever idea seemed best at the time and suffered any residual consequences of her actions.

"One; she doesn't want you seeing her, or the Bistro's, financials."

"Possible, but by now she knows I've seen them. Two; it has to do with her family. She's always secretive when it comes to her family. It wasn't exactly the same as my childhood, but hearts were broken, so it hurts the same," Casey said, remembering Aimeé's words.

"Could be; family is complicated. Especially when it comes to money."

"Three," Casey continued, rolling with the thought, "she doesn't want us to get into trouble, or see the trouble she might be in."

Travis contemplated again, then grinned at his thought when he looked over and watched Casey take a big bite full of eggs. "Would that stop you from helping her or change your mind about her?"

"Not even a little." Casey smiled at the idea of Aimeé being in trouble with the law and kind of liked the edge it gave her. Even though she knew that scenario was extremely unlikely.

"Then, four;" Travis paused, taking a more serious tone, "she's worried that somehow it could come back and hurt you. If I read you girls correctly–and I think I do–the one thing I know is you'd always put each other before yourself. No matter what the cost. It's written on all of your faces. With every hello, laugh, cry, conversation, and goodbye."

Leaning back in her chair Casey let his words sink in.

Hurt us.

That was it. Had to be it. Aimeé was worried whatever she uncovered could eventually backfire and somehow affect her–or all of them. If a person could pull off what they were doing with Aimeé's money, they definitely could find ways to steal from–or do anything really–to her, or Grace and Rachel.

Casey looked over to see Travis studying her. "You're right."

"With how fast the wheels were turning I figured I might be onto something."

"Thank you."

Her words were genuine and he couldn't–and wouldn't–put a dollar amount on the way her request for help had made him feel. A billion dollars wouldn't have been enough to take the moment away from him.

"So what are you going to do?" His grin was enough to show her he already knew the answer.

"I'm going to help a friend."

Casey leaned over and congratulated Travis with a perky peck on the cheek then hopped off the chair to hustle toward her office.

"Thank you for breakfast!"

Travis heard the call through the house that let him know she had made it to the office in record time. He let his hand rest where she had placed her lips and thought it would be fun to offer a little playfulness back to her.

"Have fun! When you're done we can talk about the Spring Fling convention. Only four days away!" His exaggerated excitement earned him exactly what he was hoping for. A loud groan and the faint smack of a forehead against a desk.

Laughing, Travis got up to clean their breakfast mess and thought about what he would do that day. When it hit him, the satisfaction stretched far and wide across his face.

It was about time to pay a visit to that nice little shop that's been catching his eye when he and Casey took their walks along the lake and into downtown. He might not have that billion dollars he was thinking about earlier, but he had enough savings to cover just about anything that would fit nicely into a tiny blue box.

CHAPTER 26

Travis knew she had a long day. He heard her exasperated voice talk through every detail of the Spring Fling conference one meeting after another. More than once she reassured the chipper Carrie Bolden that he would be there with her. She was sure on a rampage about making sure their *'face of the company'* was arm-in-arm with a significant other. Even he was starting to understand Casey's frustration.

If that wasn't enough as the end of the business day neared, he looked up from his laptop where he'd perched it on the kitchen table to enjoy a day of working from their home, to see Casey run out the door with her laptop and papers in tow.

"Can't talk, firewall down. Servers down. We have backups up and trace running. Heading to office. Will call you with an update."

Then she was out the door.

He could have been concerned, but he didn't have a care in the world knowing Casey would take care of everything–including any residual data clean up. After all, her process for just that was detailed out in a PowerPoint deck that he barely understood.

It was nine in the evening before Travis heard from Casey again. He read through the text from her letting him know she was leaving the office. It was almost ten when he saw headlights flash through the house, his queue to get up and pour a glass of wine from the bottle he'd opened and set to rest.

Travis greeted her at the door and saw she was tired and worn down. People didn't give enough credit to the type of exhaustion constantly having to use your mind could bring.

"No more people. Want to be alone." It was all she could manage.

Silently, he reached for her bags to unload the physical burden from her body. He handed her the glass and gently kissed her cheek.

Travis set her bags down on the foyer table and reached for her hand to guide her in. Rather than lead her to the living room he led her to the stairs. At her resistance, he paused at the bottom and, with a simple look, let her know it was okay. That nothing more was needed from her.

Casey followed him willingly as he guided her through her bedroom door and into the bathroom. When she walked in the heavenly scent of eucalyptus surrounded her. Instinctively she inhaled to take it in. She let him set her glass of wine on a wooden stool next to the tub that was steaming and providing little popping noises from the bubbles that were nearly flowing over the edge.

Slowly he unbuttoned the flannel shirt she'd rushed out of the house in earlier that day–not taking the time to change due to the emergency. Rather than let it fall to the floor he folded it neatly and placed it on the counter. Gracefully, his hands found the buttons of her jeans and opened the line of them without struggle, then slid them off, carefully removing one leg after the other. Again he folded them and set them on her already discarded shirt.

Taking her in he realized even in her weariness, she was beautiful. The famished sink in her cheeks more prominently carved out the edges of her bones. Red curls from unkempt, tousled hair fell from their perch to frame her face. He couldn't help the movement when he slowly moved his hand to her face.

"Just one, because I can't help it, then I'll leave you be."

When his lips met hers, the softness consumed him and it was all he could do to back away and not take more than he deserved from her when what she really needed was to rest and relax.

Casey couldn't believe the tenderness of the kiss. If she'd had more energy she would have reached out to him, and held him there for even a moment longer. Instead she felt her body react with small shiver bumps as his hands slid around her to unclasp the delicate lace that remained on her body.

He held her gaze as he moved the straps down the length of her arms, set it gently on the pile of clothes, then moved his fingers beneath the satin of her panties and let his fingertips graze her legs as he stepped her out of the fabric.

Keeping her hand in his, he moved her a step closer to the steaming bath and gently helped her slip into the warmth. He placed a towel behind her head and held it as he softly laid her back. Kneeling, he kissed her hand softly, then placed her glass of wine in it so she wouldn't have to move to reach for it. Then he silently got up and walked out, closing the door behind him.

A half hour later Casey couldn't believe the magic. The bath, the quiet, and much needed wine had worked a miracle on her. She felt rested, and if not quite all the way, at least a little restored. But in her restoration, she found severe hunger.

Not much could have pulled her out of tranquility, but when the scent of hot marinara, cheese, and pepperoni wafted its way through the house her eyes shot open and widened with recognition and need. The grumbling of her stomach didn't match the serenity of the bath either.

Casey's hand slipped only once as she hurried to get out, but it was enough to splash a puddle out of the tub. Without a care she left it, dried herself with the towel her head had rested on, and didn't bother with clothes, opting for the plush robe that hung on the ornate stand next to the bath.

The sound of her slippers slapping at the hardwood floors echoed throughout the house and stopped only when she saw the most beautiful view–two extra-large pizza boxes stacked one on top of the other waiting for her on the edge of the island.

Rushing down she found herself face-to-face with the square cardboard. She took two seconds to read the note taped to the top of the box:

Pizza saves lives!
Love, T

"I love you!" Casey whispered to the ceiling as she looked up in thanks.

Searching for the biggest slice, she pulled and a string of melted cheese stretched long and gloriously. She wondered if there were ever a more perfect moment. Then she took a bite, and immediately topped it.

"Mmm." Casey's groan of satisfaction drew a smile to her face. The *one* thing that could make this better, she thought as she took another bite and took a tentative step to the fridge. And there it was. A can of ice cold Mountain Dew. It was the first time in her life she nearly cried of happiness.

Once slice down and two more on her plate, she wandered to the living room to stretch out and enjoy her second and third rounds. At the sound of her shuffling slippers her smile met Travis' as he looked up from a book he looked to be about half way into.

"I didn't think I'd still be up by the time you made your way down here. That's why I left the note." He wondered as he spoke if she noticed he signed, *Love*. Mostly because he was curious if it would bother her or not. By the looks of it, pizza was well worth the L-word, as she didn't look the least bit fazed.

"I didn't think I would either, seeing as I was soaking in bliss upstairs. But then you brought in my weakness. Carbs drenched in cheese."

"This is good to know. I'll file that away for future use."

"I'm finding I'm thanking you more than I'd like to be, but, *thank you.*"

"You're welcome. I feel it should go without saying, but it's what people in relationships do–natural or contractual."

"This is good to know. I'll file that away for future use." Casey grinned, appreciating her own wit while continuing to devour her meal. It was the first time she made a comment about their future, and it was the first time she didn't think twice at the thought.

CHAPTER 27

It was the day before the conference, and seeing as Casey needed new shoes to go with the dress she'd picked out for the evening dinner, it wasn't hard for Rachel to convince her and the girls to head to the mall.

"He drew you a *bath?*" Rachel couldn't believe the romance in the gesture. Everybody within a fifteen-foot radius could hear the longing in her voice.

"He did."

"Oh the *heaven.* Did you immediately make love to him?"

"He undressed me, kissed me, then left me naked and relaxing in the glorious, slippery velvet bubbles," Casey boasted, then looked at the cashier and smiled. "I'll have a tomato and mozzarella panini with an iced tea."

The cashier blushed and nodded too fast to be casual, trying to ignore what he heard, fingers fumbling as he attempted to capture her order correctly.

Aimeé grinned at the sexuality of it, Rachel giggled, and Grace smiled sweetly as she was up to order next and feeling pity for the poor boy who couldn't have been more than sixteen.

Not wanting to put added pressure on the kid, Grace smiled innocently and said, "I'll have the same, please."

Half way through lunch, when all had appropriately swooned at the all-too-real business relationship Casey and Travis were having, Casey offered her friends a rare opportunity.

"I need help," she began, getting the attention of the three girls who all stopped mid-bite or sip, "and it won't be easy. But seeing as I've come to accept...*feelings* for Travis, I now feel the need to pay a little extra attention to my attire for tomorrow's conference dinner." Casey continued to eat as her friends stared in astonishment.

Because she didn't say anything more and each was about to fall off the edge of their seat in anticipation, Grace prompted, "And?"

Casey deliberately lingered in her bag, not rushing to find her phone, but moving diligently. She pulled it out and opened it to show a picture of a stunning, shimmering gown.

Rachel snatched the phone and ogled the picture Casey had taken of herself standing in the dress before heading out that morning.

"Oh my *God!* You have been blessed with the gift of *curve* my friend."

Casey let her eyes roll and a slow grin play at her lips. She watched Rachel zoom in and take in every detailed inch of the dress.

"Do you think she's going to show us?" Grace asked Aimeé.

"Perhaps, one day."

"Give me a minute, I'm drooling. Is it flowing? It looks like a river of silver and blue sequins. The long sleeves are dramatic, but that neckline!" Rachel's gaze traveled from Casey back to the picture. "You're going to have pre-dinner sex. There's no way he'll be able to keep his hands off of you."

"Is that *all* that's on your mind?" Grace asked as she snagged the phone out of Rachel's grip to look for herself.

Aimeé and Grace leaned their heads together to get a look for themselves.

"Tu est belle."

Grace only nodded. Though she didn't know to which comment, that Casey was beautiful, or that she would most likely have pre-dinner sex.

"Thank you," Casey said, acknowledging only Aimeé. "I have the dress."

"Yes. You. Do." Rachel wholeheartedly agreed.

"But," she said, not quite able to believe she was about to say this, "I need your help with, well, everything else."

Rachel's gasp was audible.

Unable to believe the request herself, Aimeé questioned, "What do you mean *everything?* "

"I mean, I need shoes, earrings, maybe a necklace, and I need help with what to do with my hair."

"Are you saying you need *the works?* " It was Grace's turn to question.

"I am."

"This is the best day ever!" Rachel shot out of her chair and hurried her tray to the trash.

"I guess that means we're starting."

Casey looked at Grace, then to Aimeé who followed Rachel's lead. She knew she needed them for their great taste and their honesty, but as the three huddled to conspire about their shopping plan, Casey wondered if she'd regret the decision to enlist her friends' help just a little before the day was through.

CHAPTER 28

The Spring Fling Conference wasn't at all what he expected. Travis assumed it would be all flowers, rainbows, hearts, and a few too many mushy stories that would bring a world of matchmakers, matchmaking companies, and singles from all walks of life together in one big love-fest.

When he found a seat in Casey's first session–different sessions were hosted by all of Match Me's leadership throughout the day, each presenting on a different topic–he laughed at the eager students as they pulled out notepads, iPads, and laptops to take notes. He shook his head and wondered if he would regret agreeing to join Casey for the entire day.

Then the unthinkable happened. Not even ten minutes in, after Casey had given her introduction and began to dive into the science behind love, he found himself reaching for his phone to take his own notes. His movements were quick so he could safely stow his phone when he was finished and none would be the wiser, but as he did he received a whisper from the man sitting next to him.

"Isn't she fascinating?"

Travis took a moment to follow the man's eyes to Casey, and immediately thought, *yes, she is.*

"I've been to this conference three times–" the man paused briefly to ensure he wasn't missing a critical piece of wisdom, then continued, "– once when I was single, and twice more after I met my wife. I always leave with a deeper understanding of what my wife needs. And, amazingly, how I can communicate my own. You know," the man's head bobbled in Travis' direction, "us men aren't always the greatest at communicating."

Not wanting to let the man down, Travis only agreed and tried to match the man's guilty look. "Isn't that that truth."

When it seemed he was left alone again he let his sight linger on Casey once more. He watched her speak in a way that showed him another side of her.

This was a professional woman who he knew was nervous–he'd seen that much when she was getting ready that morning. Too stubborn to admit it, sure, but he saw it in her quiet concentration. The way she smoothed out her jacket and trousers more than once. And the way she fussed with her hair before settling on pulling half of it back into a bun while letting the other half flow in prepared curls down her back.

But watching her now, to the eager strangers' eye, she was everything they wanted her to be. The confident founder of MatchMe.com. The woman who had single-handedly given them the opportunity to find love. The woman who built the template of a successful dating website and was willing to share it with other startup companies who were looking to do the same. And she was the woman who offered the science-backed hope to singles who were longing to find true love.

It was interesting to him that much of her presentation had to do with the individual themselves, and not as much about the partner they had found or were looking to find. It had everything to do with self-awareness and the readiness to find love. It was, after all–Travis repeated Casey's words in his head–*what was the most attractive part of a person.*

He couldn't have agreed more. Casey was obviously smart, capable, loving, and perfectly content with herself when Travis had met her for the first time. He wondered if that wasn't part of what had attracted him to her in the first place.

"Well, what did you think?" Casey finally found him when the room cleared out and she'd given adequate attention to each patron as they asked questions when she was finished.

"Delighted, and surprised. I have to admit, I was a bit skeptical, but somehow everything you said made sense." Travis nodded to the doorway where everybody had filed out. "And they were hanging on your every word."

"You weren't?" Casey pretended to be offended.

"No. You mostly just reiterated and confirmed that all of my feelings for you aren't simply love fluff."

Casey's laugh was loud and beautiful.

"Love fluff?" she questioned, unable to contain her humor.

"Yes, love fluff."

"Well, I'm happy you were able to make that determination. Will you stay for another session?"

"No," he said lightly looking down as if to study the brochure he was handed as he walked in that morning.

"No?" Now she was curious.

"No. I think I'm going to divide my time between Mrs. Sasha or Ms. Carrie. Though I think I'm leaning toward Sasha. I'd like to hear what a lawyer has to say about love. Then maybe I'll go refill on love fluff."

"As much as it pains me to say this, Carrie's session on fluff is actually very good. I would suggest catching her act before lunch."

"Very interesting."

"What's interesting?"

"It's interesting hearing you promote the likes of a woman who seems to drive you mostly insane."

"Oh, she drives me insane. But it doesn't mean she isn't the best. She can love-fluff the shit out of people."

"Ah, there's my girl."

Travis pulled Casey in for a swift kiss that smothered her laughter. When he finally let her inch away, he asked, "I'll see you for lunch?"

"Unfortunately, you might be on your own. How do you feel about mingling?"

"I'm a great mingler. When will I see you again?"

Casey put on her best puppy dog face, to ask for forgiveness for what she was about to say.

"Dinner."

Travis contemplated, then nodded. "Something to look forward to then."

Wondering how it was that he managed to be just what she needed, she realized she may never know.

Without finding the words to say just what she was thinking, she pulled him back in for a kiss that was meant to show him she would miss him every minute until then.

"Or, we could just blow off the rest of the afternoon and head up to the room?" he offered, feeling the need in her kiss that sent shockwaves through his body.

Casey leaned in and trailed a string of kisses along his jawline to his ear and whispered, "I'll see you at dinner, Mr. Mavens."

Then she backed away and turned to walk out of the room leaving him helpless for her. And, he thought, he never looked forward to dinner more in his life. Or, to be more accurate, *after* dinner.

CHAPTER 29

Travis wasn't one for naps, but when he found he'd crammed every possible piece of love knowledge into his brain by three in the afternoon, he decided he'd earned a break. He woke to Casey sliding out of her patent leather oxfords and unbuttoning the blazer she wore over only a sheer bra.

Watching her walk to him with the jacket swinging freely he grinned. She leaned on the bed and over him, taking his mouth as she had earlier. All of the same feelings of longing rushing through him. When she paused, his hands found her body and traced its curves.

"Why don't you head down and get us a pre-dinner drink to share?"

"Right now?"

Casey couldn't help her smirk, but nodded. "Right now."

It might have been cruel, but she had plans of her own. She needed to–what had her friends said? *primp?*

Travis looked down at his situation and fell back. Casey leaned in to kiss him to show pity but he stopped her. "No, you can't come near me. Any more kisses from you and I won't be able to leave. My unfortunate situation will worsen."

"You're funny, Mr. Mavens."

As much as it was killing him not to touch her, her complimentary words were all he needed to oblige her. "I'm not funny, I'm honest. Now let me be, I need to pull myself together and get my woman a drink."

He looked longingly at Casey and the fragile fabric covering her breasts. His hands reached for the flaps of her blazer, closing them, and said, "And cover this up, it's hard enough having to look at a beautiful woman. Much less a beautiful, undressed woman."

Pushing off the bed, determined not to look back, he slid on his shoes and marched out the door.

Casey knew she'd have about an hour. The lines for drinks during cocktail hour were horrendous, but they were perfect for mingling and getting people talking. She personally dreaded them, but most seemed to enjoy it. And selfishly, it would give her the time she needed to properly prepare to knock Travis on his ass when he saw her again.

It took twenty minutes to shower, lotion, dry her hair, and get Rachel on the phone.

"I have about forty more minutes."

"Okay, no time to waste. Start with makeup so it can settle while you do your hair. Then if any touch ups are needed or you want to change anything, you'll have time."

"Is that really a thing?"

"Makeup settling? Of course it's a thing," Rachel confirmed, not knowing if it was or wasn't a *thing,* but it's what she did so she went with it. "Hey, show your video, I want to see what you're doing."

"Fine, one second." Casey shifted her phone, turned on her video, then propped the phone in front of her on the bathroom vanity.

"Wow, check out the bathroom. Are you sitting down?"

"Yes."

"Your hotel room comes with a sitting vanity section?"

"Are you going to help me or not?"

"Right! Yes, helping. First the primer. Just like we did yesterday."

Casey followed Rachel's instructions straight through makeup and into hair. She kept an eye on the clock and saw she had fifteen minutes before her hour of prep would be up. When she moved her head to glance at the clock she heard Rachel's gasp.

"What is it?" Concern immediately shot a sinking feeling to the pit of her stomach.

"It's you. You're a vision. Stand up and look at yourself."

Casey didn't think, just stood and looked at her reflection. Her face was dewy and flushed. A hint of creamy blush softened her cheeks to offset the dramatic dark brown rimming her eyes. The paint on her lips was neutral with a touch of pink gloss. And her hair rolled in heavy waves off of a dramatic part that seductively covered the side of her face while leaving the other side dangerously open and her neck exposed. As if to welcome a touch from a hand or lips.

"It's not too much, is it?" Casey analyzed, turning from side to side.

"Understatement of the century. It is way too much, and absolutely perfect. Now let's get you in that dress. Actually, start with the jewelry."

"Any particular reason?" Casey was curious as to the order of things and their purpose in the event she ever had to repeat the process on her own.

"Sometimes honey, there isn't a better feeling than being in sexy lingerie and diamonds."

"Okay." No point in arguing a feeling at this point. She'd trusted her feelings until now and they hadn't disappointed.

The teardrop diamonds swung low, tickling the top of her shoulders that would be bare due to the wide, plunging V-neck line of the dress. Next came the matching necklace that would rest between her breasts, perfectly angling with the dress as it draped her curves. She thought the earrings and the necklace would be too much, but trusted her friends. Then when she'd seen it all together the day before she knew they were right. It was a statement, added a little more cover to her bare skin, and just enough dazzle to draw attention away from the dress.

When the door clicked, all Casey could do was turn as she heard Rachel squeal in the background and encourage her to hide so Travis wouldn't see her yet. There was no time and nowhere for her to go.

"You wouldn't believe the lines down th-"

Words fled as he came around the corner and saw Casey standing barefoot in front of him. Why he noticed her bare feet was more than he was willing to analyze, but something about the innocent way her feet naturally met the floor, with the woman they held wearing jewels and lace, might have had something to do with it.

"Casey." Low and gruff, Travis was barely able to get out her name.

His throaty, deep tone, seduced at the sound. She had never felt more exposed, or more anticipation. She watched as he set the stemmed wine glasses on the granite kitchenette and moved to her.

Slowly Casey picked up the phone and whispered, "Rach, I need to go. Love you." With a click they were alone.

When he reached her, his hand stopped her from unknowingly playing with the diamond that hung at the end of her necklace. His hand covered hers as he placed them both on her chest.

With his hand over hers, he lightly moved her fingertips over her body. When he led her hand to her breast encouraging her to touch herself, her breath caught at the erotic feeling that sent pins to her aching center. She felt herself moisten at the movements of her delicate hand and was unable to fathom the sensation he was causing as he guided her, showing her the beauty of her own body.

When her free hand found his shirt and began with the first button, he moved away only slightly to stop her. This was about her. Every movement needed to be about her. His free hand captured hers, linking their fingers together.

Leaning into her, but careful not to touch her, he whispered, "Let me show you how beautiful you are."

As he guided her hands, they massaged, caressed, and idolized every inch of her skin. When they found her breasts once more her head fell back. On a moan her eyes closed at the unbearable feeling of need throbbing through her. She could feel her heartbeat pulsing, pounding on her center, screaming for more.

"Look at me, Casey. Let me see you. I want to see you. I want to watch you see what you can do."

Obeying his request, her eyes were like fire as they met his, and it only intensified his need for her. He couldn't believe the radiance illuminating her body. He hoped he could contain his own desire to finish what he set out to do.

With their eyes locked, she let him move her hand down the line of her waist. It played and cupped dangerously low on her bottom before he steered it to her front.

When he moved her fingers, lightly but deliberately, so they played at the edges of her wet center he felt the drip from her hand to his as a light whimper escaped while pleading desire begged with her eyes.

He wanted to kiss her, but resisted his own need to touch her. Instead, he held firm to her gaze, and guided her fingers inside.

Casey screamed in the pleasure of release and the indescribable sensation the friction her fingers and his caused. It crippled her body until the only feeling she had was the craving to feel more. When her legs went limp, he wrapped an arm around her body, and with the other he led her to a perfect release of uncontrollable pleasure.

—

Casey eyed Travis in the elevator as they took the long ride down to dinner.

Without looking over he grinned, showing her twitch of his lip.

"What?" he asked, without turning.

She turned her body to him, facing the profile. "Why didn't you take me to bed?"

"You didn't like what we–you–did?" He angled his head slightly to look at her eyes, eyes that were impossibly dark with the makeup she was wearing.

"I did." Casey offered a smile of her own. "I found," she paused, "myself wanting more."

Travis found her hand at her side and linked his fingers with hers. He looked at her and said, "I will give you everything you want and more. But in that moment, you were so beautiful, I couldn't bear to touch you. I didn't want to ruin the perfect way I saw you."

It was something she'd never heard before. Something nobody had ever said to her, or probably could ever think of saying. It was completely perfect. Completely Travis.

"You make me feel beautiful."

"You are beautiful."

"Thank you."

He squeezed her hand as she turned to face the door when it chimed, letting them know they'd arrived at their floor.

"And thank you for not making me have to redo my makeup. It was torture."

—

Casey tended to ignore the camera but it seemed Carrie Bolden was bound and determined to get as many pictures of her and Travis as she could while they maneuvered around the ballroom after dinner. The press they invited–and the three they let stay without invitations–asked questions of Casey and Travis as if they were royalty.

Even with the distractions and the gallivanting, everything seemed to be going fine, until one reporter shouted above the rest and asked how Casey managed to run such a successful matchmaking business when she'd grown up in a broken home.

The question didn't so much sting as it threw her off balance. Her parents had never come up. Not in the near decade she'd been answering questions as the head of her company.

Casey stared blankly at the man she couldn't pinpoint–one of the members of the press she hadn't recognized, or invited. And as she delayed her response, the room grew quiet.

"I-ah, I…"

There was nothing. For all of the millions of data points in her head, she couldn't formulate a response. They would expect something genuine, from the heart. Nothing about her parents, or her opinion on love was from the heart. It was all science. All timing.

"Ms. Saunders?" the man questioned, "Would you like me to repeat the question?"

His face an evil smirk as he egged her on.

"What did you say?" Her tone was relayed more accusation than question.

The sneer grew. "I asked if you'd-"

"I heard you."

If the sound of three innocent words could have threatened a life, those were it.

Casey looked down when she felt Travis' hand find hers and immediately he was by her side. When she looked up she saw him smiling at the crowd and at the reporter she wished would swiftly find a boot up his ass.

"Casey," Travis began, "is passionate about her work, about all of you. It might come as a surprise to most that she didn't grow up in a family where life was perfect."

Travis stole a glance at Casey and she wondered if it was for show, or if he was trying to speak to her rather than the room.

"But if any of you can tell me that your parents were perfect, meet me at the bar and I'll buy you a drink."

Laughter filled the room and silenced again, the onlookers hoping he would continue.

Even Casey found it in herself to smile at the truth of his words, and forgot just a little that he was saving her from what would have been a very public humiliation.

"I think what's important to remember is, relationships aren't easy. Sometimes they can be frustrating and at times seem impossible. Sometimes, and it's an unfortunate truth, they don't work out. But Casey, or *Ms. Saunders,"* Travis heard the soft rumble of laughter but thought, *that's for you, dick,* as he looked directly at the reporter, "has done the research, put in the time, and found a way for two people to come together in a relationship that's built on a solid foundation of love, trust...and I can't believe I'm saying this...science."

The crowd smiled through approving comments and whispers amongst themselves, then allowed him to finish.

"At the end of the day, it doesn't matter where we come from, what matters is how we decide to love. And that's what Casey allows us to do."

Travis leaned into Casey and kissed her softly on the cheek then pulled back and offered one more bit of advice.

"Oh," he drew the room back in then made sure all of the focus was on the reporter, "I suggest if you want information on Casey's parents, you go to them. There's no need to ask irrelevant questions here."

The applause roared and the cheers erupted, all seemingly more than satisfied with Travis putting the reporter in his place. And the vast majority sent approving looks in the direction of the stage as Casey and Travis walked off hand-in-hand.

Carrie found them at the base of the steps and Casey immediately knew she wasn't ready for the onslaught of praise. What she really wasn't ready for was the kick in the gut as Carrie wound her arms around Travis, nearly tackling him, and telling him he was perfect. And even that wasn't as bad as Travis dropping her hand to return the hug, leaving Casey vulnerable, and accepting the praise that was lavished upon him.

Then it was her turn.

"Casey, I had *no* idea." Carrie gripped Casey's hand when she finally tore herself away from Travis. "You must have been mortified. Had I known he was going to ask such a demeaning question I never would have let him stay. I thought more press would be great. I'm *so* sorry."

"I think we survived."

Casey pulled out of Travis' reach and turned her body just so.

"I'm getting a drink. Please, you two," Casey's sweet smile was like a knife blade at the edge of a throat and Travis felt her shift in tone, "by all means, stay."

Carrie was oblivious. Travis feared the worst. Something in Casey had changed in a split second. In an instant all of her emotion was gone.

CHAPTER 30

"I can't believe I'm saying this but, I am vicariously living through *Casey.*" Rachel said her name as if never in a million years would she have believed she would be envious of that particular friend. Grace? Sure. Aimeé, absolutely. But Casey? Never.

"Why wouldn't you, she's a millionaire–of the multi-sort." Grace twisted her lip, knowing what Rachel meant.

Casey acknowledged Grace's bait with a twitch of her brow, but kept her fingers moving over her keyboard with precision as she waited for Rachel's explanation.

Rachel's longing sigh reached across the empty morning Bistro. "Money is one thing, sex is another, but love?" She huffed out another exasperated breath. "Love is another. She feels love–whether she's admitting it or not–and he for sure is head-over-heels in love with her."

Rachel spoke to her mug of coffee, not to anybody in particular, mostly to herself, "I would take love over either of those things, or anything else, really. It's the best feeling."

Snapping her fingers that finally stopped typing during Rachel's comment saga, Casey tried to bring her back to the table. "Hi, welcome back. I'm not in love. I feel nothing."

"Oh, come on now, can't you just let her have her moment?" Grace asked, laughing a bit through her words.

"Sure. According to our business arrangement she has about a month left of daydreaming, then Travis and I will be going our separate ways."

The *tsk-tsk* came with a smacking of Aimeé's lips in disapproval. "What? You too?"

Aimeé put a carafe of fresh coffee on the table and sat long enough to put in her two-cents before heading back to work. "Your arrangement is more than business. Do not pretend otherwise."

Casey let her gaze follow Aimeé back to the counter and thought, *you didn't see what I saw last weekend–he's just like the rest of them,* then turned. "One more month."

"You're sure?"

"Rach, we made a deal. Yes, it has been nice, but I'm not going to fall into the illusion it could be more than that. After analyzing our time together, I've let myself feel long enough. For the remainder of our business agreement it will be *only* business. It was a safe amount of time to allow myself to be reckless. With the deadline looming, this is a good time to put a stop to the recklessness and ensure we will come to a safe end and neither of us will be hurt."

"I'm not so sure you can assume Travis shares the same…" Grace tried to think of the right words to use, "pragmatic logic."

"I agree. He seems to have feelings for you that will go beyond your *deadline.'"*

"Then he'll have to deal with that when the time comes." Casey closed her laptop, stashed it in her bag, and refilled her coffee. "For now, I have a lot of work to do before lunch with Linette."

"That's today?" Rachel's surprise halted Casey's movements.

"Yes. Why?"

"Aren't you nervous? Do you want to talk about it? What's your plan?" Concern filled Rachel's voice and Grace's face.

"Of course not, nervousness is just a natural response to being uncomfortable. I don't need to talk or have a plan, Travis is going with me. I'll be fine."

Grace and Rachel exchanged looks as Casey walked out the door and headed up to the office to check on the weekend staff before heading out. Like it was just another day.

"Something's off. Casey isn't acting the same. Something happened at the conference," Grace said, with a hint of worry tugging at her words.

"I think she's filtering through her whole head mess." Rachel whirled her finger every which way in front of her head."

"Maybe." Grace still wasn't convinced.

"You do realize that she basically denied feelings for Travis, then said that *because* of Travis, she would be fine around the one woman who consistently has the ability to make her *not fine."*

It was a statement, not a question. One that Grace had been thinking to herself for some time.

"We can only be here for her when she realizes she loves him. But knowing Casey, love might not be enough. Their business agreement is just the excuse she needs to escape her feelings."

"Her feelings, or his? Either way, I hate that you're right," Rachel agreed, and leaned back taking another glorious sip of uninterrupted coffee–thank the Lord for weekends. Even with the heartache that Casey was destined to feel if she ended things with Travis, Rachel still felt envious of the love her friend was receiving from one of the best men she knew.

CHAPTER 31

"Ready?"

"Ready!" Casey called down from the top of the stairs to Travis who was waiting patiently by the door.

"You're sure you're not nervous?" His voice echoed throughout the house to reach her.

"No, of course not." Casey's voice lowered as she neared him, walking calmly, without a care in the world.

He eyed her, remembering the anxiety she'd felt just by looking at her mother's name on the caller ID on her phone. It would have been normal for her to feel just a little anxious as she was about to confront the woman face-to-face. But then again, this was the new Casey. This was the Casey that had, in an instant, turned cold as ice and acted as if none of the past two great months they'd shared had even happened.

"Anything I should know about?" he offered, changing his method. Why add nerves that she didn't feel. Might as well keep her thinking positively.

Casey pondered his question before pulling the handle down on the door to open it, then nodded to herself and turned. "Yes. She's probably insane."

Unable to help the snort of laughter, Travis grinned at the seriousness of her comment. "Insane?"

He followed her out and climbed into her vehicle waiting for her response. He watched her movements and saw nothing out of the ordinary. She seemed...fine.

"Yes. I've long thought my mother could be diagnosed a narcissist. I know what you're thinking, typically it's a trait held by men, but she views herself as far superior to others."

Travis sat back and thought, *yeah, that's exactly what I was thinking,* and kept his smile to himself.

"That's what makes it difficult for me to converse with her. I'm a logical realist. It's why I asked you to come with me."

"You mean it wasn't my handsome good looks and my manly charm?"

It got Casey to smile and that was all he needed. But she was all business.

"That *and* you're good at making people feel important when you speak to them. It makes you the perfect candidate to speak to my mother with me. You will make her feel like the important person she thinks she is."

"Should I be offended?"

"You should feel honored."

Travis tried to not let her comments simmer and turn his mood. He wanted to be there because Casey needed him emotionally. To be her support system. To be the one person she could count on. He should have known her mind wouldn't have defaulted to emotion. Logic was her way to navigate through life.

"Honored. Right." He played it off as he would have any other comment. How he felt she would have expected him to act; with a sense of wit and confidence. Then he sat the rest of the way in silence, not really wanting to hear any more of his questions responded to with sane rationale.

—

The way Casey linked her hand with Travis' as they walked into the lakefront restaurant was more purposeful than playful. Though he couldn't deny the way he was drawn to her even with the simple, calculated touch.

You'd do anything for her. And now you're losing her.

The thought was instant as he analyzed the deliberate action.

As Travis took in the room full of sun, great smells, and an energy only the verge of summer could bring, his eye caught on the gleam of a camera. Stumbling as he craned his neck to get a better look he thought–no, it couldn't be.

"Casey, I think that–"

"There she is."

Casey's words were barely audible, but he heard the uncertainty behind the strained control. Her wavering was enough to cut him off and decide being one hundred percent with her, in this moment, was more important than an unfortunate run in. They could deal with any residual fallout later.

Travis didn't typically like to judge a book by its cover, but he'd be lying if he wasn't giving Linette Whitley the third degree as they approached without her having yet to see them.

She looked, Travis thought as he took in the toned, overly made-up woman, like a high maintenance version of Casey.

She was beautiful, he had to admit, but the kind of beauty that looked like money. Her makeup was thick and her hair spilled out in long red waves from beneath a hat that looked like something you'd wear on a yacht–not out to lunch.

As their approach slowed, Travis took in the curve of Linette's brim and how it dipped below her eye as she scanned the dining room. As if preparing for somebody to notice her. *Wanting* them to notice her.

Interesting.

Then he looked at Casey, who took in one final breath before they were spotted. *This* was going to be interesting.

"Casey!" Linette exclaimed, too loudly for their close distance. "Don't you look absolutely gorgeous."

Linette looked her up and down.

"You *are* my daughter after all."

Travis couldn't help but notice the compliment sounded more like a compliment for herself rather than her daughter, and somehow managed to make it a little demeaning on top of it. Like she didn't normally approve of Casey's looks.

He wasn't given long to evaluate the comments. As soon as she moved in to offer Casey light, unaffectionate European kisses on each side of her cheeks, Linette saw Travis and zeroed in on their linked hands.

As if Casey was an innocent bystander who was getting in the way, Linette moved her aside and began her swoon.

"Why, Casey!" Linette said, without even the faintest look in her direction. "Who is this gorgeous man? And why didn't you tell me you were bringing a date?"

To alleviate Casey's need to respond, Travis offered his hand and his best formal introduction.

"Mrs. Whitely, it's nice to meet you." He couldn't find it in himself to add a *very*. "I'm Travis, Casey's boyfriend. I've heard a lot about you."

Casey looked on in utter fascination and in an instant knew bringing Travis was a great idea. It wasn't often she embodied over-the-top, instant feelings. But when the tone of Travis' voice was gentlemanly *and* sounded a bit like 'I've heard about exactly the type of woman you are and it's not good,' Casey fell in love.

Since the timing was terrible, she forced the feeling away as soon as it came in, but in the seconds it lasted, it was perfection.

"Oh, well." Linette sounded as though she'd been caught off guard. "All good things, I hope."

Linette turned to find her seat and smiled charmingly at Travis, then to Casey, but her eyes bore into her daughter's and held just a bit too long to be comfortable.

"So Linette," Casey began, getting down to business. "What was the big emergency getting me here for lunch?"

Looking offended, Linette moved her hand gently over her heart letting a mass of gold bangles slide down her skinny arm clinking as they fell. She held her hand in place and looked as if she intentionally angled her hand to show off not one, but two enormous diamond rings.

"Oh, Casey." Linette's tone sounded wounded. "Let's just order and enjoy our time together. I want nothing more than that."

Casey stole a look at Travis that implied, *'Just wait, it will come. And I'm sorry if it's not pretty.'*

He found her knee under the table and gave it a reassuring squeeze, he was here for her–in whatever capacity she needed him to be. *That was the deal*, he thought as he let his hand linger and noticed hers didn't repay the gesture. The look of relief that flashed across Casey's face had to be enough.

The conversation offered Casey and Travis rare opportunities to speak. When they'd asked what Linette and her family had been up to, she capitalized and went on about her wonderful children, doting husband, and the grand adventures they took together.

"Speaking of Hailey," Linette leaned back casually as she spoke of her eldest daughter, "she's getting married next spring. Isn't that just wonderful?"

Casey knew whatever she had waited for was coming. She saw it in Linette's body language and the casual shift in her mother's tone. It's how she began every time she was about to ask for something.

"Congratulations," Travis offered, reading Casey and preparing himself, "you must be thrilled."

"Oh you have no idea! The wedding will be grand. She's marrying a Shetland, you know?"

Casey knew who she was talking about. The high society family circulated in politics in a couple different states and had ties to previous Presidents. But it took every bit of Casey's control not to ask if he had any relation to a pony.

Travis saw Casey stifle a grin and jokingly widened his stare, letting her know he was on to her and that he nearly lost control himself.

"I am happy to see you are both so thrilled with the news," Linette said pointedly. "And that you clearly know why this is such an important day."

"Yes, absolutely." Casey nodded. "You *must* show your new family ties how important you are. Put on a glamorous wedding–oh! and shower too, I presume?"

"Family ties or not," Linette scoffed, but recovered and let her eyes narrow defiantly as if she knew she was about to win a battle at any cost, "it's not every day your first born gets married."

Casey sucked in the quick breath. *First born.* Like she was nothing. She was no more a daughter to her mother than the young women at the next table.

"I think you mean, second born, if I'm not mistaken?" Travis asked pointedly, trying not to get sucked into Linette's web but feeling the steam rise in him at the clear dagger that was meant for Casey. He didn't realize how much it would hurt him to see Casey suffer.

"Oh, goodness, right! I just get on such a roll sometimes, wrapped up while talking about the wedding." Linette lifted her mimosa. "And aside from getting to see your beautiful face, that's one of the reasons I thought lunch today would be so nice."

Here we go, Casey thought.

"Wouldn't it be lovely to, well, for the first time, get the whole family involved in the wedding?"

"By whole you mean…" Casey couldn't get herself to finish.

"Well, to include you in the wedding festivities, of course." As if Casey was oblivious to her involvement in the family and Linette couldn't figure out why she was being so dense. "The shower, too, obviously."

"Obviously," Casey said dryly.

Travis couldn't believe he'd missed it before, but out of the corner of his eye he caught the same man he'd spotted earlier snapping pictures of their table. The same who had questioned Casey's family matters at the conference. He began to push away and excuse himself when Casey found his hand and held on as if her life depended on it.

"Wouldn't it be just wonderful if you were involved somehow?" Now Linette was going to steamroll through. "Say, what about the shower? Wouldn't that be so perfect? Maybe you could host?"

"I don't think-"

Linette went on as if Casey hadn't even started speaking.

"It could be at your house, in tents overlooking the lake. It could be evening, there could be candles, and an abundance of stunning flowers. It's the perfect setting."

"You don't know where I live."

"Oh honey, *everybody* knows where *you* live."

There it was, Travis thought. She just gave herself away as she was lost in her daydream. She didn't realize what she'd just said.

"Only if you look, though, right?" Travis found his annoyance growing.

"My daughter is highly regarded and is known by many people." Linette tried to recover. "Of course people would know where she lives."

"And isn't that pretty convenient for you? I mean, with the type of clientele that I'm sure will be attending this momentous occasion."

Travis stole a look to his right to see the lens and the man behind it had moved closer.

"Well, it would be very nice and convenient if my daughter would agree to host." Linette turned to Casey. "You have been decidedly absent from our lives for no reason at all."

"For no reason?" Casey couldn't help it, the sting was too much. She knew her words would somehow be used against her. She knew Linette wouldn't feel them the same way a normal person would. She'd play the victim, then find another way to get what she wanted without reminiscing on this conversation for even a second.

"You think I've avoided you for all of these years *for no reason?* Did you forget that you made my childhood miserable? That you cheated on my father after he gave you everything he had when you begged adolescently at his feet? Or how about that for every major moment in my life you were too busy gallivanting around the world with your new family–formed, by the way, with the same man you cheated on my father with–to even give *me* a second thought?"

"Casey," Travis began calmly as he tried his best to lean forward and shield Casey from the angle of the camera he was sure was capturing the scene, "would you like to leave? We can just go and forget this ever happened?"

"Leave? Just walk away and let this *woman* move on with her life as if she did *nothing* wrong?" Casey eyes bored into Travis, "She ruined my life. Ruined my family. Took what should have been a carefree childhood and put herself first."

Now the tears threatened and there was nothing Casey could do to hold them at bay.

"You," she turned back to Linette, "are the most selfish, self-centered person I've ever known. I can't believe I was born from such a narcissistic human. I'm ashamed that I can even admit to being your daughter."

"Excuse me." Travis stood, having let the photographer have enough material for one day. "I'll be right back."

Casey sucked in a breath as she watched Travis leave her side.

He was *leaving? Now?* Not realizing how much she needed him there, she felt an ache in her chest, like she'd just taken a punch. More than her mother could ever hurt her, Travis walking away from her in this moment tore her apart. And now, the tears streamed.

Looking back to her mother who had a sly, knowing grin on her face. She slowly returned her gaze to Casey after watching Travis walk away.

"You are a terrible woman." Casey huffed out an audible laugh, ignoring the onlookers who were close enough to see the fallout. "And here I thought–against my better judgement–that you might actually just want to see me. Joke's on me."

Linette sat, staring coolly at her real first born, digesting the unfriendly comments made towards her but already finding ways in her head to dismiss them. To find a way to justify why, of course, they weren't true. And, she let the thoughts of her rebuttal build, allowing the words that would cut the deepest to form.

When Casey mistakenly glanced Travis' way before forcing her eyes back to Linette's she knew she'd made a mistake.

"Ah, yes," Linette said, nodding slowly with an evil glint in her eye. "I saw it the moment you walked in." Her long body leaning forward and resting her elbows on the table, excited about the words she could deliver in retaliation. "You try so hard to pretend like you don't care. But I see it. I was that woman once. I know you love him, I can feel it burning in you and I know it's killing you. The only difference between you and me is I was smart enough to take matters into my own hands. I found somebody new before I let my heart crash and burn. You," Linette turned her head, tracking Travis down and forcing Casey's eyes to follow, "dismissed his love too many times. Tsk, tsk. Now he's the one that's decided to find another person.

"And," Linette smiled cruelly, "it seems he's already well on his way."

Casey didn't want to turn her body. The sick feeling growing inside told her she wouldn't like what she saw.

The flash of a camera stunned her into blinking to regain focus. Seeing the same man who had targeted her at her own conference was standing before her, capturing her humiliation. Putting her family turmoil in still portrait, presumably to put it somewhere where it could haunt her forever.

Then she saw it. Linette's dagger.

Beyond the lens, down the stairs to the patio that led to the lake, was Travis and Carrie Bolden sharing an embrace.

Unblinking, Casey stared. Unable to fathom what she was seeing. Not wanting to admit her mother was right. And doing everything she could to keep the nausea at bay.

They held for what seemed like an eternity, then before they broke, Carrie let her lips press to Travis' cheek in a gentle kiss.

"My, *my*. Don't *they* look friendly." Linette smacked her lips together and brought her face close to Casey's profile, and in a low snarl said, "I really must run. It's too bad you weren't willing to make yourself a part of this family. It really could have been nice. I assume you have this taken care of." Linette motioned to the table and didn't hesitate to stop to see if Casey turned to see to what she was referring. Casey wouldn't be able to walk away without paying. And what was an extra meal with her millions?

Casey stood alone and let the tears flood her eyes and cascade down her face, streaking her makeup.

She'd let her mother walk all over her. Allowed the uninvited press to continue snapping pictures. But what hurt the most, was watching Travis take comfort in another's arms.

"Miss?" the waitress approached slowly, unsure of how to request payment from Casey.

"Cash in the fold on the table," Casey whispered, not turning to watch.

The waitress hesitated and sidestepped to the small clutch and lifted one end.

"Miss this is two-hun-"

"Please take it all," Casey confirmed, "I'm sorry for the disruption."

"Th-thank you."

When the waitress walked away Casey stood for another minute to let the tears slow. She watched the animated conversation and the laughter shared between Travis and Carrie. She let another couple flashes spark to her right. But the last one got her attention.

Casey's head slowly moved from Carrie to the man behind the camera and back again.

Her initial thought was, *she wouldn't. Would she?*

Then, because if life had taught her anything, there was no such thing as coincidences, she had no choice but to believe the worst.

Carrie was trying to sabotage her, her company, and her relationship.

Travis motioned to the top of the patio mid-conversation and both he and Carrie looked directly at Casey. When they did, she saw a smile on Carrie's face, and a look of dread whiten Travis' to a ghostly pale.

Casey turned, methodically maneuvered around the strewn chairs, grabbed her clutch, and walked out, leaving Travis and her feelings for him behind.

CHAPTER 32

"We're coming over."

Casey listened to her friends insist on joining her at the lake for the fifth time and rolled her eyes. She knew she never should have called them.

"I'm fine." Her words were sharp and jagged with the threat of another round of tears.

"You're not, we're coming. Unless you'd like to explain to us over the phone what has you so upset?" Rachel questioned, the usual peppy tone replaced with concern.

"No."

"Then we'll be there in an hour. Aimeé a little later."

"Fine."

Casey clicked the phone off deciding there was nothing left that needed to be said right then. She wiped at the single tear that trickled down her raw cheek. She needed to be ready for Travis when he got home–no, to *her house*, she corrected. Not his home. It never was. It was a place for him to lay his head, that was it.

Ten minutes later she heard a car door slam from the driveway and the front door open. Casey was ready, seated at the head of the dining table with a glass of wine in her hands.

"Did Carrie drive you here?" Casey's voice was void of emotion.

Travis heard the low question as he walked, but waited to answer until he entered the kitchen, until Casey came into view. "She did. She was concerned."

"I'm sure she was."

"What do you mean by that?" Travis questioned.

"You think I'm stupid?"

"Far from it." Travis took a step forward, his irritation growing.

Casey sipped and nonchalantly shifted her gaze to him, not having made eye contact until then. "It wasn't a coincidence the paparazzi was there today, was it?"

Travis was trying hard to put together what Casey thought she was on to.

"I assume not."

Casey nodded. Glad he was admitting to at least that small detail. She wasn't under the impression he would admit to much more.

"And what about Carrie?"

"What about her?"

Casey tried to read his tone, to see if he would give anything away, irritated when she found nothing. "You don't think it was a coincidence she was also there today?"

Then it clicked. "You think Carrie had something to do with that man snapping pictures of your family drama?"

"Wouldn't it be convenient?"

"Your mom got into your head."

It was a low blow, but she could take it.

"She's not anywhere in here." Casey motioned the glass toward her head. "I haven't let her in in a long time. What I have learned is to trust my head. What I can see, and lately, what I feel. What I saw today was a little too planned out." Casey paused. "And what I felt, I'm sad to admit, was disappointment. I let you get too close to me. I let my feelings cloud my better judgement of keeping you at arm's length."

"You're going to have to explain that one, because even I can't keep up, and I'm pretty sharp." Travis let the heated words slide out like ice on water.

"I saw you and Carrie. I saw her kiss you. I saw you not back away."

"You...*what?*" His fury turned to confusion.

He replayed the series of events in his head. None of it coming together to form the ending Casey thought she knew.

"It's fine. You are free to enjoy any woman you'd like. But I would no longer like to do business with you."

"Hold o–"

"I'll finish out the rest of my contract with Thomas and Jane." Casey cut him off. "As for this," she motioned a finger between the two of them, "your services are no longer needed. Please gather your things and move out."

"Casey, this is a huge misunderstanding." He realized as soon as he let the breathy laugh fall out he made a mistake. "Let me exp-"

"You think this is funny? You think getting to be a part of a day in the life with Linette, letting her share with me how much of a disappointment I am to her, how much she doesn't want me, makes *you* the perfect candidate to write everything off as a *misunderstanding?* And that's not even starting on Carrie.*"

"You know that's not what I meant."

"And when I needed you most to stand by me," Casey didn't want the tears to come but she couldn't control them, "you walked away and left me alone with that-that *witch.* And when I finally worked up the courage to walk away I found you in Carrie's arms. Giving Linette just the ammunition she needed to break me into a million pieces." The last words came out in sobs.

"I had no idea. I tried to-"

Travis stood, now speechless, as watched the woman he loved break apart in front of him. When he tried to move to her she pushed back and moved away from him.

"No! Don't come near me. Just go."

Travis fought an internal battle of sadness and fury. He didn't want to see her hurting, but he couldn't believe how such a smart, rational woman could be so *irrational.* How could she not know? How could she not see how much he loved her? Why wouldn't she just listen?

Anger won out at the thought.

"You honestly think, after all the time we've spent together–the great, amazing time–that I could possibly want any woman besides you?"

"Just-"

"No, it's my turn." Travis pointed a finger at her, then turned, exasperated and needing to gather his thoughts. How did a man tell a woman how he felt about her in a way that would make her understand? Especially when she was hellbent on not wanting to understand. He ran his hands through his hair and made his way towards her once more.

"I have wanted you from damn near the time I laid eyes on you. Before I knew you were sarcastic, stubborn, and would obviously make my life miserable."

"Is this supposed to be helping?"

"Just, stop." He held up a hand and shifted his weight from foot to foot, placing his hands on his hips. Travis dropped his head and sighed. Then he stopped everything, his thoughts, movements. Really, of all the things he could say, there were only a couple of words that mattered.

"How could you not know that I am in love with you?"

CHAPTER 33

"Say something."

Casey stared at her friends who were sitting on the edge of her bed staring back at her. By the time they arrived she had finished her third glass of wine, poured another, changed into sweats, and found her way under the fluffy covers of her bed. It seemed safer there than out in the open.

"I…" Rachel started and lost her words. She shook her head, not trying to regain them.

Casey watched her eyes fall on the two additional bottles of wine on the nightstand next to the bed.

"I planned on sharing." Casey rolled her eyes.

"I can't seem to find our glasses," Aimeé commented disbelievingly.

"Like you would have gone all the way back downstairs once you were in sweats next to your bed."

Not paying attention to the conversation, Grace still couldn't believe what Casey had told them. And of all the details, only one piece of the puzzle stuck in her mind.

"He told you he loved you?"

Casey lifted her glass in a toast to Grace for hearing her correctly. "That he did."

"And you…" Rachel began, leaving the open-ended sentence for Casey to finish.

"Told him to leave."

"Right."

Rachel lifted a brow and pushed off the bed eyeing Grace and Aimeé. "I'll get more glasses."

Grace slid from the edge of the bed to sit next to Casey with her back against the headboard, then took her free hand.

Casey stared at it, remembering what it felt like to have her hand in Travis'. She had felt so safe. Even when she tried not to feel anything, she felt comfort. Then in mere seconds everything changed.

"I'm not asking to make you angry, I'm trying to understand." Grace led with what she hoped was a rational introduction. "There isn't any part of this that really could be a misunderstanding? A crazy, or terrible coincidence?"

Casey had tried to see other avenues. She even considered Linette was the one who hired the press junket. But her mother would never do anything that put her own image at risk. And at work, too many things were lining up. Carrie constantly pressuring Casey to show off her boyfriend, hinting at ways the company could be taken away from her, putting her in precarious situations that seemed to be no-win.

Then there was the conference. She doted on Travis when he'd seemingly come in and saved the day. And now, the same man, in the same place, where she and her mother were supposed to meet? And Carrie was there? It was too much.

The part she hadn't been able to say out loud, that possibly hurt the most, was Carrie would never have known they would be there if somebody hadn't told her. The only person that could have done that was Travis. The sliver of a chance Carrie had been their dining of her own accord was just too coincidental. Wasn't it?

Rather than explain herself, Casey simply said, "No. There's no way."

Grace had seen the wheels turning in Casey's mind as she thought through the scenarios. She wouldn't make her say it out loud. But that didn't mean she agreed with Casey's logic. She had gotten to know Travis, and he was a good man–a great man. From what Luke had told her, Travis had been through his own set of heartbreaks with his parents, then his ex-girlfriend. She couldn't imagine he was the type of guy that would put somebody else through the same pain. But maybe that thought was best shared at another time.

"You know, I was thinking about it." Rachel walked in with three stemmed glasses. "He just doesn't seem the type to me. I can't see him putting anybody, especially you, through that."

So much for holding off, Grace mused. Thank God for Rachel.

"Have a couple drinks and I'll explain it to you again." Casey sneered at her friends who weren't listening and taking the side of the man who had crushed her. And went on making it worse by telling her he loved her. As if that would have changed her mind. What an ass.

"What will you do now?" Aimeé questioned, not wanting to press too much.

Casey finished her fourth glass by tipping it high and making sure every drop fell into her mouth.

"Now," she reached for the bottle Rachel just opened and poured, "nothing."

"Nothing?"

"Nothing."

Rachel gently grabbed the bottle, limiting Casey's intake, then poured and handed Aimeé a glass and sat next to her. "I don't really think that's how feelings work."

"Exactly. I don't *plan* on feeling. I plan on going through the motions, same as I have for years. Nothing like a good routine to help you get back on track."

"That's it? Just forget about it? The dates, the lazy weekends, the generous nights, the sex."

"Don't," Casey's voice cut like a knife, "you dare talk about the sex."

Casey let the anger fall off her face as quickly as it came. She started to slink down into the covers and held her drink up in Grace's direction. Grace snagged the misaimed glass of red before it tipped and spilled on the bed.

"Let's just all go to bed and have a nice day tomorrow," Casey mumbled drunkenly through her pillow and was snoring within seconds.

"It's three o'clock." Rachel wasn't the only one who had glanced at the clock on the nightstand.

"Let's let her sleep. She'll be miserable enough tomorrow."

"What should we do?" Rachel asked.

"I saw ingredients for your American nachos in Casey's refrigerator," Aimeé offered.

"First of all, yes. Second of all, nachos don't have *ingredients.* That's too fancy. And you probably don't have to label them *American.* But my dear friend," Rachel threw an arm around Aimeé, "you can call it whatever you want as long as you give it your amazing French touch."

"Nachos and a movie?" Grace asked.

"Is it wrong I'm enjoying this?"

"No," Aimeé said, "we can enjoy while she's sleeping. Because when she wakes up we will all be miserable."

—

The next morning the sound of laughter and the scent of coffee filled Casey's kitchen. The girls were sitting on their own stools at the island and talking about the different things they could do that day to keep Casey's mind off of Travis.

Rachel's tone was adamant as she said, "Nothing cures heartbreak like shopping. Shopping and chocolate."

The sound of Casey's phone buzzing on the counter cut her off again.

"What in the heck is going on with Casey's phone. It won't stop going off."

"Why in God's name are you all yelling?"

The three women turned to see Casey standing at the top of the stairs holding her head with one hand and her stomach with the other.

"Oh sweetie." Rachel consoled at the disheveled sight. She picked up Casey's phone and brought it to her, thinking she could kill two birds with one stone: shut the damn buzzing off and help her friend down the stairs, as she didn't look like she'd make it on her own.

Casey felt like she'd been run over by a freight train. Obviously that would have killed her, but then again she thought through the throbbing pain, this did seem a little like death. Normally she would have shooed away the help, but seeing as walking was seeming an impossible task she let Rachel come to her.

"Oh honey, let me help you. Here, take this." Rachel handed Casey her phone. "It's been going off nonstop."

Even through the nausea Casey couldn't help but look. When she saw what was coming through, the gag reflex was instant.

"What the…*shit!*" Casey took off down the hall and slammed the second floor bathroom door, causing an echo throughout the room.

"Perhaps shopping can be an afternoon activity?" Aimeé suggested as she got up to refill their mugs with fresh coffee.

CHAPTER 34

Travis sulked in his office, unmotivated and unwilling to do anything. His emails were piling up and it was only nine. He groaned at the chime of another email coming his way.

"Don't you people know it's only Monday? Give it a rest." He glanced at the top of the list and rolled his eyes. "Seth."

Then he groaned again knowing if it was an email from Seth he should probably look at it.

"Aren't people just the worst?" Maggie grinned through her words as she sailed into his office.

"Yes."

"Isn't falling in love *the worst?*"

Travis paused and looked up, squinting. "Yes."

"Though, being with the one person who was made for you, right by your side throughout life seems nice too."

Travis dropped his head to the desk with a thud as Maggie sailed right back out.

"I've never seen you look so good, my man." Luke strolled in behind Maggie and sat in a chair across from Travis.

"Go away."

"Seen the news today?"

"No, go away."

"It's pretty interesting."

Travis lifted his head to find himself inches away from Luke's phone screen. "I said no, go a–"

Travis' eyes registered the first line. "What the fuck is this?"

Luke let the phone go when Travis snatched it from his hand.

"You think you're miserable," Luke started, "imagine how Casey's feeling."

Travis scrolled his finger quicker than he could read, but he didn't need to read the details to catch the headlines and the images that followed them.

"Where is this posted?"

"Everywhere. Seems like her mom really is a piece of work."

The protective rage building inside Travis was something he'd never felt before. His immediate instinct was to find that reporter and beat him to a pulp. But more than anything he wanted to talk to Casey. To make sure she was ok.

He stopped at the next headline and read it in detail:

Family in turmoil—mother suffers heartbreak as she tries to rekindle relationship with estranged daughter, multi-millionaire Casey Saunders, before throwing the wedding of the year for soon-to-be Mrs. Hailey Shetland.

Travis didn't know it was possible to physically hurt for somebody else, but he supposed that's what love did to you.

"I have to go."

"Get outta here. I've got you covered."

"Thanks."

—

Aimeé had heard the Bistro door open and close enough times to know when a person was casually sauntering in and when they were coming in determined and on a mission. Usually the latter had less to do with food and more to do with friendship.

When she looked up she found herself staring at Travis' distraught face. He looked worn, ragged. The unshaven stubble looked tired, and the bags under his eyes looked pained. He wasn't sleeping much more than her friend.

Sympathy wasn't a practice Aimeé considered herself to be good at, but it fell upon her and showed in the dip of her head as she lifted a hand to Travis' cheek.

"How are you?"

"I don't matter. How is Casey? I saw…the news."

"She will not return our calls. She needs time alone."

"What can I do?" Travis asked.

The door behind them slammed and they turned to find Casey looking as if she was prepping for war as she processed the view of Aimeé offering her support and compassion for the man who had destroyed her. Not from his actions, but from the feelings he'd caused in her.

"You've done enough," Casey snapped an answer, letting her confused feelings show through anger. She didn't care how she was perceived, she just knew she was hurting.

Casey walked passed Travis as if he was no longer there and slapped a manila folder on the counter in front of Aimeé. The sharpness of the action and the snap of sound caused her friend and the patrons around her to jump and take notice.

"What is this?" Aimeé questioned, already fearing the worst.

"It's your cousin. The money is in a couple of accounts located in France. Looks like I'm not the only one with a fucked-up family."

Casey saw the pain in Aimeé's eyes and quickly turned so she wouldn't have to look at the result of her reckless actions. She stopped and looked at Travis, then Aimeé once more. "You think he's so great," she didn't have to explain who she was talking about, "against your wishes, *Travis* advised me to look. Guess we all know each other's dirty little secrets now."

Their eyes followed Casey as she walked out without looking back. After a moment of disbelief, Travis turned and found Aimeé looking down at the folder.

"I'm so sorry," he offered, not knowing what else to do.

"I'm fine," Aimeé said, steadying her voice with each word, pulling in the tears, only leaving a gloss to rest over her eyes. She picked it up as if she didn't want to touch it and offered it to Travis.

As he gently took it from her she said, "Would you please give this to Chris? You're staying with him for a short time?"

"Of course. You're sure I can't do anything?" Travis realized he hadn't only fallen for Casey, but he'd come to care for each of these women as if they were his family–sisters he would have loved to have. And seeing another one of them hurt seemed to hurt him just as badly.

"That's all. Thank you."

Aimeé turned, ending their conversation as she busied herself with work, adjusting the bakery items and interacting with customers as if nothing at all had just happened.

CHAPTER 35

The Bistro was finally empty as the last customer walked out the door, into the warm night. The end of May offered a slight breeze but also the promise of summer. It allowed for the patio to sit open and the girls to enjoy the rest of their time alone taking in the weather.

"It's been two weeks and she won't return any of my calls. I haven't gotten a response to any of my texts or emails." Rachel leaned back. "She wouldn't even let me in when I went to her house."

The knock on the door had all of them turning. When they saw Travis on the outside Aimeé quickly stood to let him in.

"Travis, hello. Come in." Aimeé moved to the side and motioned to the table where they all sat. "There are croissants and we just opened a bottle of wine."

They all noticed the slowness in his step as he searched for Casey around the table and the drop in his shoulders when he didn't find her. He thought he'd find her there. Rather than mention it, they offered him a seat and poured him a glass.

"I didn't want to have to be the one to tell you this, but you look terrible." Grace grinned at her comment and got the result she was looking for.

The girls laughed lightly and Travis sighed, then let a low laugh escape on his exhale. He shook his head and looked around the table.

"I have no idea what to do. I'm lost. And I'm usually very gifted directionally."

Rachel elbowed him at his small joke.

"I'm usually pretty fucking–sorry–good at reading people. I thought I knew what Casey wanted. I wanted to–want to–give her everything. Anything at all. She would just have to say the word, hell, she'd only have to mention it."

"We know," Rachel soothed. "Travis, can you tell us what happened?"

Travis laid out the chain of events. Everything from the start of their relationship, or *business deal,* to the second Casey asked him to leave her house and never speak to her again.

Aimeé filled the silence of letting the story sink in with her question. "You're in love with her?"

Travis looked down at his wine and gave a slow, deliberate nod. "From the minute I met her. I don't think I knew it until later. But when I think about it–which now seems like every minute of the day–that's when it started."

"What do you intend to do?" Grace asked.

Rubbing his face, Travis looked up and began, "There's nothing I can…"

He hesitated as he saw the three women glare at him, then straightened and cleared his throat. "I'm not going to give up."

"There's my guy!" Rachel clinked her glass to Travis' at his better judgement answer and took a swig, feeling rejuvenated that her friend–with a little help–just might end up with her man after all.

"Is she always like this?" Travis hinted at Rachel with a slight tilt of his head.

Grace smiled and asked, "You mean overly optimistic with full faith that everything always works out? Especially love?"

"Yes," Travis pointed to Grace, "exactly."

After a short pause Grace and Aimeé answered together, "Yes."

CHAPTER 36

Travis looked around and tried to embrace his new living situation. Unlike the rest of his friends, at their recent poker night Christopher had taken pity on him and offered his office as a make-shift bedroom Travis could stay in until he found a place. A blow-up mattress he'd used for camping might not have qualified as a bed but it was the easiest thing he could pull out of storage on such short notice.

He took a swig from his beer bottle and dropped his head. How had he not been ready for this? Yeah, he anticipated the best, but he knew he should always to prepare for the unexpected. He hadn't even begun to look for a new place to live. Now he was starting his search from scratch.

That, he thought though, wasn't his biggest regret. Sure, the girls had a plan, but it didn't mean he didn't miss Casey every time his brain got a free minute. Somehow he'd really fucked this up.

"The guys'll be here in ten." Christopher walked in and plopped on the chair next to the couch and turned on ESPN.

Rather than respond, Travis lifted his head in acknowledgement. "You worried?"

Travis looked up and stared blankly at his new roommate and blinked a couple times. "You mean am I scared to try and surprise the smartest woman in the world, in public, to confess my unending love?"

Christopher smiled and took a sip of the water he brought with him. "Yeah." Christopher inhaled sharply for effect. "Yup, that's what I'm talking about."

"Why on earth would I be worried?"

"What's the worst that could happen?

Thinking about it for a minute, Travis realized there really was a *worst.* It was Casey, tech extraordinaire. She could freeze his accounts and ruin his credit in less time than it would take him to get another beer. And after that thought, Travis stood and walked to the kitchen, deciding not to answer Christopher. Might as well not put the bad juju out there.

By seven, the small dining table had four bodies, three full beers, and a deck of cards dealt to its players. Christopher had turned down a drink from each player at least once. He didn't like taking a chance when he had plans to work a morning shift the next day. Luke was up, winning the first three of four hands. And William was confidently talking trash, sure he'd get all of his money back and then some.

"Nothing to say for yourself over there? Just going to sit and sulk all night?" William asked through a shit-eating grin.

Travis stared at his hand. "I just realized that I'm homeless, I'm sleeping on an air mattress in a borrowed office, and the woman I love is miserable and hates me." He threw in his hand and leaned back in his chair. "Oh yeah, and you assholes are taking all of my money."

"C'mon," Luke chided, "it can't be that bad."

"I was sleeping with the beautiful love of my life in a damn-near mansion three weeks ago. Now I'm…here. Sorry, Chris. No offense."

"None taken. I'd rather live with Casey, too."

"Well, hopefully this will help." William slapped a key on the table.

"What's that?"

"A key to your mansion."

Travis leaned forward and examined the worn brass. "No shit."

"Yes, shit." William drank from his bottle and continued. "Think there's anything you might be able to do with that?"

Smiling a little, for the first time in weeks, Travis swayed his head. "I might feel a small plan forming."

"I thought you might."

Luke looked to Christopher. "This isn't breaking and entering, is it?"

Chris looked to William. "She gave you the key?"

"She sure did."

"Then I say enter at your own risk. The law won't be the one to get you in trouble."

Travis picked up the key and happily tossed it to himself before sliding it into his pocket.

A plan indeed, he thought.

CHAPTER 37

Casey had no intention of letting her friends in. Not when they were banging on the front door, or when they had separated and each found a window to peer through and knock incessantly on. But Aimeé had seen her trying to sneak to the kitchen for a Mountain Dew and delivered the twist of the knife.

"You can't not let me in after deceiving me and going behind my back."

Casey hunched as she listened to the words that tried to be strong, but she heard the hurt that lay beneath the façade. She turned and stood opposite Aimeé and let her head drop. Flicking the lock to one of the French patio doors, Aimeé slowly moved inside.

The women found themselves face-to-face. One saw the weary lines of heartbreak, and the other saw the hurt and sadness caused by betrayal.

As Casey whispered, '*I'm sorry,*' Aimeé pulled her into an embrace, holding her close so any tears that needed to fall would have a place to land.

"I know," Aimeé soothed, and rocked them back and forth as the two other friends found their way in and joined in the hug.

The sun was setting before Casey realized the day was nearly gone. She didn't know how long they hugged, talked, ate, and shared drinks, but somehow the time had passed. Closing her eyes, she found herself wishing every day could be like this. Because for the first time in nearly three weeks the time had gone by quickly. She didn't feel every agonizing second that went by due to the ache that was suffocating her heart.

"I'm sorry you're hurting."

Casey looked up to see Rachel examining her face, reading it like she'd always been able to do.

"I am not good at admitting when I'm wrong."

"No," Grace grinned, "you're not."

Sighing out a laugh, Casey threw a pillow in Grace's direction.

"Jerk." Casey offered a small smile. *"But,* I can't help but feeling like I am."

Wanting to press, but also wanting Casey to be able to go at her own pace, Rachel offered a question. "Wrong about Linette, or wrong about Travis?"

"Not about my mom. She really is a terrible person. Sometimes I get confused, wondering how she could have loved my dad one minute then hate him the next."

The girls' moved eyes from one to the other as Casey's thoughts drifted.

"She doesn't seem capable of love."

"I've never heard you talk about love as though you thought it existed before." Aimeé wasn't the only one who noticed the different way Casey seemed to be approaching the topic. "It seems more than a science to you now?"

It could have been the wine that had her guard down. Or a way to offer her heart some reprieve. Maybe if she said it out loud it wouldn't hurt so much?

"It has to exist."

Rachel edged closer to Casey and pressed, "What do you mean?" She was practically begging Casey to finally admit she was in love. It would mean there was hope. Hope for their plan. Hope for her friend– both of her friends'–happiness.

"I can't find a logical, reasonable explanation for why my heart physically aches. My chest feels as though it's caving in, like my lungs can't catch a full breath. I can't eat, I can't sleep. I've thought about it– often to nauseating degrees over the last couple of weeks. It doesn't go away, just ebbs and flows. Sometimes not so bad. But other times," Casey pressed a hand on her heart as if the pressure would ease the pain, "it's so bad I think I might be suffocating. Those are the times–the really bad ones–when I think about Travis, and not being able to see him anymore. And it's my fault."

It wasn't the response that Rachel wanted, but it was close enough to proof. As she listened, there was one thing she knew for sure: that she and her friends definitely loved each other, because as Casey spoke, they were all feeling the same pain knowing she was suffering.

"Are you sure it's over?" Grace prodded. "And what about him hurting you?" She knew the answer, but Casey needed to be the one to come around to her own conclusions.

"He hasn't reached out to me since I ran into him at the Bistro."

Casey offered Aimeé an apologetic look at the memory of her hurtful encounter, only to be given a look of dismissal and forgiveness in return.

"I, um…I." Losing her words, Casey didn't know how to explain her emotions without feeling like she was an idiot. She had seen her dad suffer enough. Constantly letting her mother run all over him time after time, constantly forgiving her out of his love for her.

If she forgave Travis, knowing he'd hurt her, wouldn't that make her just the same?

"I don't want to be like my dad."

"I don't understand."

"He loved my mother so much it caused him pain. She was terrible, and he still loved her. I was hurting so much that day, and I still loved him. I still loved Travis."

Rachel sighed, "You love him."

Casey looked up. "More than anything."

CHAPTER 38

Pacing in front of her laptop, Casey had planned her speech and carefully crafted how she would deliver her resignation. She had weighed the pros and cons of staying. Eventually, it all came down to not being able to deal with Carrie on a daily basis.

No, she thought, *that's a lie.*

The truth was–and she was working damn hard on the truth–it would hurt too much to see other people falling in love all around her. By something she created.

So she'd let it go.

Wow. Let it go.

Casey fell back to rest on the corner of her desk with the heavy realization of what she decided to do, and let the words sink in.

Let it go.

Bringing her hand to her chest she was surprised at the sinking feeling it created.

Pushing off the desk, she paced the room once more and couldn't believe what she was about to do. She picked up her phone, selected her dad's name, and made the call.

At the sound of his voice Casey almost teared up.

He answered. He always answered for her.

"Hi, Dad." She hated how small she sounded.

"Hey, sweetie. Is everything okay?"

"I, ah, Dad?"

"I'm here."

"Can I ask you about Linette–about mom?"

Casey could have sworn she heard a sigh of relief from the other end. As if her dad had waited years for her to ask about them. About what had gone wrong.

"I'll tell you anything you want to know." The sturdy tone sounded safe. It offered security and confidence.

"You loved each other." It wasn't a question.

"More than anything."

"How could–or–why did it stop?"

There was a long silence. Casey found her way to the couches in her office and sat, willing to wait as long as she needed for an answer.

"I would have tried forever," Ian finally admitted. "I would have waited a lifetime for your mother to love me again."

"But you fought. All the time."

"I wish you wouldn't have grown up like that, but yes."

"Why?"

"I was fighting for her. Fighting to be understood. We both were. But one day it changed. That's when I knew."

"What do you mean?"

She felt him searching for the right words to say.

"Your mom stopped fighting for things that she wanted. She started fighting to leave. That's when I knew that my love wasn't going to be good enough. I had to let her go. It was the hardest thing I've ever had to do–aside from realizing I'd lost my daughter along the way. That's the one thing in life that's hurt me the most."

Tears threatened her eyes, but she pushed on, wanting to hear everything. Wanting to *know* everything.

"You would have stayed?" she asked.

"I would never have given up on us."

"Why?"

His answer seemed to come so easily. "Because when you love somebody, truly love them, you never give up."

"You make it sound simple."

"Love is simple. We make it hard." Ian's voice hesitated before going on. "Case, sweetie, are you okay?"

Nodding at first, Casey finally spoke. "I'm in love. And I'm terrified."

Hearing the small smile in her dad's advice, she listened. "Don't be afraid of love. Of anyone, or anything you love. It took me a long time to learn that lesson. Sometimes love does mean letting go. But Casey?"

"Yeah?"

"When you find it, try to fight like hell to keep it."

The conversation didn't last much longer, but when it was over Casey realized she didn't love just one, but two things–Travis *and* her job.

Circling her desk, she eyed her laptop and said aloud, "Well, let's just handle one at a time."

CHAPTER 39

Confidence wasn't something Casey struggled with. It was a byproduct of being a realist; of having a scientific point of view when it came to beauty and attraction. She understood that she found Travis attractive because he mirrored certain qualities she herself possessed.

Casey looked at her reflection and studied her face. It was symmetrical, curved in nicely at the jawline, and sat on a neck that seemed proportionate to her limbs. Her eyes, nose, and mouth were evenly spaced and all just about equal in size. Her body, from top to bottom, curved and angled in the right places, and her breasts stuck out just as far in the front as her butt did in the back.

Her brow twitched at the last observation. Okay, maybe that wasn't scientific, but it did seem to add a sense of proportion to her look. And, she thought as she turned, it let the gown her friends had chosen for the night fall nicely over the curvy mound and drape to the floor. She never would have chosen the sunset-red, off-the-shoulder dress herself, but she had to admit as she turned, it was beautiful.

"Are you coming out, or what?"

"I'm coming," she said, adding extra drab to her voice to get a rise out of Rachel. She grinned when she heard her friend mumble through the door.

"It's like she doesn't even care this whole night is about her."

Casey pushed through the door and received the praise she didn't want, but knew would come.

"You're like a real-life," Rachel halted mid-thought, "well shit. What's that redhead's name from *Who Framed Roger Rabbit?*"

"Jessica." Grace obliged her with an answer.

Aimeé waved it off and offered, "I don't know who you're talking about."

"This," Grace pointed to Casey, "but bigger boobs."

Aimeé nodded as if she understood completely.

"Well?" Casey asked, "Will it do?"

"You'll knock 'em dead."

"Have you decided what you'll say?"

Casey thought back to the phone call with her dad. She loved her company. It was hers. Every detail was hers. And it was successful. In the end, she didn't resign, she wasn't willing to give it up.

Looking at her friends, she hesitated at a thought that had been nagging the back of her mind since she decided to stay. She wished Travis would be there with her.

"We know," Grace comforted.

Casey simply nodded.

They all shuffled down the stairs, each carrying something for Casey. Aimeé held makeup she would touch up once more before Casey left for her evening. Grace carried the gold clutch that would serve as a makeup bag and phone storage. And Rachel held matching gold heels and a shawl.

Gathered by the door, Casey hugged each one and asked, "You're sure you can't stay? Be here when I get back?"

"Sorry, Case. I've got a day filled with work tomorrow and I promised Luke I'd be home tonight for dinner and a movie."

"I have to go spy on them through the window to make sure they're every bit as cute as I think they are. Oh, and I have to volunteer tomorrow at the school. I can't be hung over for that. Imagine hundreds of screaming grade-schoolers with a throbbing headache."

"That sounds terrible without the headache." Casey grinned, then let Rachel kiss her cheek.

"What's your excuse?" she asked Aimeé. "Actually, never mind. I don't want to hear what time you're getting up to go to the Bistro tomorrow. It'll make me sick."

"Then I'll not give you the burden. But come in tomorrow and we'll share a coffee and breakfast."

"It's a date." Casey looked to each of her friends, thankful they hadn't given up on her. Thankful, she grinned, they were just annoying enough to get her to cave in and let them help.

"I love you."

"We know." They all took Casey in their arms. "We love you, too."

CHAPTER 40

The driver pulled up to the old hotel that had served as host for their gala as long as they'd hosted one. It had the perfect combination of old charm and modern luxury. Every year they upped the ante on aesthetic and service, and Casey noted this year was no exception.

A red carpet stretched from the circled drive to the ornate double doors. Men and women in perfectly tailored white suits stood at the ready to help guests out of their cars as they arrived, and ushered them into their evening. Upon walking inside, another set of hosts waited, offering a choice of champagne or wine, or as a guide to the bar for a mixed drink of choice.

Carrie had outdone herself this year, Casey noted as a nice young gentleman took her shawl and replaced it with a small card that would ensure she could retrieve it again at the end of the night.

Carrie, she thought, sighing. Casey had been rude to her on their call and now, after, she wished she could take it back. Especially when she'd learned the truth about the infamous paparazzi.

Irritated with herself, Casey couldn't believe she hadn't looked sooner. It's what she was good at. It allowed her to make smart, educated decisions about nearly every aspect of her life. Yes, this time she was a little distraught, but that was no excuse. She was smarter than that. But, she supposed, love did crazy and irrational things to a person.

Casey wandered down the hall toward the music she heard coming from the ballroom. As she walked she sorted through the information she'd found when she finally decided to take matters into her own hands. It didn't take long to find the emails and phone calls Linette had made to a local entertainment journalist. A *well-connected* local entertainment journalist. From there the web began to form and spread quickly, his reach was far and wide.

The journalist hired the photographer. The photographer sold the photos to every contact in his arsenal.

Her own mother.

Casey leaned her head back and shook out her arms at the tension that started to form at the memory recall.

"Casey?"

The question came from behind her. A familiar voice with an unfamiliar lack of spirit. Casey turned to see a wary and timid Carrie hesitate before making the final move toward her.

"Carrie, hi." She knew what Carrie was going to do, but Casey knew she had to take responsibility for her own actions. "I know what you're going to say."

"No–I–I'm so, so–"

"No, Carrie, please. Don't apologize. I need to apologize. I misread a situation, and worse than that, I was rude to you last week when you've honestly," Casey was surprising even herself with the realization that was forming as she spoke, "been nothing but nice and supportive to me over our years here together. So, I'm sorry."

A small squeak came out in what Casey assumed were the words that got caught up in Carrie's shock.

"Ah, thank you. I hope you understand I don't expect that from you. I'd like to share something with you. I think it will make sense when I–well, you know–share it."

Casey was seeing a version of Carrie she didn't know existed. The usually peppy to the point of nauseating, happy person, was nervous. It made Casey feel worse for what a jerk she'd been.

"You don't need to–"

Carrie stepped aside and Casey realized there had been somebody with Carrie and she hadn't noticed.

"This," Carrie said, taking the hand of a pretty brunette and holding her closely, "is Angela Boston. Angela is my fiancé."

Casey couldn't hide her delight at both the happiness in what Carrie shared and the humor in the mix-up. What had her so upset when she saw Carrie and Travis together was nothing more than a friendly hug, smeared by the words of her awful mother.

"No!" Casey said too loudly, realizing the horror in Carrie's face at her laughter. "No, no, no. Carrie, I am so happy for you. I was laughing at *myself.* I was–oh God–Carrie, I was jealous of you when I saw you hugging Travis. And my mom, and the situation, I just–I was all wrong."

In a rare display of emotion, Casey folded both of the women into a hug.

"This is great. So great." Casey let them breathe and turned to Carrie's fiancé. "Angela, it's so nice to meet you. I'm sure I don't have to tell you you've found a beautiful woman in Carrie."

Angela smiled as she looked at Carrie and agreed, "Beautiful in every way."

"I hope you enjoy this night, and I'm happy you're celebrating with us. I can't take credit for any of it. Carrie does all the heavy lifting, but I hope it makes it that much more enjoyable for you. I'm sorry, I should…" She rolled her head toward the door of the ballroom and shrugged.

Casey didn't want to leave but she was expected to speak and put on a brave face to a room full of people who believed in bringing love to the world. And they believed in her, and the company they worked for. So they deserved to see her at the top of her game.

"Yes, please, go. You'll do great. But, dang it, sorry." Carrie stopped her before she turned away completely. "I feel like you should know, even though I'm sure you already do. Travis was the one who encouraged me to share my love story with everybody. I was hesitant, but he," Carrie looked at Casey, then reached for Angela's hand, "he reminded me that love is, well, love. And it's beautiful in every form. And that's nothing to be ashamed of."

Casey nodded once and smiled. "I've never heard truer words spoken." Then turned and walked through the large ballroom doors.

CHAPTER 41

It wasn't so much the gala that had him nervous. Travis liked to think he did well in public settings. He got along with others–most of the time. He was relaxed enough to enjoy casual conversation, and curious enough to be genuine when sharing words with a stranger.

Yeah, the gala would be fine.

What he had planned for after the gala? That's what had him worried.

The part where he and Casey would be alone. Where she could reject him, not hear him out–or worse–not truly listen to the words he would say because she already made up her mind. *That,* he thought, would be the worst.

Luke walked into the room and found Travis hunched over the office desk that served as his flat dresser for the time being. "You ready?"

"Don't I look ready?"

"Look like shit, but your suit's nice." Travis turned to see Luke smiling like a punk teenager who'd appropriately razzed his friend.

"Fuck you."

"Hey, it can't go wrong."

"Actually, it can." Travis closed his eyes and reworked his initial scenario and thought aloud, "Very publicly, extremely wrong."

"But your suit's nice."

"Fuck you."

William laughed from the hallway behind the door.

"Really? You're all here?"

"Don't know why we wouldn't be. It's only appropriate for us to give you a proper send off. Especially since it could be your funeral."

Luke smiled again, this time at the new laugh William offered to his words.

"Hey," William said, turning into the opening and pausing a beat for Christopher to make his way down the hall to get a look for himself, "when you get ahold of one of these girls you gotta do what you can to keep her."

"Amen." Chris nodded absently, then looked up at the three faces staring at him. "What? You think I spend every waking hour at the Bistro for police work and pastries?"

Unable to disagree with the sentiment or hide his grin, Luke offered his agreement. Then thinking of his own strange love affair with Grace, said, "Just always be ready. They can be unpredictable."

"Why do you think I've been walking around with this damn ring in my pocket for a month?"

"Go big or go home," Chris said, not at all surprised.

"Technically I don't have a home."

"If she turns you down, your self-pity will earn you another month free of charge."

"Gee, thanks."

"Go knock her dead, buddy."

———

A red carpet.

Travis had just walked down a literal red carpet. Fully equipped with flashing cameras, which he supposed were more for his million-dollar love interest than himself. There was enough publicity around her current affairs to make one of the front pages that would come out the next day.

A light snapped just before he walked through the door causing him to blink away the blur that stunned his sight. As he did a hand found his arm and pulled him away from the door and out of the line of fire.

"Travis? Are you okay?" Carrie's voice sounded concerned, and he had a hunch the question wasn't in regard to the paparazzi.

"Why do you ask?" He sported a boyish grin and received one in return.

"She's here."

"Your *she,* or mine?"

Carrie wrapped her arms around him like a sister would an older brother. "Both, but yours in particular."

Pulling herself away he could see she was fighting back tears. "Thank you for encouraging me to share my own love story. It seems like something that should be so simple, so natural. But I was worried. For what?" She shook her head. "Now I don't know. It feels so good having Angela by my side. To share in this with me. And I have you to thank."

Carrie turned and leaned her head motioning for Travis to follow her, so he did.

"I have a feeling you would have come around to it in your own time."

"Maybe," she looked over, "but waiting any longer would have seemed like too long. Know what I mean?"

Looking at Carrie, Travis wondered if she could read his mind? All he could do was agree. Any time spent from here on out without Casey would be too much. "I know exactly what you mean."

As they walked toward the ballroom, Travis tried to pay attention to their small talk and make sure he greeted everybody he'd met during their previous engagements. Unfortunately, the grand décor and the elegance of the evening had him taking in details he would have normally ignored. In all the times he'd been to this hotel, had he ever noticed the gold molding on the ceiling, or the deep reds–burgundy, he thought proudly, coming up with the name–of the flowers painted on the paper-covered walls?

His head scanned upwards and he found himself staring at a line of chandeliers that led to an arched doorway that was sure to be the ballroom.

The ballroom.

He folded his hands together and wondered when they'd gone clammy. Was it when he saw the entrance to where he knew he'd find Casey? Or had they been that way the whole time?

As they approached, the doors opened and he found the last ten seconds he had to prep himself before seeing Casey were stolen from him as she walked through. By the time she looked up and stopped, he had already been staring at the vision she made.

Casey stole a glance at Carrie and nodded pleasantly. So pleasantly it pulled Travis out of his trance to make sure it was Carrie she had sent the *nice* silent gesture. But when he looked back to Casey all thought was lost again.

The long dress flowed, hugging the angles of her body he knew intimately, and had the intense desire to explore once more. Her hair waved over one shoulder and the need to run his fingers through it pulled him toward her.

"You're here."

"I'm here." Travis recognized it wasn't a question, just a curious observation.

"You didn't have to–I mean–after the way I treated you, I didn't expect you to–"

Holding out his hand in offering, Travis cut her off, "We made a deal."

A deal.

Casey nodded and placed her hand in his. They'd made a deal.

She noted he said nothing about the way he felt. Nothing of the love he confessed before she'd told him to leave. He didn't show any emotion beyond a man seeing an attractive female. He didn't even show anger, which would have been welcome and something she could have dealt with. But the slow, cool response he gave cut her to the core. She'd gone too far, and she knew it. He was only there to fulfill his end of their deal. Because, Casey glanced at his handsome profile then pulled away before he could see her longing, he was a man of his word.

—

Throughout the start of the evening there were moments when they forgot their feelings. Allowed themselves to simply be in the company of each other and the rest of the guests. They laughed at jokes, told stories of old flames, and listened to others share what drew them to the company and what encouraged them to stay. The theme was almost all the same–people wanted love in any form they could get it: through relationships or work.

Travis couldn't help but see the way Casey listened intently as people spoke. Still trying to understand and learn after all these years.

Then it hit him. She was stubborn–more than anybody he'd ever met. But she was also constantly evolving and learning. And, he stared at her as she leaned into a conversation, willing to change if it meant improving.

Unconsciously, he moved his hand to his pocket. If she was willing to change, to accept, he was willing to put in the time it would take for her to love him.

Before long, Casey excused herself. She would be moving to the stage to speak to the masses that made up her company, then she'd quietly find a way to make her escape. Being there with Travis had given her confidence, but it also tore at her heart knowing she pushed away the one man she had ever loved–probably ever would.

Glancing at their table, she stole one more look at Travis before the entrance music came on, cuing her to start her ascent. As she climbed the stairs a voice boomed above the beat and introduced her to a roar of clapping hands.

This is amazing, she thought. *Look at everybody. I created this.* Holy shit. *I created this.*

Scanning the room, she locked eyes with people at the tables as the spotlights shifted and allowed her vision to clear. She noticed Travis looking around the room in awe, or maybe pride, before turning back to the stage and letting out a two-fingered whistle.

Her smile was genuine as she took in the act and admitted, he was good at this.

"Thank you," Casey said, leaning into the microphone. "Thank you very much."

Her next inhale and exhale was audible, showing nerves, but it quieted the crowd so you could hear the faintest sound of the ceiling vent and the creak of a chair as somebody adjusted their position.

"You might find it hard to believe, but this won't be long. And, I'd like to take a moment to talk about love."

The crowd laughed heartily as they stared at their charismatic leader, most knowing she wasn't much for words if prior years had proved them right. And love. Why wouldn't it be about love? It was their meal ticket after all.

Casey smiled. "Love. It comes in many different forms, doesn't it?" she began, as if she was asking herself that question. "But ultimately, it's a feeling. A feeling each one of us controls. Oftentimes," she paused momentarily and thought of her dad, "it's a choice."

Picking up the microphone, Casey moved from her perch behind the narrow stand to sit on the edge of the stage. "I'm going to need a little help here." She and the crowd laughed as one of the members of her accounting team helped her take a seat.

"Thanks, Daryl." She shifted once, then started again.

"When I thought of all of the things I could say today it wasn't hard to come up with hundreds of topics. And if you've ever had a conversation with me you know how my brain works–often faster than you'd like to hear me talk." Casey grinned at her truth. "But nothing that filtered through my mind seemed genuine. They were all true, good topics, but they weren't *real*. They lacked feeling. So I'm going to share two things that I've realized in the very short term.

"The first: I love this job. I love what we do. Admittedly, I probably get more joy out of the science behind it than the overly romantic–" small chuckles escaped those who knew her well, "–but the end result, what we do and what we are able to create for people…"

Casey sighed letting an unexpected bout of emotion pass.

"I really love it. And when the wheels started turning," she wound her finger on the side of her head, "I realized it's not just me. It's bigger than that. *We* are bigger than that. And something happened in that moment. I found that I loved more than just this job–this *thing* we do.

"I love all of you. You are the reason we're here. *You* are the reason I get to continue to do what I love. So in wrapping up the first of my lessons, I want to say *thank you*. *Thank you* for letting me love you. And for giving us this."

Casey's arms stretched out as she motioned to all of the people that sat in front of her who were now standing and clapping.

"Enough of the mushy stuff, we want to hear number two!"

The crowd and Casey laughed at the voice that shouted from the back.

"Okay, okay. Number two. This one, at one point probably could have cost me my job. But I'll share it with you now that my rehabilitation seems to be nearly complete. It wasn't long ago that I didn't believe *I* was capable of falling in love."

CHAPTER 42

She was holding the train of her dress in one hand and her shoes in the other, standing barefoot in her driveway. The driver had gone but she wasn't sure how long ago he'd pulled away.

Casey had admitted her love for Travis openly, only to look down from the stage and find he wasn't there. Though, she thought, sinking into a slouch, she supposed he'd done what he needed to do. He'd fulfilled his end of the deal by being there. It shouldn't have surprised her that by the end of the night he was ready to hang it up. No need to stick around for awkward goodbyes, especially after openly professing her love. It was probably for the best that he didn't hear it.

An exaggerated groan escaped as she began to trudge forward. Might as well go inside. No use being crabby and sad in her driveway.

If the girls were here they would have poured her wine and probably had ice cream waiting. But they had their own lives to live. And God did she loved them.

Casey rolled her eyes. "Aren't you just filled with all the love today?" she asked herself as she unlocked her front door and let herself in. She dropped her shoes on the doormat and flicked on the porch light before moving to the back of the house.

As she approached, a small flicker of light caught her eye. Walking slowly, she squinted and moved to the wall of windows that looked out over the lake. Pausing on the inside she put her hand against the pane as she took in the sight. Her friends were amazing.

Lantern lights glowed in the night on what seemed an unending path to the lake. Excited, she reached for the handle of the French door and flung it open. She laughed as she noticed the bottle of David Ramey

225

wine sitting in a tin pale when she made it halfway between her house and the lake.

Scooping it up she wanted to hurry but couldn't find a reason to rush the beautiful walk. As the deck came to a small peak she saw a fire blazing on the beach and a single figure standing, an outline in the fire light.

Casey's arm dropped, the bottle hanging at her side, and she slowed to a stop as she realized it wasn't her friends. She held her breath as Travis slowly turned at the sound of her footsteps stopping on the wooden path.

For a moment she stood, processing the moment as she aligned the night's events in her mind. But for the first time in her life, she knew what she wanted to say, and none of the thoughts that filtered in and out mattered.

Without going to him, Casey shrugged, lifting the wine with the movement and said, "You left."

"I," Travis hesitated and tentatively moved closer before continuing, "I needed–no–I wanted…wait, just wait." He met her face to face. "I couldn't wait. I didn't want to wait another minute. This," his hands motioned to the lantern lit walk and the fire, then between the two of them, "couldn't wait."

"You missed it," Casey said, calmer than she thought she'd be considering the moment.

Shit, Travis thought. She was being calm–that wasn't good. Calm meant she'd made up her mind. Calm meant no matter what he said she wouldn't budge. He knew that because her stubbornness was one of the sexiest things about her. *Shit.*

Might as well get on with it then.

"You're right, I'm sorry. I missed it. I missed the end of the night. But really, I thought, I wanted to do this. To have this moment with you, alone, without the crowd and the lights."

Casey tilted her head at his nerves. A rare and adorable quality she hadn't yet experienced.

"See, the thing is, I know you don't believe in love. I know you don't believe in marriage. But I do. And I believe I've found the one person in the whole world that I want to love and I want to marry."

"Travis, I–,"

"No, please, let me finish." Because after today, he thought, it would become pestering. He wasn't going to give up, but this was his moment, damnit.

Casey nodded and again he saw the unnerving calm.

"You're not wrong."

Casey's eyes narrowed in confusion wondering where he was taking this.

"Your parents loved each other. My parents loved each other. But they ruined it. They made a vow–a deal–and they broke it. They gave up."

Hearing him acknowledge her feelings, his agreeing with her, caught her off guard. It wasn't a subject people tended to dwell on. To admit that her parents were at fault. But he would–he did. Nothing to Travis was off limits. That's probably why she trusted him. Why she loved him. If she could just get him to stop talking.

"Travis."

"I'm never going to give up on you."

The words flew out, catching her by surprise, stopping her slow smile. She had made her decision. She didn't expect anything he could say would rock her. But those exact words shot straight to her heart.

"I love you, Casey. Every part of you. There will never be a day that goes by where I will not actively express how I feel about you. I will pester you, and taunt you, and use our friends against you."

It was dark out, but he didn't miss the lift of her eyebrow at his comment.

"Yes," he said, defending his words, "they are *our* friends now, not just yours. And I will, if I have to, use them against you–in a good way. Because I know that they know, we are good for each other.

"I will irritate you until you realize I'm not going anywhere. And if it takes a day, or a lifetime, it makes no difference to me. Though," he looked up in thought, "it would be nice if it were sooner rather than later, because I'm choosing to love you for the rest of my life."

His chest lifted with his inhale and fell with an exasperated exhale.

"I love you. That's it." Travis finished, lifting his hand giving her the floor. "Now you can go."

Travis dropped his head and rested his hands on his hips, then waited for disappointment, knowing with what he just committed to it could be the first of many disappointing conversations. But hell, like he said, he wasn't giving up.

"You missed it," Casey said again.

"No, no, I think I covered just about everything."

"No, you missed my speech."

"I, ah," Travis looked up at the setting he'd created for what was supposed to be a romantic moment that seemed to not be going at all as planned. Though, if he really thought about it, did he really think it was going to be all that perfect? Really?

"I had some things to do. You know: set the mood, try for romance, express unending love." He might as well quit while he's ahead. "Never mind. What did I miss?"

"It was very good. I talked about love. I meant to only talk about my love of work, but somehow I got into the love of friendship, love of family–well, not really in my case–but you get the idea. I really rambled."

It took a minute for Travis to catch up but finally realized she was talking about her speech again.

"I think I surprised a lot of people. Hell, I surprised myself. And by the time I'd gone around and around, and finally got around to telling everybody I loved you, you were gone. Of course the people who thought we've been together for three years found it a little strange."

"I know, I'm sorry, I should have stayed and not left but…what did you just say?"

"You were gone." Casey shrugged and tried not to let her grin slip.

"No, before that."

"I'd gone around and around."

"Damnit, Casey. After that." Travis moved his hands to Casey's arms and wanted to shake it out of her. He'd do anything to hear those words again.

"Oh, that I love you?"

When Travis pulled her into his body and held her, the wine fell to the sand with a gentle thud and she laughed. She wrapped her arms around him and felt his warm breath kiss her neck as he burrowed into her as if he never intended to let go.

"Tell me you love me again," she whispered, and felt his smile at her request.

"I love you. I love you." Travis pulled away just enough to look at her. "I love you."

Casey pulled him into a kiss that felt like fireworks.

She wondered if it would always feel like this, or would it fade? But as he brought her closer to him yet, she realized this was exactly what he meant when he said he wouldn't give up. The fireworks, like love, were a choice.

Casey leapt into another hug deciding she'd start right now, so she wrapped her arms around his head and as he did before, held so tight she hoped her love for him would cascade into him.

"Hey," she whispered into his ear, "you said you're pretty good at making deals?"

"I am. Being my latest venture–aside from some minor missteps–I think you can attest to that."

"Then how about you make me another one?" Casey leaned closer yet and kissed him just below the ear before saying, "You should marry me."

Travis paused before stepping back.

The air between them nearly took Casey's breath away. Hadn't he just said he wanted marriage? Love *and* marriage? Now here *he* was backing away?

"That's a heck of a deal to make." Travis slid his hands into his pockets as he took another small step backward.

Casey's heart dropped.

Then he fell to his knee and removed one hand to hold hers, and with the other, pulled out a small box.

"I thought you'd never ask," he started, "literally. Like in a million years, or at least as many in our lifetime. Never thought you'd–"

Casey laughed and brushed at the tears with her free hand while reprimanding his comedy. "Yeah, yeah. Travis Mavens, if you don't get on with it, I'm going to change my mind."

"Well, I only say that because I figured I'd be the one who'd have to ask. Which is why for the last month I've been carrying around this damn box with me everywhere."

Travis took the moment to look at her–truly look. He took in all of her beauty, inside and out. He wanted to see her in this moment so he could try for the rest of their lives to get her to feel like this every single day.

"Casey Saunders, yes, I will marry you."

Leave a Review!

Did you love it? Leave your review with Amazon,
or the retailer from where you purchased
In the Business of Love.

Then, continue reading…

Continue to the next page for a special excerpt of ***Postmark Christmas,*** a magical and fun holiday romance.

POSTMARK CHRISTMAS

A Holiday Romance Novel

KATIE BACHAND

MINNEAPOLIS, MN

CHAPTER 1

Harlow Hill had been listening to Christmas music since July. She told herself it was because of the job. Her clients started putting together holiday commercials, print advertisements, and plans for their festive – and usually over-the-top – holiday parties even before their Independence Day events were over.

But she knew, even without the big-ticket clients and events, she would still be yearning for Christmas. She would be sneaking in a holiday music session while working out, or turning the air conditioning up at The Hill – her inherited Victorian mansion on Summit Avenue – and throwing on some cozy winter pajamas, opening a bottle of eggnog, and settling in for the Hallmark Channel's *Christmas in July* event.

Thank God somebody out there had the right mind to air adorable, romantic Christmas movies when the temperature outside was ninety-eight and the air so humid your glasses would fog up just moving from inside to out.

Sally, who was preparing to give her weekly project update, was just as excited about it as Harlow. Though she was usually a little less restrained and reserved in her presentation.

"Hi! Good morning! Are you ready for our update?" Sally asked as she bounded into Harlow's office, her words a mixture of singing and shouting.

Sally, Harlow noted upon her entrance, was wearing the same winter white color of the walls and the same red accent. Only instead of concrete, her sweater was a chunky knit, and instead of red picture frames and vases, her earrings and necklace were a mixture of berry-red beads and feathers.

Harlow couldn't help but smile at the enthusiastic young woman. Sally wasn't unlike Harlow had been as a young marketing and advertising executive. Maybe that's why she'd always had a soft spot for the vibrant, and ambitious brunette.

"I am absolutely ready. Come in. Who else is joining today?" Harlow gestured to the leather chesterfield sofa across from her desk, and Sally sat.

Harlow knew Sally wouldn't need any of the staff to help in the breakdown of every excruciating and finite detail of their plans, but Sally – and Harlow too, admittedly – loved having the room filled and hearing from the team as they recounted the status of the projects they owned. All of them were competitive, but overwhelmingly supportive.

"We'll have Ryan and Vanessa. Jacquelyn is on-site setting up for her skating event this weekend. Which, if I might add, is amazing." Sally said, while her hazel eyes grew two sizes, letting a dreamy haze cloud across them as she looked off into the distance. "Her decision to go with *A Log Cabin Christmas theme* was dead-on. The evergreens she brought in are the perfect pine green, and they are adorned with these chunky amber lights, fragrant cinnamon pinecones, red robin ornaments, and the presents are wrapped in buffalo-check paper. Seriously, it's like walking into an LL Bean catalog."

"Oh my God, are you talking about *A Log Cabin Christmas?*" Vanessa asked, catching the last couple words while running through the door. Attempting to be on time once this week, and to not spill her coffee upon entry. "It is glorious and rugged perfection. It makes me want to live in a cabin and dress in plaid."

Vanessa plopped next to Sally on the chesterfield as Ryan sauntered in, completely cool and unfazed that he was five minutes late. He took one of the wooden chairs that bordered the couch, sliding effortlessly in and offering a killer smile.

Oh the hearts he would break, Harlow thought, and the pining hearts he was creating. Sally, the ever put-together professional, had to force herself to concentrate just a bit more when Ryan walked in.

Harlow watched the three sit expectantly, and loved everything about them. All so different, but all of them beautiful, passionate, and driven.

She'd heard friends and colleagues from other companies tell her that millennials were lazy and ruining their corporate drive. Harlow had seen first-hand that was far from true. She'd never seen individuals have so much fun and try so hard to produce results in her lifetime. They embraced the old, and she loved that they understood and drove them toward the new.

"Okay," Harlow began, "let's get started. It sounds like Jacquelyn is on track. Is there anything she needs from me that wasn't in her recap email this morning? Does she need any assistance in set-up or opening?"

"She is on top of it." Sally took the lead. "All decorations are in place. Props – like the wooden toboggan sleds and the hay bales for on-ice seating – arrived yesterday. Those should be in place by," Sally looked at her watch, more out of habit than a need to see it was ten after nine, "now."

Sally drew her chestnut hair over one shoulder, not realizing her nervous habit, and went on. "The food vendors are scheduled to arrive at five tomorrow morning. They are expecting a crowd. At least double what they had last year since it was such a hit. And it's the Saturday before Thanksgiving so it's anticipated that a lot of people won't be working next week. Jacq calculated for that, too."

"Perfect. Please let me know if you hear of anything from her. I know she'll reach out to one of you before me, but I'm available." Harlow nodded, took a sip of her coffee, and made a note that everything was on track. "Okay, Vanessa, how are you doing at the hotel?"

"Good. We are back on track after the delivery mix-up last week."

Harlow appreciated Vanessa's word choice. 'Mix-up,' to Harlow's mind, was putting it extremely nicely. The florist sent less than half of the greenery, garland, and poinsettia order. And what they did send went to the wrong hotel – in the wrong state. Apparently, Minnesota and Michigan were easily interchangeable.

Vanessa had simply gotten on the phone, redirected the shipment, got a refund for the undelivered items, covered the charge for the delivery, worked with a local flower and garden shop, and had the rest of the delivery the following Monday.

"I've confirmed with Sasha – the hotel's event planner – the room will be set up by tomorrow morning. We're talking over-the-top blues and silvers – on and in everything. Bulbs, flowers, tassels, vases, and even the food. The caterer is prepared and we've confirmed the headcount. Entertainment was set up last night and they'll arrive by three tomorrow. That's four hours before the seven o'clock start time. And their equipment – silver."

Vanessa looked around and saw her comment received smiles from the room. They knew it was ridiculous too, but it was just the right amount of obnoxious.

"Hors d'oeuvres will be served to the five hundred guests upon arrival – cute, dainty finger-foods. There will be holiday cocktails, beer, and wine available for beverages straight through the night. A plated dinner will be served at eight with light holiday music continuing to play in the background. At nine the dessert bar will be set up. The Bistro will provide the treats and do set up and break down. I've seen the spread – they look delectable. And if any of you make it, they are making extra dinner plates for emergencies, it's roasted rack of lamb with blueberry glaze." Vanessa moaned as she pretended to faint falling to the tufted back-rest. "There are no words."

"Music will pick up at that point, offering a more festive beat." Vanessa sat up and went on. "It will hopefully encourage dancing *and* for those in attendance to open their wallets. There is a raffle for prizes large and small. All proceeds going to Heritage House. It's an orphanage in downtown St. Paul."

Heartfelt *ahh's* made their way out of Sally and Ryan at the generous gesture.

Vanessa agreed and went on to tell the group it was the first party thrown by two accounting firms that joined forces in October. There were good feelings all around and she couldn't wait to celebrate with them – they'd invited her as a guest to her own party.

Ryan then lived his own bit of excitement as he recounted the details of his event taking place at the NHL hockey arena in St. Paul. It was all-man, or all-fan, appropriate.

Miniature hockey gear ornaments took over the trees that would be lit up all around the rink and near the concessions areas on every floor. Over four-hundred of them. Minnesota's team had donated signed jerseys, posters, sticks, and pucks to the event.

"Everything is good. The only thing I might need help with is the final walk-through for the charity executives. They are hoping for a picture at the opening of everybody who came together to make the event happen. Harlow, are you available for that?"

"Friday, December 13th?" Harlow asked, mostly for Ryan's sake, to let him dictate, but she knew their schedules inside and out.

"Nailed it. Could you be there around six?"

"Perfect."

Ryan smiled proudly, and Sally and Vanessa nodded at themselves for an update well done. Their pride lasted until Lisa, the busiest one of them all, ran into the room.

"Did I miss it? I missed it. Shit." Lisa asked and answered her own question, then plopped herself on the chair across from Ryan, and sank in exhaustion.

Harlow, and the rest, attempted to hide their amusement as they watched the new mom chug coffee like she would water after running a marathon through the snow. And by the look of her boots that hadn't yet been changed into heels, she might have done just that.

"I'll give you the update. Everybody is executing perfectly." Harlow sent appreciative and proud looks toward the group then continued, "We are on track and it seems it's going to be a very Merry Christmas."

"Thank God. What is Christmas again?" Lisa joked as she looked up, pretending to be confused, then added, "I'll meet up with each of you in our one-on-ones to make sure there isn't anything else you need from me, or last-minute details you'd like my help with."

"Sounds great, Lis." Ryan said, the first to get up and walk out with a wave, then he answered a phone call from one of his clients he greeted by name.

"Lisa, you're stunning. Even in your frazzled, no-sleep, new baby world. It's making you sparkle like a fresh, fluffy snow," Sally said as she followed Ryan out and tapped Vanessa on the shoulder, a sign that told her she should follow suit.

Vanessa stood, reached over to squeeze Lisa's hand, winked, and followed Sally. The women walked out organizing a trip to a coffee shop for their next meeting. And they'd need it seeing as they'd be putting in a long couple of weeks, and many days with hours that would reach well into double digits.

Harlow looked at Lisa and smiled sympathetically but with as much joy she knew Lisa's new baby brought into the world.

"How is sweet baby Layla?" Harlow asked.

"She's great. The most precious, unsleeping human on the planet."

"What if you just took a couple more weeks off. I promise we will be fine here." Harlow didn't have the heart to tell Lisa that when she was gone things trudged forward, but barely.

It was hard losing the one person who knew everybody's schedule; scheduled all the meetings, job interviews, client interviews; had relationships with the event planners from the hotels, local, and national caterers; knew where to get the best deals, and understood the ins and outs of tailoring your mood and correspondence to appeal to the right people for the right occasions.

"Not a chance. I need a break. Even if it is so I can sleep at my desk. But if it gets to that point, I promise I'll book one of the mother rooms. Might as well hook myself up to the pump if I'm going to be still for more than ten minutes," Lisa said, pointing to her boobs like they were feeding objects rather than an appreciated and appealing part of her body.

"Okay, but if it gets to be too much, you tell me. Before we get too into work, what can I bring for Thanksgiving?" Harlow asked, excited about the holiday that was now only six days away.

"Yourself and your favorite bottle of wine. Nothing more, nothing less. You know how Mom and Steve get. They rule the kitchen and no outsider must enter."

Lisa and Harlow both understood the term 'outsider' was affectionately used for any person who wasn't her mom or her doting husband, which included family.

"Understood." Harlow saluted.

"Did you call them?" Lisa asked, changing the subject, knowing Harlow's family had been on her mind.

Harlow thought of them constantly, but more so around the holidays. Lisa knew the Hills came from money. She'd known since she and Harlow were childhood friends going to the same elementary and high schools. But as people do, they had drifted apart during college and the first couple of years back in St. Paul. It wasn't until Lisa had applied for the Executive Event Coordinator job that they had reconnected.

They'd hit it off again immediately and filled a void in each other's lives they hadn't realized was missing.

When they rekindled their old friendship, Harlow had confided in Lisa that the money was still there, but the once-close family had begun to jet-set around the world and hopping around to live in different states. Vincent, Harlow's brother, had moved his wife, Catherine, to New York to open a branch of their marketing and advertising company there. And Harriett, her sister, had done the same but had taken her skills to Nashville. Her parents, Walter and Vivienne, had since retired and liked to spend the holidays in France, Italy, or any other picturesque European country.

This year, Harlow had waffled and wavered on reaching out to them to see if they'd all come home for Christmas to spend it together like they used to.

"I haven't." Harlow's head dropped, showing disappointment in herself and readied for a stern talking-to from Lisa.

Lisa got up and sat on the coffee table so she could sit and reach across Harlow's desk to take her hand.

"I promise it won't be hard. Just a quick call. Or even a text. Just send a quick feeler out there to get everybody's schedules?"

"It's not the schedules I'm worried about. And calling or texting isn't the hard part. It's the answer that I might get in response. I'm afraid to hear they won't be able to make it. Or, that they offer I go to them – which would be really nice – but it's not home." Harlow shook her head.

"I know. I understand," Lisa said, letting out a sigh for her friend. She understood, because even though her parents and extended family were always around and she had them for all holidays and special occasions, she couldn't imagine how sad she would be if one day she didn't have that. "But promise me you'll keep thinking about it. Your family is wonderful. I bet they just don't realize how much you all would love it. How much you all need it."

"I promise. Lis, you are amazing. And you do actually 'sparkle like freshly fallen snow.'"

The women laughed at Sally's description from the meeting, but only out of appreciation. And, if Harlow wasn't mistaken in her friend's glow, it was the truth.

CHAPTER 2

"Thanks, Brandon. Yeah, if you could have that ready by the time I get up that would be great. We aren't wasting any time on this."

Harris Porter stomped his boots, shook out his tailored winter coat, and tenderly smoothed and brushed the flakes out of his styled hair upon walking into the building.

He continued to listen to Brandon, his number one product manager, confirm he'd be able to have information ready on the feed company they were looking to collaborate with by the time he made it up to their offices.

Hopefully the collaboration he was working on would happen in the *very* near future. Very near if he could convince – probably more like beg – his dad. Maybe by the second quarter if he pressed hard. And fourth quarter if he let it happen organically and didn't come up against any hurdles along the way.

"Perfect. Just walked in. Be up in five," Harris said, before he swung the second set of doors open that led to the completely modernized Creamery, Co.

Harris looked around and smiled at the angled, black strips of wood that paneled the reception desk, noting it looked modern but balanced out the white walls and the concrete desk tops, floors, and pillars. It was a remodel his dad had let him take on only a couple years earlier. Now, it matched their website and appealed to the younger generation – who were going to be their new customer and employee demographic.

He grinned but was baffled by the thought that the 'younger generation' no longer included himself. There was an entire youthful generation coming up behind him. They were ready to work, and ready for their work to make the world a better place. That's why this feed collaboration was so critical to their success.

Yes, he thought, he'd use that in his pitch to his dad. Charles Porter had made his own father's creamery business into a billion-dollar company. Harris had helped Charles turn it into a multi-billion-dollar company. And there was so much more they could do.

Harris jumped at the clank that sounded from behind him. When he turned he saw two boxes, at least six-feet-tall, trying to cram through the oversized double doors.

"Wait, wait!"

Harris whirled around once more to see Nancy Lawson, their front desk receptionist yell, while waving her hands to try and halt the delivery man.

"Good morning, Harris. How are you today?" Nancy asked as she whooshed by.

"Great," Harris responded quickly, hoping to get it in before she was out of earshot. "How are you?" he asked, letting out a smirk knowing she was too nice not to keep the conversation going.

"Oh, really," Nancy huffed, "really great." She turned her head slightly and lifted her voice. "The kids and grandkids all made it in last night."

Nancy huffed out another couple of breaths as she and the delivery man continued to reach opposite sides of the box in their repeated attempt to find each other.

"Can you imagine, ten adults and seven kids, all under the same roof? For a month. More actually. They are staying until the New Year." She shook her head stopped her tilting and put up a finger in Harris' direction, showing she'd be right back with him.

"Sir," Nancy greeted the driver after hovering on one side long enough to finally catch him, "good morning to you. I hope you are doing very well. You are soaked to the bone. We'll have to get you some coffee or a hot chocolate. But before then," she continued without letting the driver respond – and he seemed okay with that as long as he got the hot chocolate, as that's when his eyes and eyebrows perked – "you'll have to take this back outside. We have a delivery entrance and it will be much easier for you there. I promise. No squeezing through doors or scuffing my floors. Once you have it in, you come find me, and I'll have a hot cup waiting for you."

"Yes ma'am." The young driver nodded, gave a little salute, and was pulling the gigantic boxes back out the small opening he tried to jam them through.

Nancy turned on a dime and Harris watched the fit grandmother of seven speed walk back to her throne.

"Nicely done." Harris said, genuinely impressed.

Nancy nodded firmly, but added a smile that let Harris know she was back to their original conversation.

"What are you all doing for the holidays?"

"I'm probably working straight through. We've got some big opportunities knocking on our door." Harris wasn't lying about either, there was a good chance he'd miss the holidays this year.

"Harris." Nancy's motherly tone sounded like his own mom's disapproval of his working habits. "You have to make time for the holidays *and* for family. It's what's most important."

"I am – I will," Harris agreed, but his agreement wasn't as truthful, "But this is setting us up for the future. We will never have a want in the world. And, we'll be helping a lot of people."

Nancy looked at Harris. He was the same age as her youngest son, and she adored him just as much. She, like Harris she supposed, remembered a time when his father, Charles, had been frugal and unwilling to spend any of their hard-earned money. Charles hadn't been much different than Harris himself. As a result, they'd grown up humbly. It wasn't a bad thing, but she imagined Harris had felt the impact and never wanted to say he couldn't afford something. Whenever she pressed, it was always 'one more deal' or 'one more sale or collaboration," *Then* there would be enough. *Then* he would settle down.

She wished she could shake some sense into him.

"As long as you promise to at least take the important days off. Thanksgiving, Christmas Eve, and Christmas day. If for no other reason than realizing that you won't have anybody to work with." Nancy smiled at the laugh she got out of Harris. "You have very kindly given the company twelve holidays and those are three of them. Four if you include the day after Thanksgiving – so you might as well add that to your list too."

"I'll do my best," Harris agreed. It was genuine, and it was true that he'd be hard pressed to reach anybody on those days. He'd think about it more seriously since she brought up that point. And, if he showed up to the holidays it would make his mom happy – and maybe make his dad loosen up to the feed collaboration idea.

"Hey Nance," Harris said, his curiosity getting the best of him, "what was in those boxes?"

"Oh, one of them was a big tree and as many lights and ornaments we could fit into the empty spaces. The other was a giant post box for your dad's *Postmark Christmas* campaign. It's so wonderful, that idea."

"Don't we have at least twenty other trees in storage?"

Without missing a beat and without giving the chance for him to argue, Nancy looked Harris in the eye and smiled sweetly, "Now, we have twenty-one."

Harris laughed and nodded, accepted that apparently one office building can never have too many Christmas trees, then waved and headed to the elevator to make his way to the top floor. A floor, he had noted earlier that morning, that was already decorated, and exploding with Christmas reds and greens.

CHAPTER 3

Snow had been scarce in early November, but the cool flakes that fell now warmed Harlow's heart as she watched them fall while rocking Layla in her second-floor nursery.

Lisa and Steve had decorated it with plush blankets, fuzzy animals in whites, tans, and browns, and soft gauzy curtains that were just the right amount of precious baby-girl. The delicate chimes of a *Baby's First Christmas* snow globe were already filling the sweet little room. Some things just couldn't wait, Harlow thought, as she closed her eyes and listened as Layla slept in her arms.

When the music stopped Harlow looked down and envied the peacefulness of the darling face as she slept. She could have put Layla down minutes ago but the feeling of holding the sleeping baby tugged at her heart and amplified her longing to love. So she would love, hold, and rock this borrowed baby even if only for another ten minutes.

When Harlow had finally separated herself from Layla she stepped out and stretched, thankful she'd decided on an oversized sweater for the day. She'd eaten more in that one Thanksgiving meal than she typically did in a week. She vowed to never eat again as she pushed away from the table earlier. And wouldn't you know it, she was almost ready to go back for round two.

"If you're thinking what I think you're thinking, you go first, because then I won't feel as guilty."

Harlow laughed at Lisa's ability to read her mind and nodded as though she'd been caught.

"I can't help it. It was too good. I was actually wondering if I had it in me for seconds on green bean casserole and stuffing before dessert. That is just so disgusting," Harlow groaned.

"What do you think I was doing when you took Layla up? I snuck seconds so I could be ready for dessert by the time you got out. Now you have to do it just to make me feel better about myself." Lisa wrapped an arm around Harlow and they walked to the stairs together. "How'd she go down?"

"Like a doll. She's beautiful. Perfect and beautiful," Harlow said, thinking it was an understated version of the truth. Layla was even more than that – she was a precious gift. After years of trying without success, Lisa and Steve had been blessed with a miracle.

"I'll call you tonight when she's up at one and four, we'll see if you still feel the same way," Lisa said with an eyebrow raised, but her smile was full of pride and joy.

"Forever and always."

"Yeah, yeah. Do you think you'll stick around for the movie tonight? Mom said she was watching the baby so Steve and I are getting a two-and-a-half-hour night out on the town. For a movie. With the rest of the family," Lisa said, slowly playing out the words to make it seem less exciting as the thought dragged on.

"As appealing as that sounds, I think I'm going to head home. I love the idea of sweatpants and curling up on the couch with a big blanket. And I know your mom already has leftovers packed up for me – the saint – so I'll shamelessly sit surrounded by reheated Tupperware and relish every minute." Harlow grew more excited as she foreshadowed her evening.

"You sure?"

Harlow knew Lisa was asking out of care and concern. Lisa knew going home might be hard, especially on the holiday. But she'd be fine. She might even work up the courage to call her parents or text her brother and sister something more than the usual *Happy Thanksgiving, I love you and miss you.*

"Definitely." Harlow was determined to be independent and find a place in her heart to love the holidays and be thankful for everything she had – not just the pieces of the family she didn't. Besides, she was luckier than most. She had a family. They might have been scattered around the world but she'd take that over any alternative.

"Okay, but if you change your mind, you know where we'll be. Now, let's sneak in and stuff ourselves some more."

—

The snow had left a sparkling dust of white on the sidewalks and streets. It found its way into the creases of signs and stop lights until wintery gusts of wind would come and swoosh it around to land in another nook or cranny.

The beauty of the street lamps had illuminated the ground, causing it to glitter as Harlow drove by. It had drawn her out into the evening for a walk on Grand Avenue after she'd made it home.

It wasn't late, maybe only six or six-thirty, but the sky was dark and she needed those street lamps to light her way.

Tomorrow, the sidewalk would be bustling with Black Friday shoppers loading up with gifts, and lining up outside of the delicious restaurants after working up a hunger from all of their racing around. She loved it here for that very reason.

It hadn't been hard to be the one to stay. To purchase the home that had been given to her and her siblings. It was the perfect house in the perfect neighborhood. Now, looking down the softly lit street that looked like a scene out of a 1940's Christmas movie, it reaffirmed her decision to stay.

But tonight, she'd had the same feeling that had been creeping in over the past couple months, a certain loneliness when she walked through the mansion. *The Hill,* she thought. An immaculate Victorian with endless charm and character.

Growing up it was her haven, her excitement, and her playful escape. That was when she shared it with her family.

The first couple of years after everybody had moved out were nice. She had redecorated, keeping only the furniture and paintings that had the kind of nostalgia that tugged at your heart when you sat on them or looked at it. Everything else – that wasn't of great value and nobody else wanted – was sold in an estate sale, with the profits donated to local charities.

All-in-all, Harlow considered it a win. But after the redecorating and making it her own, the walls seemed too hollow and she found herself longing to have people shuffling around the kitchen, kids running through the halls with their feet stomping and echoing from the floors above, and something other than a blanket keeping her warm at night.

Harlow wrapped her arms tightly around her body at the thought, and the brisk wind swirled around her. As she did, the world around her came back into focus and she noticed a red, round man, opening a box that was nearly the size of himself.

She walked the two short blocks to get closer. She wanted to see what Santa was doing out on Thanksgiving night. Surely Mrs. Claus wanted him home. Surely *he* wanted some of Mrs. Claus' cookies. Harlow chuckled at her thought and shook her head.

"Santa? Hello, can I help you?" Harlow asked, holding back a giggle at the round body tugging at the industrial staples holding the box together – in what seemed to be a steel hold.

"Oh!"

Santa jumped then actually gave a "Ho-Ho-Ho" – the closest thing she'd ever heard to the sound she imagined the real Santa would make.

"Well, didn't you give me a startle." Santa laughed, grabbing his belly. "I would welcome the help if you aren't too cold out here on this beautiful night. It's like the weather knew a little snow would make my day."

It had been a long time since Harlow had believed in Santa Claus, but this man might make her a believer once more. Everything about him was jolly; his voice sounded like a song, and his laugh hit his jiggling belly every time.

"Sure!" Harlow was delighted she could help. "What would you like me to do?"

"I think if you'd be willing to hold the box in place I'd get a good enough grip on it to get it open. It keeps skating in circles every time I try to pull it."

Harlow positioned herself next to Santa and readied herself to push so she could hold the box in position as he pulled.

"One, two-" Santa pulled on three and the staples sounded like tiny fireworks as they popped free from the side of the box. "We did it!"

Santa held his hand high for Harlow to slap it for five as they cheered.

"What's in here?" Harlow asked, trying to peek around the now opened flap.

"Oh, this? This is a miracle maker," Santa said as he rounded the box, removing the rest of the cardboard and foam. "It's a Christmas mailbox."

"For letters to send you?" Harlow could feel herself being drawn into Santa's excitement.

"For that and so much more. Some people, kids and adults alike, have no place to send their Christmas wishes. For things that are more than a gift you can wrap in a box. And sometimes you can't give your wish to a parent, or in some cases there aren't parents to help you send the wish."

Harlow covered her heart with her gloved hand as it broke while she listened and thought about those children who Santa was talking about.

"So, we set up this beautiful Christmas-red mailbox for any and everybody to write and send their Christmas wishes. Some things that are wished for can't be fulfilled, but we sure try our best to come close."

"I love everything about it. It's wonderful." Harlow brushed a small tear away from her blue eyes and pushed a stray curl of red hair behind her ear.

"It really is. Wonderful, that is," Santa agreed and looked at Harlow.

It wasn't the first time he looked at her but this time he stared, pleasantly it seemed, but knowingly, too. Like he saw her through and through.

"You know," he started, "Christmas is for everybody. Sometimes wonderful, magical things can happen by making a simple wish. Perhaps you'll be back. You never know what miracles Christmas can bring."

Harlow smiled at the wise man and his rosy-red cheeks and delicately wiped another tear away.

"Thank you, Santa. I just might."

Harlow leaned in, gave Santa a kiss on his warm cheek, and turned to head home. Thankful she was blessed enough to have one.

If you love **_Postmark Christmas_**, head to
Amazon.com for your copy today!

ABOUT THE AUTHOR

KATIE BACHAND is the author of contemporary romance and sweet holiday romance novels.

KATIE lives with her husband, son, and golden retriever in beautiful Minneapolis, Minnesota. She hopes in her novels, and in life, you find great friendships, great love, and great appreciation for our wonderful world and the people in it.

Visit Katie on her website at
https://katiebachandauthor.com

Visit Katie on any of your favorite social media outlets by following the link below, or searching **KATIE BACHAND** on Facebook, Instagram, Pinterest, and Twitter.

https://linktr.ee/katiebachand

CPSIA information can be obtained
at www.ICGtesting.com
Printed in the USA
BVHW030950240820
587132BV00006B/60/J

9 781733 432672